KIN

KIN

Stephen Goodwin

HARPER & ROW, PUBLISHERS

New York, Evanston,
San Francisco, London

This book was completed with the assistance of a fellowship from the National Endowment for the Arts.

FIRST EDITION

Designed by Janice Stern

Library of Congress Cataloging in Publication Data

Goodwin, Stephen.
  Kin.
  I. Title.
PZ4.G6583Ki [PS3557.0624]   813'.5'4   74–1886
ISBN 0–06–011608–0

For my mother,
Jeannette Goodwin

1

One

They reached Ewell, the seat of Manspile County, the southern extremity of Alabama's Black Belt, in the late afternoon of Friday, the sixth of September, 1968. Parker Livingston had a vivid consciousness of date and place, for the occasion did seem historic despite the uncanny familiarity of the landscape. He anticipated the shapes of pastures and ponds, fence lines and houses, creeks and hills, even the placement of grazing cattle and the depth of the day's waning light, so that recapitulation preceded fresh sight. "We do not change," said the complacent fields, and the Montgomery radio station, WBAM, or the Big Bam, said *Ka-boom* with its famous cannon, just as it had always said. Without a determination to cling to his own sense of significant absence, Parker might easily have slipped into the emollient fancy that he'd been gone only two hours, not two years.

Because of his determination, however, and because Arthur Kin was beside him in the Volkswagen, Parker took offense at the inertia expressed in almost every detail of the slovenly landscape. The South, the South—he'd known he was in it last night when, somewhere in Carolina, he'd pulled off the highway and driven toward a stupendous orange moon, the airborne bulletin of Union 76, that rose above the trees. Midnight, but he was sweating, his shirt sticking to the ridges of his back, when he stopped the car and stepped out into the rank air. He smelled swamp gas, heard the croak and grumble of nocturnal insects and reptiles, the raucous hoots of night-preying birds, the splash and hiss of creatures he couldn't identify but had listened to for most of his life. A drowsy fat man, rubbing sleep out of his eyes with a fist like a potato, wobbled out of the station, passing beneath the sign that bore his name, L. P. "Buster" Everly. He was missing most of his front teeth— lost them, probably, trying to live up to his nickname—but that didn't prevent him from turning a dazed smile toward Parker. "Traveling late, good buddy. Fill er?"

"If you kindly would," Parker said in his best Alabama accent. He was surprised at the sound of his voice, but why not? He was close enough to home to revert to the idiom.

"These little foreign jobs don't take but a thimbleful anyhow," Everly opined as he cranked his pump and went to the fender. He saw Arthur then, Arthur's sleeping head against a jacket jammed for a pillow between the seat and the window, but the interior of the car was dark and he didn't make out the color of Parker's companion. "You boys going off to school?"

Arthur stirred. He lifted his head and looked about him, and Parker was sure that he knew from the odor and feel of the air on his face and from the sight of big Buster hunkered beside the car that they were in it, the South, that climate which sustains much that has perished elsewhere. Everly, however, occupied with heaving himself upright after setting the catch on the nozzle, failed still to get a proper squint at Arthur as he turned and reached for his sponge and squeegee.

"Nope," Parker said. "On our way to Alabama."

"Alabama, huh? Wherebouts in Alabama? I got some people down there."

And he turned back to the car just as Arthur issued from it. He missed a beat or two, and the sponge dripped upon the belly that stood out like a marquee, when Arthur flattened his hands on the small of his back and arched toward the sky, a casual nigger gulping the air of Carolina. With his fingertips Arthur plucked the material of his shirt from his damp body before he steadied his glance on Everly, and then, only then, did the proprietor remember himself.

"It's lots of bugs this time of year," he said as he bent over the windshield. "Look at em all squorshed here. Sometimes it gets so bad you can't hardly drive for the goddam things. It's worsen a snowstorm out there on the road. Fucking moths everywhere."

"Where's the gents'?" Arthur interrupted, and before Everly could reply, he slouched across the station yard in the direction of a roughly lettered sign, MEN, at the corner of the building. Everly left off discoursing about moths as he watched him go. His brooding became as palpable as the other emanations of that night, and after he'd rammed the gas cap on, rocking the car with his vehemence, Parker apprehensively followed him inside to pay him. Surrounded by stale Twinkies and Nabs, green pickled eggs afloat in a gallon of vinegar, plastic worms and frog and spider poppers, TNT and cherry bombs, and all the other usual junk, Everly fiddled at the buttons of his cash register. He probably had a pistol hidden somewhere in the merchandise, and the longer Parker waited, the more anxious he grew. Among his wares, reminded of his station in life, Everly was breathing hard and trying to interpret the insult that had taken place.

They got away without incident. They hopped into the VW—that is, Parker hopped in and started the engine while Arthur sauntered back across the lot—and beat it back to the main road before Everly came to any conclusions. It occurred to Parker that the only threat might have been the one he imagined, but he was inclined to believe that it had been actual; that particular Buster wasn't the first Buster he'd seen, and he thought he knew the man's state of mind as well as he knew his own. Maybe better, for he didn't understand why he couldn't bring himself to speak to Arthur about Everly. They'd pushed on through that night and the next day, one driving and the other dozing, deeper and deeper into the South, neither saying much, while the stitching sound of the engine and the lyrics of "Ode to Billy Joe," a ballad they heard at least once an hour on the Blaupunkt, were coded on their brains. Parker's body was numb with weariness, but his consciousness felt as alert and trapped as a mouse that had fallen into a grain bin, and after that little midnight drama the chief enterprise of his homecoming was to brace himself for the worst.

When they exited off the interstate onto U.S. 31, the seamed, patched highway of his youth, Parker's umbrage grew with each mile. Clabber Girl, Nehi, Red Man, Jax, Buell's Bungalows, and even Burma Shave—nailed to trees, wired to fenceposts, the same signs were still there, and they advertised principally the marksmanship of Manspile County. Every *o* had been penetrated, every *i* emphatically dotted, every period duplicated by rifle fire, and the riflemen had been followed by men with scatterguns, plainer fellows who just liked to hear the thwang of birdshot on tin. U.S. 31 had the look of a shooting gallery as it ran toward Ewell through the plantations of the Lightman Lumber Company, the thickly ranged pines so nearly of a height that they might have been trimmed by a celestial scythe. It crossed the iron bridge over Murder Creek, upon whose superstructure many of the county's passions were recorded: Carlton Loves Mavis, Beat Lanier, War Eagle, and Roll Tide Rolllll. It passed deserted, stove-in tenant houses and several places which had burned, leaving brick chimneys with gaping black mouths which looked as though they had sucked up the contents of entire households, pots and crocks and shoes, the grandma and baby along with the bedsteads. Then, as it neared Ewell, coming alongside the Louisville and Nashville tracks and into view of the water tower, where the numerals of high-school classes, including Parker's own, were daubed in gigantic red, it was planted with the heraldic crests and badges of Kiwanis, Pilots, Rotary, and Lions, organizations joined in sentiments of greeting. "Ewell, huh?" Arthur said as they came into the city limits, pronouncing it correctly, ee-well, the way any southern black man would. Ewell A Friendly Community And A Nice Place To Live Drive Safely We Love Our Children. And next the cross of corrugated tin, man-sized:

J E S U S
    A
    V
    E
    S

Yes, indeedy, Parker thought, and we are all His children, or if not His we are all the governor's, whose grinning face on the campaign poster was larger than the cross or the Volkswagen: Y'ALL COME.

"Ee-well," Arthur repeated, making sure that he had it right. Did Parker hear in that single word a hint of entreaty? It sounded almost as if Arthur was soliciting him to join in an attitude toward the place, but he was too busy glaring at the Elite Cafe and the Victorian courthouse—there were cannon on its lawns, a few men lingering on its benches, and a Confederate monument at its entrance—to pay much mind to an ambiguous supplication. *Feast your eyes on this,* he wanted to announce to men and monument, for he too was a citizen of that town and he had his own right to decide what traffic could pass the muzzles of those decorative cannon. He also had a right to decide what traffic passed the threshold of his house, he thought as he turned into Jefferson Street, and he doggedly set his chin in preparation for his meeting with his mother. He had telephoned her that morning from Athens, Georgia, to say that he was on his way, and he'd mentioned that he was bringing home a companion, but he had not found the nerve to tell her that Arthur was black. Why should he have to identify a guest in that way? He shouldn't, and yet the omission made him testy, for his mother was not particularly enlightened—but with that opinion Parker reached depths in which, for him, there was no standing. His mother was a widow, and her husband, Parker's father, had killed himself. Parker wasn't sure of the circumstances of his father's death—he'd been only eleven years old at the time—but he knew that a black woman figured in the story and that his father was supposed to have had a son by her. It was the oldest and most inevitable of all southern stories, and also the most grievous in its consequences for the survivors—how, please God, was the wife, son, mistress, or bastard of such a man ever to find a place in the community, in a family? To Parker it often seemed impossible that such a history was his, and the father he remembered, the man of flesh and blood, was blurred by the guilts and lusts his son had learned to impute to him. Philip Livingston was as imperfectly conceived as a character in a dream, so that Parker believed himself less the issue of an individual father, the chromosomal sum of a particular union between that man and his mother, than the get of a racial principle. Nevertheless, the fact remained that his father had been capable of launching sperm into his mother's womb and into other wombs as well; his father was now dead and his mother was alive, at home awaiting him; he was bringing to her a black man, whom he had announced merely as an Army friend. But if a son can muddle through, he thought, why should not a spouse? If he could act a friend to Arthur, shouldn't his mother be capable at least of courtesy? These and the other questions that he framed as he drove the last half mile, along the shaded, placid street where he had grown up, were all barbed, for he did not want his mother to be merely civil, as he knew she would be, he wanted her to be improved by the opportunity.

The Livingston house was not columned, porched, or galleried, but it stood in spacious and well-tended grounds, and it had a spare sort of elegance. There was a crescent of cut glass over the front door and the walls ascended to an entablature and cornice of the strictest Revival purity. At that hour, with sun on the western panes, dusk in the magnolia, and an unseen mockingbird plagiarizing the notes of lesser singers—they heard it when Parker switched off the engine and extinguished the Big Bam—the house was plenty imposing, a bijou of the post-bellum South, a civilized hall, tranquil edifice (it was dumfounding to hear that bird, to cease hearing the motor of the VW), and also, indubitably, it was the master's dwelling. Bow down, Kin, and wipe yo feets—Parker couldn't suppress a twinge of that satisfaction.

Before Parker had time to emerge from the car and stretch, the side door of the house opened—and in the slam of the screen door, a characteristic sound composed of whoosh, creak, and bang, a composition that had punctuated his life, there was a seduction of the past—and his mother strode toward him down the brick walkway. If she took in Arthur, who had also stepped from the car, nothing in her demeanor revealed it. She looked fit and tanned, younger even than Parker remembered her, for her hair was cut short and close to her head, and she wore trousers that showed off the figure she worked resolutely to preserve. Except for the portion of gray that muted the blond of her hair, no inroads of age appeared to have succeeded. There were blushes of applied healthy color on her cheeks and she was smiling at Parker, but the smile was under restraint, as were her kiss and the embrace in which she kept a buffer of space between them, so that she was as light as and scarcely more tangible to her son than the waft and fragrance of a breeze. More weighty, even as Parker kissed his mother and received her cheek against his, was the looming presence of Queen Iva, announced by another report of the screen door. Advancing through the boxwoods in her bearish walk, she wore a dress that seemed as big and white as a parachute, and her face expressed joy and disapprobation together.

"Hello," said Mrs. Livingston, retreating, to Arthur. She

extended her hand to him and he had to walk around the car to take it. "I'm thrilled to have you here."

"Just look at you," said Iva to Parker, "if you ain't a mess."

"I've been traveling for three days."

Iva did not slow down, nor did she hurry, but came across the paved parking area in her turned-over slippers, chuckling in happy puffs. She enfolded Parker with such energy that he nearly left his feet, and over her shoulder, in the midst of that whamming embrace, he saw the patient and studiously empty faces of Arthur Kin and his mother.

"Lemme step back and get a better look at you," Iva said, adjusting the gold wires of the spectacles that had come unseated. "Was that a mustache I felt up against my cheek? And look at that hair. It's enough of it to go into business with. But I believe I see you underneath it, the same old Parker."

"Iva, did you meet Parker's friend?" Mrs. Livingston asked. "It's Arthur, isn't it? Arthur Kin?"

"Yes'm."

"Uh-huh," grunted Iva.

"Arthur lives in Biloxi," Parker felt obliged to say. "We took the same plane from Germany, and he needed a ride home."

The two women seemed to expect an explanation and Parker realized that he felt he owed them one, though he disliked the note of apology which crept into his account of the journey down. Assigned to the same Army unit, bunkmates in the same barracks room, they had met by chance in an Amsterdam café long after their discharge, and they had joined for the trip home. The Army conveyed them only as far as New Jersey, and since Parker was driving to Alabama anyway, and Arthur had to get to Mississippi,

Parker had offered him a lift. As he talked, Parker couldn't help making his gesture sound more innocent than it was, more innocent too than either of the women listening to him believed. His mother nodded diffidently; the diffidence was genuine, and Parker knew that it would prevent her from any remonstrance, but she would retire into the forms of civility for the length of Arthur's visit. As for Iva, disapprobation would soon get the better of joy in her expression, and she would, in her own time, deliver her reproach. If they were provoked, Parker thought, it was their own fault, not his; it wouldn't harm them to suffer a black man under that roof. So he was both abashed and defiant as he concluded his explanation, and he forced a note of cheer into his voice when he said, "Is there any hot water in that house? Any ice? I've been dreaming of a shower and a drink."

"It *has* been a muggy day for a drive," Mrs. Livingston said, and as the travelers removed their luggage from the car, she addressed a number of polite questions to her son, which he answered just as politely. She told him that the guest room had been made up and she preceded him to the house, holding the screen door open for him and Arthur to pass. Parker led Arthur across the dining room—under their combined weight the floor trembled enough to make the cruets jingle in the silver cradle on the sideboard—and up the stairs to the guest room, hearing as he went the contending, though not heated, voices of the women. Queen Iva, it sounded, was being stubborn, and Parker, as soon as he'd left Arthur in the room off the landing and deposited his luggage in his own room, hurried back down the stairs.

"I wish you'd let me drive you home," Mrs. Livingston was saying, "after you've stayed this extra time."

12

"I can catch a ride down the street. It was you I stayed to see," Iva said to Parker. "What you mean staying gone two years and then don't call up till just a few hours before you get home? I didn't have time to do nothing but bake a ham."

Her combativeness had degrees, and this seemed serious enough for Mrs. Livingston to excuse herself tactfully, leaving Parker and Iva alone in the kitchen.

"I couldn't call up from Germany, now could I? I've only been back in this country twenty-four hours."

"How come you didn't call yesterday, then? Ain't they got phones up there, wherever it was? How come you didn't give some warning, when we hatn't seen you for two years and been just waiting for this day?"

"I didn't want to call until I knew when I'd arrive. I thought that might keep you from going to trouble over me."

"Trouble? What trouble you mean? Fixing something for you to eat? It's nothing in the house but that ham, fixed the way you like it."

"No cake?"

"It would of been some if you hadn't come slipping back like a stranger. Friday afternoon too, and me not coming in tomorrow, so I wouldn't even seen you till Monday if I hadn't stayed."

"I'll look better by Monday, I promise. I'll be cleaned up by then."

"It won't do a bit of harm," said Iva, not to be deflected from her pique by any attempts at humor. "It's past time for me to go. Mose setting at home, waiting on me to come get his supper for him. I only stayed where I could see you when you got here. It's a long while since you been together in this house, you and your mama and Amsy."

"Where is Amsy?"

"Out somewhere. She sposed to done been back."

"She wouldn't even wait for me?" Parker said with false indignation.

Iva forbore answering. She was sitting, removing her slippers and replacing them with street shoes, and when she stood she drew on a garment more like a wrapper than a coat—it was too hot out for any sort of covering, but she never left the house in that white workdress—and hooked her purse over her arm. She tilted her head back and looked him over; when she focused in that way, her fragile spectacles used with a dowager's pomp, she seemed to scrutinize minutely, and Parker had the uncomfortable sensation that she saw more than his mussed and sticky exterior. Finished with him, she arranged her summer hat, a pinkish thing that had the shape of a tam or an old-fashioned water bottle, carefully upon her head, upon silver hair that in patches was bright as chrome.

He was relieved when she left, even though the promptness of her departure was a plain affront. She did not like having Arthur Kin in the house; she hadn't mentioned him, but there was no mistaking the source of her dudgeon. Well, he hadn't expected her to be pleased, and while he wished that his arrival might have given her a less blemished joy, he didn't suppose that her sense of injury would be lasting, and Arthur would surely be gone when she returned on Monday morning.

In fact, the understanding was that Arthur would leave the next morning on the first bus, and Parker sought out his mother to tell her that. She had gone to the room they called the library, where she was busy setting out ice and bottles. "Has Iva gone?" she asked, and knowing the answer to her own question, she said, "She's really gotten more touchy these last two years, but, Parker, she was so excited when you called this morning."

"She seemed a little upset that I hadn't given more notice."

"She gets put out by things, but she'll be over it in a few days."

Parker blurted, "I hope it's not too inconvenient—bringing Arthur along with me, I mean."

"Oh no, of course not."

"He's only going to stay the night. He'll be leaving in the morning."

"Well, if he hasn't been home for two years, he's probably anxious to see his family, just as they are to see him."

"I'll call tonight to ask about the bus schedules. I just thought he'd want to break his trip and get at least one night's rest."

"It's no bother if he wants to stay longer. And don't worry about inconveniencing me—I don't have any plans for the weekend."

"I hope you didn't cancel anything on my account."

She shrugged.

"You shouldn't have gone to any trouble."

He left it at that. They both knew that the exchange had been freighted; she had expressed as much displeasure as she would express, and he had expressed as much regret. He then went upstairs to his own room, past the closed door of the guest room. He heard the shower running, and he thought it was fortunate that the guest room had its own bath.

After his scrub-up, damp hair still lashed to his head, Parker went to retrieve Arthur and take him downstairs. Approaching the now-open door from the main upstairs hall, Parker thought at first that the room had been vacated, that Arthur must already have gone down without him. The light from the windows had become very obscure and no lamps were on, but Parker made out the live silver patch of the mirror, the luster of a maple dresser, the glint of gold thread that ran through the bedspread. He could see only the foot of the bed until he descended the four steps to the landing and entered the doorway; the sharp lines on the spread might have been graven in stone for all the impression Arthur Kin made upon the bed. He was sitting forward, elbows on his knees, dressed soberly in dark trousers and knit shirt, but he appeared as wary, as lightly poised, as prepared for immediate flight, as a sparrow at a feeder. It occurred to Parker that this visit was as taxing to Arthur as it was to him, but he asked in a jocular voice, "Feel better now that you washed some of the dust off? Ready to go down and get a drink?"

"Sho."

"That shower woke me up just enough to keep me going for another couple of hours."

"Mine made me tireder."

"A drink will help."

"I don't know. It seems like we been moving for a long time. I was liking just sitting still. It's all kinds of birds been singing that I hatn't heard for a while."

"Oh, the birds," and Parker stopped for a second to listen. "The damn things will drive you batty if you stay here long enough. My mother puts out feed for them."

"It's nice to hear um for a change. This is a nice place you live at."

Parker liked the subdued humility he heard in Arthur's voice, and as he led him from the room, he was pleased that the occasion was decorous. This, the evening of his return, was being treated ceremoniously, but he didn't mind letting Arthur suppose that the Livingstons, few as they were, foregathered at the day's end to refresh themselves with iced drinks in the paneled library. He might have become quite expansive had his mother's courtesies not seemed patronizing enough for one family. She'd brought out the silver ice bucket and the Jefferson cups, and she was prepared to drink to their safe trip home. Arthur, however, declined to accept a bourbon and requested instead a Coke. She had to go to the kitchen to fetch one, and Arthur, now embarrassed to have put her to any bother, said that he'd just as soon drink from the bottle. Mrs. Livingston seemed bent on serving him in a cup and she prevailed, but as soon as she handed it to him he drank it off in a gulp, forgetting that a toast had been suggested. Mrs. Livingston lifted her own cup in a silent salute to her son, and she then propelled herself into conversation with Arthur about Europe. "You lived in Amsterdam for three months! I do envy you. It's the loveliest city. And did you go to the flower fields? They were so beautiful when I was there—that was on a trip with Parker's father, years ago. There were fields upon fields of tulips, every color imaginable. Did you see them?"

Did he see them, those *tew-lips*—even his mother's accent ran against the grain of Parker's sensibility. He wondered how Arthur would have answered if anyone else had asked him that question. But Arthur said only, "No'm, I passed up the flowers."

"Of course the spring is the time to see them, and you were there later, weren't you? Still, how wonderful to have all that time in Amsterdam. You'll certainly have something to tell your people in Biloxi."

That was correct, Arthur would have something to tell

his people—but it wouldn't be the sort of thing that Mrs. Livingston appeared to have in mind. He'd tell them about the girls, the bars, the clothes, but not the flowers. Parker couldn't make out if his mother meant to sound condescending or whether she just couldn't help it, but that's how she did sound and she knew it. She looked at Parker once as if to say: *You might at least, if you had to bring one to this house, have chosen one I could talk to.* Yet the difficulties of the conversation spurred her on, and her increasing desire to extend honest hospitality to their guest only made her seem more affected. Parker, who failed to hear the current of hospitality in everything his mother said, watched Arthur huddle deeper in the claret-colored leather chair, a weary black soul who must have been reminded by everything he saw and heard that he was out of place, and Parker was far more pained on his guest's account than he was on his mother's. *Mama, leave him alone,* he wanted to say, *he is being as polite and agreeable as he knows how to be, and he's behaving that way for your benefit alone.*

"I didn't realize you were roommates all that while," Mrs. Livingston said.

"Yes'm, we lasted it out."

"Parker, I don't believe you ever mentioned in your letters that Arthur was your roommate. I wondered so about you—your letters were always so short. I never knew what you were doing with yourself while you were over there."

"I'm sorry, Mama. I'm home now."

He spoke rather sharply, as if the fact should cancel failures of the past. *Home*—he had to repeat the word to himself to take the full effect of it. Was this really his home? This woman his mother? Had he crossed an ocean and driven a thousand miles to listen to her interrogate Arthur Kin? Was this room, subtly lighted and deliciously cool, containing his father's books and objects in their accustomed order on the shelves, the space above all others on the great globe where he was properly enclosed? The answer was yes, much as he wanted to doubt it; the voice did for a certainty belong to his mother, the gracious lady resuming conversation with the black fellow slumped in the chair. How was he to join those two lives, and his own to them, in a room filled with his father's relics? He didn't know, but the enormity of that question made him grateful to his mother for talking. It might have been nothing more than manners that sustained her, but still it was more than he could find to sustain himself.

And he felt a special gratitude that Amsy returned at that moment. Her arrival was noisy—a beep on the horn of the car, another bang of the screen door, a dash through the kitchen and dining room—and he hardly saw her before she was in his arms. Affectionate, demonstrative, impulsive, Amsy was sometimes a little too gushing for her brother's taste, but he was happy to see her then, happy to have his face in her shining hair, her body pressed against his. And then—this took the merest part of an instant—he was conscious that she was wearing a skimpy halter and pair of cut-offs, that his own arms joined behind her back touched bare skin, for beyond the broad yellow ribbon that held her hair in place he saw the appraisal of his visitor. Amsy hadn't even noticed Arthur yet, but if Parker had been asked at that moment would he want his sister to marry one, he'd have said no, and certainly not that one. Though he wished he could repent them, those were his thoughts while she was in his arms, her firm body and entire weight entrusted to him in greeting.

Amsy didn't give the least sign of confusion when he introduced her to Arthur, and she was so full of questions about the trip and about the Army that Parker didn't have a chance to answer her at first. Her inquiries came quick as hail, and Mrs. Livingston used the flurry of talk to excuse herself. She'd get dinner on the table, she said, and she hoped that a cold meal would suit their appetites. Amsy offered to help her, but Mrs. Livingston refused, and as a special dispensation she told Amsy to help herself to a drink. Amsy put on an exaggerated look of long-suffering for her brother's benefit: "You see what I've put up with while you've been gone."

As she poured herself a tonic with a splash of gin, she made Parker repeat the account of his journey, and she too seemed to be fishing for an explanation of Arthur's presence. "You weren't traveling together this summer, then? You just met up in Amsterdam? That seems so strange to me—I don't even run into people I know when I go to Montgomery."

"I was glad to find somebody to share the trip," Parker said, not with entire candor.

"Not as glad as I was," Arthur volunteered. "I was kinda stuck over there. They give you a travel allowance when you get separated—"

"Separated?"

"Discharged. Demobilized. Liberated," Parker explained.

"They give you this allowance," Arthur continued, "and I had done been separated from the money when Parker came along."

"What were you doing in Amsterdam?"

"Just living there."

Amsy pouted. "I want to travel. I want to be able to say, Oh, I was just living in Amsterdam, or Paris, or Rome, anywhere. Ewell is the end of the world."

"What have you done with yourself all summer?" Parker asked.

"I taught May Millicent Page to count to twenty in French. That's been the main thing. So let's not talk about my summer—tell me where all you've been. Why didn't you send for me? Ashamed to travel with your little sister?"

The question touched more closely than she intended, for Parker had traveled with a German girl named Erika, of whom Amsy had not yet heard. "I had picnics in the Alps, went swimming in Corsica—"

"Swimming? You can swim in O'Bannon's wash-hole. You don't have to go to Europe for that."

"What do you want to know, then?"

There was plenty she wanted to know, and she managed to prompt her brother, and also his guest, into fairly lively speech. Amsy had always been ironically deferential toward Parker, an attitude which two years had not changed, and under her spirited quizzing he actually began to enjoy the report of his journey. It didn't matter whether he described olive groves or goat cheese, *Fasching* or *le mistral,* for Amsy's responses gave value to all he could say. Although she deplored a bit excessively her own provincial routine and wasn't above feigning artlessness, her animation did not seem insincere, and it warmed Parker to his own form of hyperbole. He embellished his observations for her benefit, inviting her to needle him. He was surprised at how easily they slipped into this familiar rhythm of talking—it was the conversation he had always had with Amsy, resumed now as if it had never been interrupted. The content was different, but not the stances or the emotions.

"When you go to Italy," he said, "you can understand why Germans have such a good opinion of themselves. They look around and say, *Gott in Himmel,* this is a parody of a civilization, and the people—so little, and so dirty."

"That sounds about like Conrad," Arthur said.

"Who's Conrad?"

"Just a German, you know, any German—like Ivan is a Russian."

"That's the GI name for them," Parker added.

"Where do they get off feeling so superior?"

"Italy is beautiful, but it's not efficient, and beauty doesn't compute."

"Why do all these German tourists go there, then?"

"Because it's cheap."

"And Conrad will save a penny whenever he can."

"Ungrateful," Amsy accused them, "both of you. You live in Germany for two years and turn around and talk about them like that. I wouldn't mind putting up with them for a while. Beer, elves, cuckoo clocks—what else goes on in Germany?"

"You left out Volkswagens and Mercedes."

"Knowing that," Arthur said. "They got the cars over there, and it seemed like every last one of um was out on the Autobahn going a hundred miles a hour every time I wanted to drive somewhere. They drive so close together it looks like they been welded, a Porsche to a BMW to a Mercedes, and each one of um flicking his lights wanting to pass the one in front."

"Death-defying," Parker said.

"I don't believe you two. Wait till you've been here for a while. I tell you, you will pine for Germany, you will positively waste away you will pine so. You seem to forget that you've come back to a pretty pokey place."

"I'll make out," said Parker.

"You've even gotten to look like some kind of German," Amsy exclaimed. "Blond hair, blue eyes, a mustache like one of those duelers, and you've gotten a little chubby too, haven't you?"

"What about me?" Arthur said. "I always thought I could pass for a Bavarian. You ought to see me in my leather short pants and the hat I wear to yodel in, got a little red brush in the band of it. Yes indeed, I was often mistaken for a Bavarian when I wore that outfit, and all sorts of people pestered me, asked me directions, what time it was, where was a good restaurant, till it got so bad I had to give it up."

"What did you tell them?" Amsy asked, laughing.

"Mox nix, I always said, it don't matter. I never did get the hang of that language. Now French, I like that better. Sounds like a bunch of pigeons cooing."

"Do you pass for a Frenchman too?"

"Do I sound like a pigeon?"

"How's your French, Parker? Did you use it? Or were you too shy? Didn't you wish, just once, that you had me along to interpret for you?"

He said gallantly that he had often wished for her, particularly on those occasions when his vocabulary was not equal to his irritation with innkeepers or waiters. Amsy asked about the food, and they got into a discussion of the apparent willingness of the French to eat anything, but somehow Parker's relish for the talk was dulled by the way his guest shouldered into it. Although Arthur was amusing —some Bavarian he'd make—his contributions were transparently flirtatious. He was eyeing Amsy in a way that Parker didn't like at all, and Amsy wasn't discouraging him. Immodestly dressed, her legs, belly, and shoulders bare, she talked with too much wriggling and laughed with too much abandon to suit her brother. She wasn't deliberately leading Arthur on, but Parker thought she should have the sense to squirm a little less. Didn't she see the effect she was having? And while he was at work censuring her, Parker acknowledged that he was envious of the way she was able to engage Arthur Kin, and that his censure was mean-spirited. How did she plunge into such frankness with Arthur? And what kept him from it? He realized that he did not care to know the full answer to that question.

For dinner they ate potato salad and sandwiches from the ham that Queen Iva had baked. The dining room was an intimidating chamber in which to eat a cold meal, but Mrs. Livingston had set their places at the big table, four small plots on the vast polished plane of cherry, four little homesteads in a forbidding geography. The plates—she hadn't used the best china—bore scenes of farmers and livestock, and bottles of beer had forced their crass way into the room, standing beside tall slender glasses, and of course the humble ham was present, but otherwise the scene was elegant in its most general appearance and in its fine detail. There was the finely wrought cradle for the condiments on the sideboard, which itself was worked in various woods, and the pure lines of the antique candelabra, holding new but unlighted candles; there was the curved glass of the china cabinet on the opposite wall, and the cut glass of the chandelier overhead; there were the painted flowers on the backs of Hitchcock chairs, floral patterns on the wall, and actual flowers in vases on the serving table. The room was, in all, rather daunting, and Amsy asked directly, "Why are we eating in here?" For the dining room was ordinarily reserved for high occasions, important holidays or large entertainments, and they usually sat down as a family at the smaller table in the kitchen. Mrs. Livingston said that the four of them would have been too crowded in that nook, and she asked if Amsy wasn't chilly without a blouse. Taking the hint, Amsy went upstairs and quickly changed into a chaste shift, and during her brief absence, before Arthur could embarrass himself again by a premature consumption, Mrs. Livingston offered the terse blessing that was the customary prologue to all meals in that room.

Yet the meal went off without any particular awkwardness, and even Mrs. Livingston seemed willing to take part in the chatter that Amsy stimulated. Parker praised the ham and claimed that the unadorned pig rivaled the most sophisticated dishes they could concoct in Paris, and Arthur chimed in, but Amsy protested again; she'd eaten French food in New Orleans, and she appealed to her mother to take her side against the two rubes. Mrs. Livingston was diplomatic, but she seemed pleased by the playfulness of the dispute, and Parker wondered if he was the only one at the table conscious of the authentic history taking place— a black man was sharing their board. Arthur's skin was the color of the meat of an Alabama pecan, and his features, a firm mouth and a straight nose with nostrils shaped like the wings on Mercury's heels, also suggested that a white man had penetrated his genealogy. His hair, cut just before his departure from Germany, was spruce and springy. Nothing in his appearance was menacing, and Parker should have been pleased that his sister and mother, now that she had settled down, accommodated the visitor with so little apparent strain. He should have been; he counseled himself, without much success, to be reasonable.

Mrs. Livingston did not stay downstairs after dinner. She was worn out—from waiting with so much anticipation, she thought, to see Parker again. "It's a joy to have you back safe in this house," she said, and she sounded as though she meant it. "And I'm glad to have you here, too," she said to Arthur. "I hope you'll have a good rest."

"I'll clean up the table," Amsy offered. "Don't you do it."

"Thank you. And don't you keep Parker up too long—remember that he's been traveling for days."

"How could I forget? He's practically asleep in his chair."

"I won't stay up long."

"Good night, then," she said, and she kissed both her children before she left the room.

"Do I hear any offers of help?" Amsy asked.

"This is my return. I'm not supposed to do chores."

"OK, hero, but how about clearing the table? And you can keep me company for ten minutes in the kitchen while I load the dishwasher."

They adjourned, all three of them, to the kitchen, where Amsy betrayed her first signs of uneasiness. Rinsing the plates and glasses, she began to fill Parker in on the gossip he'd missed, and for Arthur's sake she added impromptu biographical footnotes. "Tom Finlay and Joanne Head are pinned," she said to Parker, and then immediately to Arthur, "Tom Finlay still to this day has a little dent in the middle of his forehead where Parker hit him with a rock. Parker, you marked that man for life." The requirements of this sort of conversation made her seem dizzier than usual, but Parker thought he detected a series of sly moves, and he was sure of it when she said, "I just knew you'd be home tonight, even before you called. I knew you'd get here before everyone left for school."

"When does everyone leave for school?"

"On Monday, most of them."

"I can think of some of them I could do without seeing."

"You've gotten awfully hard to please," she said with

some tartness. "You used to have a few friends around here."

"I'm too tired right now to think of seeing anybody. Maybe I'll feel more like it tomorrow."

"Do you think so?"

"I don't know. Can't we wait till tomorrow?" And Parker thought, though he could not say, can't we wait until Arthur is gone?

"That's the problem," Amsy said. "Dotty's having some people out to the lake tomorrow, and she wants us to come. You'd be welcome too, Arthur," she added.

"When was this little party planned?" Parker asked.

"Last week," Amsy said vaguely and defensively. "But I told Dotty this afternoon that you were coming home and bringing a friend."

"I see."

"She had asked some people to go out there anyway," Amsy said, rallying. "It's not in your honor, if that's what you're thinking. It *is* what you're thinking, isn't it? You're awful, you know? Dotty wants to see you, but she has other interests too. You weren't exactly what you'd call a faithful correspondent." And after that scolding, Amsy gave her attention to Arthur: "You can stay over another day, can't you? Dotty's expecting to see a friend of Parker's. You don't want to get on a bus tomorrow morning. I hope you'll stay."

"I don't mind if I do. It's going on two and a half years since I been to Biloxi, and one day more can't hurt."

Tee hee, he chortled, or so his laugh sounded to Parker. It was that silly, that goofy, that ridiculous. Arthur seemed to have the idea that Amsy was courting him—and he didn't seem to be altogether wrong. Parker, who was weary anyway, suddenly felt as though he'd taken a lick over the head from a blackjack, and he longed for sleep in his own sweet bed.

"I'm glad," Amsy said to Arthur, and she at once turned back to the sink, having finished her social organizing for the evening. Parker suggested that they turn in; Arthur yawned and agreed that he could use some z's to rest up for the pick-nick. He stood, stretched, scratched his head, and Parker let him make his way upstairs by himself. As soon as his door closed, a faint sound that barely reached the kitchen, Amsy turned and asked her brother, "Do you think there'll be any trouble about him?"

"You're the one who invited him."

"I'll be furious if there is." She dried her hands vigorously on a dish towel and put a threatening expression on her face, as if to warn everyone in the county, including Parker, that she meant to look out for Arthur Kin. "Why didn't you tell us about Arthur when you called?" she asked seriously. "Why did you bring him home anyway? It doesn't seem from watching you that you're really friends."

"He needed a ride," Parker began to explain. "He was stuck over there."

Amsy joined Parker at the table and prepared to listen carefully. Her patience, her steady eyes, the hair now tucked behind her ears as if to hear him better, the curve of her cheek—Parker believed that if he could have explained to anyone, it would have been to Amsy. "Can't I tell you later? Tomorrow? I am perishing for lack of sleep."

"Why not now? I want to hear."

TWO

Parker groaned, signifying both his fatigue and his accession to her request. "Do I have to?" he complained, but he was already trying to think where he should begin.

"What do you mean, do you have to? Are you thinking of holding out?"

"No." He smiled. "It'll be easier to tell than to get pestered to death by questions."

"All right, then, shoot," she said. "How long have you known him?"

"Two years," he replied, and right away the qualifications began. He had shared a barracks room with Arthur for the duration of his military tour, but the row of standing lockers which separated their bunks might as well have been a palisade. Although there was no stated animosity between them, Arthur, who'd been at the Badstein headquarters before Parker arrived, had already established for himself a sort of routine. After putting in his duty day at G3, Arthur practiced with the post basketball team or signed out on pass, and he ate his meals at the mess hall in the company of the other black troops attached to the unit. Quiet, reserved, seldom present in the barracks, Arthur was not so much hostile as indifferent to his new roommate, and he couldn't have known that the room assignment was testing some of Parker's most prized principles.

"Bigot," Amsy said. "What was so difficult about living with him? He sounds like the sort of roommate you'd want. I'd rather have a quiet black guy than a noisy redneck."

"I had one of those too, a character from Texas, a fish named Strickland, but that wasn't the problem."

The problem, Parker told Amsy, was his own. Rather proud of his freedom from prejudice, he was determined to be fair-minded and to renounce all consciousness of Arthur's color, but he found that the most common slurs and slanders occurred to him. It didn't help that Strickland was around to remind him of the virulent proverbs they both had heard during the course of their southern childhoods. Parker regularly denied them, both aloud to Strickland and silently to himself, but he was exasperated by the power of that old wisdom to afflict him and to subvert his best convictions. Arthur was the first black man that Parker had ever lived with on anything like equal terms, and he was appalled to learn that none of his theoretical dogma—he'd been an outspoken advocate of racial equality during high school and later in his fraternity during a year and a half at college—had the force of authentic faith. All Strickland had to do was say "Moon pie" and the whole edifice of Parker's certainty began to quake, requiring the most assiduous efforts to shore it up. As a result, he'd been hesitant about approaching Arthur, and in the first several months of their tenancy in that barracks they exchanged fewer than a hundred words.

Parker had always known, of course, that when Arthur

left the barracks on pass, he was on his way to Badstein to cruise the chicks, and Strickland never let him forget that those were white chicks: "Maybe you noticed, it's not any pickaninnies in Bad-town, so who do you think he's jamming?" Parker had never actually seen Arthur with a girl, yet he made precisely the same assumption that Strickland made—what else would a girl from a German dance hall and a black GI from Biloxi have to do? Parker never imagined that they might be subject to the same trials as other pairs of lovers, and so he failed, when Arthur returned early to the room one night, to respond to an unmistakable invitation to candor. He didn't even understand the invitation until it was withdrawn, or rather canceled out by his own jittery reaction to it.

Alone in the room, Parker was roused from a half-sleep by the opening of the door. Thinking that the fourth member of the room, Davy Gentile, had entered—that row of lockers hid his cot from the door—he called out a greeting that included a reproof for noisiness. He recognized his mistake as soon as he heard the distinctive glide, a sound like a stiff broom sweeping followed by a crisp thwack of leather, of Arthur's jazzy shoes. They were imitation alligator, and they had silver buckles so big they looked like Pilgrim shoes; they were part of Arthur's stepping-out costume. The rest of it, on that night, was maroon trousers, gold shirt, and blue cap. Arthur was spinning the cap around his finger, but even in the midst of that play, even in his dashing get-up, he was manifestly dejected and low.

"Sorry," Parker said. "I thought that was Davy that came in."

"Naw. I'm back early." Arthur banged out the crown of his cap with his fist and leaned against the lockers.

Parker saw that he must want the comfort of talk, but he

was too much taken aback to offer any solace. "Been to B-town?" he asked.

"Yeah, that's where I been."

"Big night?"

"Had a pretty sorry night."

"Mercy," said Parker, "a mean-looking dude like you. Bad-town is getting *bad.*"

He meant his loutish, leering tone to suggest complicity, to reveal that he, a white man, knew what Arthur was up to when he left the barracks and didn't hold it against him. He used the barracks idiom clumsily, and he saw that his excessive heartiness grated on Arthur, yet Arthur remained in the alcove of lockers, shoving the cap in and out of shape.

"I feel used up," Arthur said at once. "This bush I been going with called it off."

"That's what's bothering you?"

"Yeah."

"There's got to be others," Parker said.

"That's the thing. I'm not looking for others."

But Parker wasn't able to believe that, and he persisted in his goony cheer. Arthur's forbearance became more apparent with each new insult—for insult, Parker later realized, was how his remarks must have been taken by a man who was feeling any real sorrow. He treated Arthur precisely as though he were not capable of sorrow, as though sorrow were not a possibility in the sort of relationship he was likely to have with a European girl who would take up with him. It was Arthur who stopped him, finally, by asking about the book, *Demian,* that lay on the floor beside the bed. The cover showed the naked torso of a woman from whom emanated two spectral males, one from her left shoulder and the other from her ribs. "What's this spook shit you reading?"

"You ought to read it," Parker urged at once. "The picture won't make any sense unless you do." In an instant he planned the development: soulful white GI introduces black barracks-mate to elevated literature and thus is formed the basis of lasting interracial friendship. He was sincere, even solemn, when he coaxed Arthur to accept the loan of the book; the role of missionary fitted him more closely than that of friend.

"I'll try it out," Arthur said. "It looks like I'm gone to be needing some reading material."

So the conversation which began with Arthur's reaching for the most standard kindness ended with that didactic charity. Arthur read the book (Parker saw it in the pocket of his fatigues the next day, and he had to check the impulse to speak out, for he had an abomination of bruised paperbacks), but his scornful reaction to it snuffed out Parker's hopes. "This is about the most ridiculous excuse for a book I ever read," Arthur snorted when he tossed *Demian* onto Parker's cot. "Tell me something: you ever see a woman rear up like a mountain and stars pop out of her head, like Sinclair sees in this book?"

"It didn't really happen."

"Knowing that," Arthur snorted again. "I tell you what the only good part was in the whole sorry book. It was right at the beginning, when that kid is blackmailing Sinclair, you remember? And Sinclair asks Demian what he should do, and ole Max says, 'Kill him,' just like that." Arthur laughed. "He don't even think it over, just says kill that nasty little mother. Scat! Off him!"

Arthur's laugh was as remote from Parker as if it had bounced off the skin of a tribal drum. He took it to be the purest expression of race, and with it Arthur Kin disappeared into the black skin that Parker could see. His plan

33

collapsed, and he didn't pursue the dialogue which had gone irrecoverably astray. He ascribed to Arthur ignorance which verged on barbarism, and though he later revised his opinion—he reconsidered that incident at compulsive length, trying to locate the moment at which the exact shape of his blunder could be descried—he was not able to win from the episode any saving lesson.

"We were right back where we started," he said to Amsy.

"It sounds as though you wouldn't have been satisfied unless he'd fallen in love with you," Amsy said, "and proposed on the spot. Maybe if you'd been able to take it easy—"

"What I've been trying to tell you," Parker said with some heat, "is that there were reasons why I *couldn't* take it easy."

"Sorry," Amsy protested.

"I wanted a more natural relationship with him," Parker said more gently, "but I didn't have—what? The right experience, I guess. Arthur's not like Commando, or Leroy's kids, or any of the people I knew around here."

"Isn't he? He's from Biloxi."

"We weren't in Biloxi, we were in Germany."

"Didn't you ever get any closer to him? Why did you ask him to ride home with you when you met up in Amsterdam if you were such strangers?"

"I didn't intend to ask him."

"What happened?"

What did happen? It was hard to account for it. Parker had to explain the complications of shipping home his Volkswagen and he mentioned, in passing, the existence of Erika. After parting with her at the Karlsruhe Bahnhof— and he refused, despite Amsy's prodding, to say more about Erika: "I'd never stay awake long enough to finish if

34

I started on that"—he delivered the car to Rotterdam. The shipper couldn't guarantee that the VW would be on the pier in Newark earlier than the twenty-eighth of August, and not wishing to arrive in New Jersey before the car did, Parker found himself with three weeks on his hands. He hitchhiked through Denmark and Sweden in pelting rainstorms, and he decided to abandon that discouraging pastime and spend his last days in Amsterdam before proceeding to Rhein Main to claim his space on a military flight to MacGuire AFB, New Jersey.

He didn't have, at the lingering end of his journey, the spirit to yield to another foreign place. He trudged about Amsterdam and dutifully aimed his vision at scrolled façades, but he saw nothing that was not alien. Feeling dull and thirsty after one of his outings, he stepped into a thronged café, and because he heard a few words of English among the languages in use, he took a seat at the bar in the hope of company. The other customers at the bar, however, were men just off work who knocked back a slug of gin, looked for its effect in the mirror opposite, drew deep breaths, and plunged again into the street. The talkers were all at the tables, and Parker turned from his own image in the stippled yellow glass to look about him.

He promptly noticed at the back of the room a blond girl accompanied by a black man. There was no reason, apart from his tiresome southern vigilance, why his eye should have alighted upon that pair in a room that presented an ethnic compendium; yet his attention passed over a glamorous Asian girl swatting her monkey, over a cluster of purple turbans that bobbed like stormy little clouds, even over a group of Africans adorned with gold and bone, to stick upon an ordinary sort of girl with straight light hair and her companion. The girl's face was almost hidden by the fall of her hair, but the man's features were plain enough and took a precise definition from the metal glasses he wore. The two leaned toward each other across the table, above the disorder of cups and saucers in which their hands were clutched, and Parker thought that it was their appearance of intimacy, rather than any sense of disapproval, which attracted and held his eye. He supposed ruefully that he would never be able to look at such a couple without remembering where he came from.

He experienced a variety of longings as he watched them, and he began a vague process of placing the black man. An American, he was sure, despite the broad-sleeved shirt of mauve Indian fabric, despite the fancy choker of turquoise beads around his neck. His hair was too political, his color too diluted, for him to be anything but American. Very likely the man was a soldier, or ex-soldier, as Parker himself was; the glasses looked to be government issue—and then the fact came to him with momentous chagrin. The man was Arthur Kin. The face was one he'd seen a hundred, a thousand times, in worse light and from less advantageous angles, a face he had studied with some deliberation. It had never opened much to him, and it was framed differently now, but still it was a face which Parker should have named as easily as he recognized his own hand, which loomed before him with a glass of beer and providentially concealed him from Arthur. He hid his face in that glass of beer and turned back to the bar and mirror to seek composure. He told himself that Arthur Kin should by now have been home in Biloxi, that the hair and costume had misled him, that no one would be on the lookout for an old barracks-mate in a Dutch café, but he knew that his lapse was indicative. He was uncertain how to act, whether to ignore Arthur or to approach him, whether, if he did approach, to pretend that his recognition was immediate or to acknowledge his absent-mindedness—not that Arthur would particularly care. Would Arthur resent an interruption of his conversation with the girl? Was his conversation as intimate as it appeared? Had he ever told the girl about the Army? About Parker? What had he told her? The questions proliferated, and Parker felt guilty, but also impatient and silly. He disliked his muddle, although muddle was the familiar shape of his attitude toward Arthur, and, as usual, he put a stop to it with a few simple reflections. He *had* shared a room with Arthur Kin, occupied the same quarters for longer than a year, and he *had* belatedly recognized him in that improbable café; it was an encounter that ought to be completed.

Therefore he rose, beer still in hand, and bore down resolutely on the couple. When Arthur saw him, he too rose, and the first word Parker heard was "Mercy," that ironic barracks cry, followed by his own name, "Parker! Hey, Parker! Hey, man, you in Amsterdam!"

His recognition was so prompt, his enthusiasm so unexpected, that Parker was embarrassed by his own mood, and as heads, including those cumulous turbans, bent toward the commotion, Parker wished that Arthur could be a little less demonstrative. "You been following me?" Arthur asked. "What you doing here?" Then Parker reached the table, and Arthur's hand disengaged itself from the girl's; Parker shifted his glass in order to shake it, but he didn't get the grip right; Arthur wanted to link thumbs, a hold Parker had never attempted but which he at once guessed to be an expression of militant sentiment. He bungled it— no solidarity in that handshake—but Arthur's good humor didn't falter. He said, "Take that cold right hand and grab a chair, then sit down and tell me where you been at."

Arthur introduced him—"Here's one of um I lived with all that time in Badstein"—to the blond girl, whose name was Katrin and who spoke a very correct, clipped English. It seemed to Parker that she was vexed by the interruption, but Arthur remained exclamatory. "You looking good," he told Parker. "Taking that uniform off was a improvement."

"And how long have you been in Amsterdam?" Parker asked, hearing how dry his own voice was.

"Since April, right after I got separated. Started out to go to Sweden and those places up there, but I never got no farther than Amsterdam. Man, this is *the* city."

Arthur reached to touch Katrin's arm, and he appeared to mean that he had stopped in Amsterdam because she was there. "I got to show you around," he said. "I know this place better'n I ever want to know Biloxi. But tell me how you came in here—you been following me, like I asked you before?"

"I just wandered in."

"Seeing you makes me think of old Gentile, crazy Davy. How's he doing? And what about Strickland, that sorry dude?"

Arthur cheerfully recalled the inkstain that was permanent as a birthmark on Gentile's tongue—Davy had a habit of licking his draftsman's pen—and Strickland's sinister wall-eye. He wanted to reminisce about Army times, the fatigues and grievances they'd shared, but Parker was less nostalgic than Arthur, for he was suspicious. He'd never seen Arthur so genial—was he stoned? There was dope all over Amsterdam and Arthur certainly looked as if he'd know the way to find it. Parker inventoried the man before him, remembering both the taciturn Pfc and the flashy spade who went out strutting in Badstein; this new Arthur, with his Flemish girl and his third-world clothes, with his good-earth jewelry and his voluminous hairdo, had adopted the trappings of the movement. His language, however, was still plain Mississippi.

"But when'd you get separated?" Arthur asked him. "It's been long enough to grow you a head of hair. Ain't it peculiar"—here he patted his own head—"the way us GIs just let it sprout? I don't care if I never hear another clippers buzzing round my head. You ought to seen that shriveled-up little mother that cut our hair at Badstein," he said to Katrin, and he described for her the chart of authorized haircuts in the base barbershop. "They wasn't no Afro in it, so I always asked him to cut my hair like the Ivy League picture." With a gesture that laid his hair flat he won a smile from the girl, who looked up from her intent shredding of a paper napkin. Parker wondered that she was able to understand Arthur's diction at all, and he waited for Arthur to veer round again to his inquiry, prepared to hold up his end of the dialogue by filling him in on his itinerary from Badstein to Amsterdam.

But the evocation of the barbershop led Arthur to thoughts of Boyles, the mean First Sergeant, and speculation about the man's outrage if he could see them now— "Boyles take one look at us, man, and they wouldn't be nothing but a little smoke and some brass buttons where he used to be standing before he burnt up"—and from there to a recollection of their insubordination on Exercise Deep Hole, when Boyles brought them before the bar of military justice. Arthur called upon Parker to witness the details of the story, but he told it for the benefit of the girl. He seemed to wish to draw her into his own mood of gaiety. Parker had the impression that the mood was willed, that Arthur was applying the chance meeting to uses of his own. What had they been talking about? What could have prompted Arthur to this performance of delight? Parker couldn't guess, but he decided to leave them to resume their own communication as soon as he politely could. It appeared that the possibilities of the encounter were the same as the possibilities they'd already had; although they were both out of uniform, and although a film of shared experience stretched over the meeting, Parker felt that the unity Arthur attempted to enact was spurious. The familiar divisions still existed. Parker agreed with Arthur that their Deep Hole punishment had been worth it, since they'd got rid of Strickland as their Room Commander, and he drank down his beer. "I'm just as glad it's over," he said. "Deep Hole, Badstein, all of it."

"Knowing that. It's a whole lot nicer to set here and think back on it than it was to do it."

"It looks like you're settled here. You staying much longer?"

"Not sure." Arthur shrugged. "What about you? You going home?"

Parker laboriously explained the complications of his forthcoming journey, concluding, "I'll drive south as soon as I pick the car up in Newark."

"So when you going to Rhein Main?"

"Day after tomorrow."

"You got a ticket on the big ceegar?"

"Going standby."

"And what you hurrying home to?"

"Going back to school."

"With all that good VA money."

"Righty-right."

"I'd like to get me some of that," Arthur said. "Maybe it's a school over here I could go to, where I could learn to talk Dutch." He touched Katrin's arm once again, but she did not respond.

"I'll be off, then," Parker said. "Maybe we'll bump into each other again."

"How come you want to run off? You hatn't seen Amsterdam," Arthur said, but the cheer had left his voice. "Let me show you this town."

Parker was standing. "Too late. I feel like I'm on my way already."

"Listen, what you doing tonight? You want me and Katrin to take you poking round?"

The offer seemed sincere enough, but the insistence annoyed Parker. What did Arthur imagine he could show him? Did he want to fix him up with one of Katrin's friends? Now there was an idea, Arthur procuring for him. His doubts about Arthur's motives had not abated, and he said blandly that he had a few things to do before he left Amsterdam.

"What you got to do? Pack your suitcase? How long does that take? You got to buy presents to carry home? I'll show you where to get um where it ain't all this tourist junk."

"Thanks, Arthur, but I really ought to be on my way."

"Mister Busy," said Arthur, and Parker was almost relieved to catch the faint sound of truculence.

"It sure has been nice," he said. He pushed his chair forward and he was about to nod a farewell to the girl when Arthur also stood.

"Hang on just one minute. You mind if I 'company you to the street? It's something I'd like to say."

Parker didn't seem to have any choice. He shrugged and made his way to the front of the café. At the door he stopped, thinking Arthur and Katrin were behind him, but

Arthur was still at the table, offering the seated girl an explanation of some sort. She listened stiffly and did not look up at him when he moved away. "She gone to wait for me here," Arthur said. "Let's me and you step outside."

Arthur led the way onto the sidewalk, turned at once into a short alleyway that was bedecked with laundry. The rusty-looking ironwork on the windows bore pots of blooming flowers which had been set out to take the air. The alley soon debouched into a calm, shaded canal street where children played on the pavements a game that resembled hopscotch, skipping through chalked squares to the chant of a rubicund Dutchman selling herring and onions at a corner stand. The sun falling in the street made a filigree of the trees and created rows of sparkling, scalloped reflections in the panes across the water. Parker was careful to stay a pace behind Arthur, marching through that placid scene as though trouble were hidden everywhere, and keeping an apprehensive surveillance on the figure moving with a jaunty, rambling walk just before him.

"Tell me this ain't pretty." Arthur said "pooty" and he smiled at the scene in a proprietary way. "You blame me for wanting to stay here? And what you think of Katrin? I tell you what, this place been good to me, and I ain't in no big rush to trade it for more Biloxi."

Out of earshot of the herring vendor he slowed down and lingered at the edge of the water. "I guess you see what I'm asking you."

But, for all his suspicions, Parker didn't see. He came to a halt beside Arthur and stared down into the canal; the water was thick as gelatin and bits of refuse were embedded in it down to the lowest visible depths. Congested, malodorous, the canal did not return even a reflection of the city which Arthur declared beautiful and generous, but if

Parker could have looked a little more toward his companion, he might have noticed how the sun laid a sheaf of silver upon the ignoble waterway. As he gazed into the unclean water—and all of Amsterdam rises out of that element—he considered the city's reputation for tolerance, its civic pride in hospitality. Amsterdam! Where a black ex-GI could smoke dope, shack up, and wear a necklace—did it come to more than that?

"Lookit," Arthur said, "I don't know when I could pay you back, to be honest with you. But I done sold my car and spent that money and I spent my travel allowance that they gave me to get to Biloxi with and I'm hurting for cash."

Of course. He wanted money. That accounted for his joviality in the café, his attempt to persuade Parker to stay in Amsterdam. He'd been improvident and spendthrift and he was corrupt enough to affect friendship to get a loan out of Parker.

"I hate to ask you," Arthur continued, "but we been living on next to nothing. Ain't either one of us got a gilder. So I'm thinking that since you on your way, and you soon be getting on the VA payroll, maybe you got a little extra left over that you not gone to be needing. Like I said, I don't know when I could get it back to you, but it would be a kindness if you could trust me."

The request was fluent and not at all imploring. For the first time Parker knew exactly what he wanted to say. "I'd help you if I could, but I've got just enough left to get home on." He wasn't really lying, even though he had a thick wallet of traveler's checks in his pocket; it was quite true that he couldn't bring himself to bestow them on Arthur Kin. He began to itemize his prospective expenses, the customs duty and taxes on the car, and he believed he sounded convincing.

"Any little bit you got would be appreciated," Arthur interrupted. "I don't plan to stay here forever, just a little bit longer. That's why Katrin is so upset, see, because she knows I got to leave soon. But we been having some bad times, and I don't want to have to run off and leave her just in the middle of um."

"I'm cutting it close as it is," Parker replied. "The excise tax—"

"Sound to me like you holding out," Arthur said calmly.

That impertinent accusation, which seemed also to contain a threat, settled the matter. Had Arthur been humble, Parker might have risen to magnanimity; at the mention of bad times, his fingers in his pocket had measured the thickness of the wad of checks. He understood rituals of that kind. But he wasn't going to be bullied and he thought he had every right to be indignant. "I told you I can't spare anything, but you can believe what you please."

"Check," Arthur replied. "I read you." Arthur turned to face him. "I'll be getting on back to Katrin. Maybe I'll see you on that big ceegar after all. Wouldn't that be a trip?"

"You think you'll be leaving soon?"

"Looks like it, don't it?"

"What will you do when you get to New Jersey?"

"Go home to Mississippi. What else?"

"How are you thinking of getting there if you've already spent your travel allowance?"

"I don't feature walking," Arthur said.

And Parker told Amsy, who had heard him out with exemplary patience, "I saw what was called for." He offered Arthur a ride in his Volkswagen as far as Alabama, and he laughed tensely when Arthur accepted by saying, "Ain't that big-hearted of you, though?" They began to stroll along the canal in the direction from which they'd come, reaching an agreement to travel together from Amsterdam to Rhein Main. They were overtaken as they walked by the sound of a thumping engine, and presently by the pert varnished tour boat which it propelled; the passengers floated by at a distance of only a few meters. Parker had the vanity to be pleased that these strangers' glimpse of Amsterdam included him and Arthur, as though he had just performed an act which did credit to the city's tradition of generosity. The viscous water did not lift much in the boat's wake, and no waves slapped the foundations. A few numb swells undulated across the water without disturbing the detritus suspended in it. When Arthur took his leave and disappeared into the alleyway, Parker walked on alone, and for about as long as the water moved, he felt he had done the right thing.

He stopped talking, and Amsy, after a pause, when she was sure he had finished, asked him, "Well? Was it the right thing?"

"I suppose it was. I only wish my motives had been a little more virtuous."

"But you did give him a ride home, and he would've had to leave anyway. You always were a tight pocket. Who ever heard of having money left at the end of a trip?"

Parker smiled. "It was sticky having to hide my wallet the whole trip home. I didn't want him to find out I'd told him a fib."

"For a price I'll keep your secret."

Parker threw a dish towel at her. "Some sister."

She threw it right back, but he caught it and stood up. "If I don't get to bed, I'm not going to any picnic tomorrow. I think I look forward to it—I want to see the expression on Tom Finlay's face when he sees Arthur. It'll be worth the trip."

"Is that why you brought him, then?"

"Sure. I thought I'd make a declaration—one of my best friends is a spade, and here he is." He flung out his arm as if introducing Arthur to a crowd.

"Have you no shame?"

"Too much. We can't settle that subject tonight. I am going to stagger up to my bed now and sleep the sleep of the just."

Three

On Saturday morning Parker was awakened by a rapping on his door. His long sleep had not refreshed him; he felt immensely heavy and dull, as though he had slept underneath a mattress as well as upon one. "It's nine thirty," a voice called, "time to get up." He opened his eyes and saw in the midst of a white ceiling a bluish light fixture. With so little to orient him, he thought of Arthur Kin before he identified the voice as Amsy's and the room as his own. "Parker? Are you awake?" He replied in a furred mutter and when he moved he found that his right arm was also furred; it had been pinned behind his head and did not respond to his command to come forward. He rolled it along the bed like a tube of clay and hacked at it with his left hand to get the blood moving. The arm felt as if it were being devoured. Amsy said that she was going down to start his breakfast and her footsteps moved away from the door. She skipped down the steps to the landing and spoke again, this time to Arthur, but her words and his answer were indistinguishable. Parker wagged his protesting arm back to sentience and managed to get his feet on the floor.

It took him only a few minutes to wash, dress, and present himself downstairs, where he was immediately scandalized. Arthur was seated at the table in the glassed-in kitchen nook, and at the stove Amsy was wearing an arsenic-green bikini. The denim shirt she wore over it was unbuttoned, and she was therefore exposed from her throat to her omphalos to the gap of her loins. "Good morning," she said to Parker, "are you hungry?" He stared at her belly and she cocked her head and waved a spatula to get his attention away from it. "You look sort of deranged," she said, but she didn't close the shirt. "Sit down and I'll fix you some eggs. Dotty should be here any minute. We have to get out to the lake early, before the others."

Parker obeyed her. He sat down opposite Arthur and found that the smile on his guest's face was sheepish and cunning. Beyond Arthur, through the window, he saw his mother at work in the garden, her back bent and her uncovered head flashing like a lens when it caught the sun. She was having nothing to do with the day's outing, and he remembered that Iva would not be in that morning. He wished that he too could absent himself so easily. Amsy kept up her talk from the frying pan and soon brought him eggs, her shirt flapping about her; Dotty arrived and coolly said hey, laughed at Parker's mustache, drank a cup of coffee, and smoked a Salem; she was reasonably dressed, but she and Amsy acted like Dixie darlings with a secret, and it seemed to Parker that they were barely able to refrain from rolling their eyes at one another. Yet he was not at all irate; he realized that he was simply resigned. A rebellious arm, his sister's belly, a black visitor, a morning that got thicker by the minute: it was useless to hold out against the day. Useless, or maybe just too late. Having come from

Amsterdam to Ewell, he couldn't call a halt to the drift that now carried them all forward.

After their eggs and coffee, they gathered up the picnic goods and stepped out the door into the sort of morning in which the sun does not bestow color upon objects but instead deprives them of it, fades them instead of vivifying them, the sort of light that hurts the eyes—but they were all wearing tinted glasses. Mrs. Livingston was not, and she straightened up in a plot of roses to wish them all a good time. She was a bit disheveled and her face was rapt and flushed. An arc of sweat glistened upon her upper lip. In one gloved hand she held an implement that looked like a claw and she waved it absent-mindedly. It did not appear to cost her an effort to turn back to the roses, to leave her children to whatever fate awaited them. She did not even bother to watch them dispose themselves in Dotty's car, an Impala convertible.

The top of the car was folded back, one more invitation to trouble. They approached it laden with baskets of food and armfuls of towels and canvas bags crammed with sunning equipment. Parker didn't think it was very prudent to take to the public highways of Manspile County in an open car, not on a steamy Saturday morning and not in the company of a black male and a half-covered white girl. But he wasn't going to send Amsy back into the house to change and he couldn't order Dotty to raise the top, and anyway he had already acquiesced. He chucked his burden of towels into the back seat and then they all looked at the pavement, four young people bedecked with sunglasses, overcome with bashfulness, getting belted by the sun, feeling the macadam soften under their feet. Finally Amsy adjusted her wide straw hat and gave Arthur a poke to get him into the car. She climbed in behind him and Dotty said,

"You drive," and handed Parker the keys.

And that was that. The black Dodge barreled past them ten miles from Ewell, a mile or so beyond Spivey's Store, on a straight empty stretch of road lined on either side with pines. Three Mile Flat—it was a famous piece of local track where every good ole boy rolled up his windows and tucked in his neck and stomped down his foot to the floorboards. The road surface was good there, but the Dodge was going so fast that as it came toward them Parker could see the front wheels slamming up and down beneath the upraised, unbouncing, forward body. The Dodge blew past them and even at that terrific speed Parker saw the bright red upholstery, the three pairs of shoulders which filled the front seat from window to window, the three heads which swiveled in unison. Sessions, Fuqua, Bates—in that instant, at that velocity, he recognized them. They were three characters who'd always been around Ewell, available at the pool hall or the barbershop, working at service stations or driving cabs—Parker wasn't sure what they did, but they were part of the permanent population, and he named them all at once without having to summon memory. It seemed to him that he'd waited years to see them arranged as they were in that Dodge. Sessions was driving and he braked immediately, first just touched the brakes and left blistering patches on the pavement, and then, when he'd slowed down enough, locked the brakes and burned two curving, smoking tracks that ended in the clay and weeds on the left-hand side of the road where the Dodge came to rest. It sounded like an accident, but it was no accident, as Dotty, Amsy, and Arthur, who all three turned at the noise, realized. Parker watched in the rear-view mirror; he saw the black rubber smoke rising, the orange clay flung out from under the wheels as the Dodge began its pursuit of them, the grille and lights of the Dodge as it plunged through the hot warps of air that rose from the baking highway. No accident, but it was no mirage either, despite the distorting shimmer. It was the thing itself, and Arthur Kin also recognized it. In the mirror Parker watched him turn back again, lower himself into the seat, fix his eyes on the road straight ahead.

Parker drove forward at a calm sixty as though it were the most innocent thing in the world to be on his way to a picnic in the sticks of central Alabama with his sister in the back seat in a tiny bikini accompanied by a black Army buddy. He even, as Sessions gained on them, let the speedometer needle fall below sixty, for he did not want to get into a high-speed duel with the Dodge, and he believed that any sign of evasion or flight would seem a challenge. The Dodge came on, closing quickly; Amsy was on her knees on the back seat, facing it, her hand raised to keep her big straw hat on her head. "Go on, Parker," she urged, "go on, go on, go on."

"We can't outrun them."

So he waited to be overtaken, and they all heard the Dodge when it braked again, right behind them, heard the tires bite when the gears changed. And they all watched— all but Arthur, whose arms were folded on his chest—the Dodge ease up until the bumpers were nearly touching, saw clearly the three malevolent grins, Fuqua's explicitly obscene signals with both hands pressed against the windshield. The Dodge tapped them, fell off a few yards, tapped them again—not hard enough to damage the cars or knock them out of control, not hard enough to snap their heads backward, just hard enough to make certain they knew they were being rapped. Their pursuers were laughing and jeering, having a rousing high time in the lurching Dodge, and they howled when Amsy's hat flew off and flapped against their windshield—Fuqua instinctively ducked it and Bates pounded him on the back—and sailed over them before drifting and settling on the road behind. That's when Amsy began to shout back at them. Bastards! Idiots! Go away! Scram! Leave us alone! Parker really didn't know what she said, but she was answering them and leaning out over the folded top and banging her fists on the trunk of the Impala. The Dodge nudged them again and her extended body fell forward. The open denim shirt blew up over her back, and when Parker reached over the seat to grab her he caught only the lower half of her green suit. He tugged, she tried to bat his hand away, he glimpsed her untanned skin and yelled, "Sit down, Amsy! Sit down!"

She was exposed, but she didn't care. "Those lousy bastards!" she hollered. "They're not going to get away with this! Don't you let them get away with it, Parker!"

She reached down to the floor of the car and picked up a heavy picnic jug and began to swing it by the handle as though she meant to throw it. Parker believed she would have thrown it too, if Sessions had touched them one more time. He didn't; he let the Dodge fall back, let Parker pull away on the first sharp curve at the end of that straight stretch, dropped out of sight in the hills and bends near Kingberry. Parker did not drive any faster, and Amsy remained posted and watchful on her knees, and she was satisfied only when they passed through the village of Kingberry, the boarded-up train station and the store plastered with advertisements. Four men—two white, two black, and Parker noticed them because their bench-sharing seemed so natural, placid, and serene—stared at them from the benches in the shade of the store's porch, and Amsy slipped down onto the seat.

"We can't let them get away with that," she said, leaning

52

forward and speaking into Parker's ear. "We ought to call the sheriff or the highway patrol as soon as we get to Dotty's."

He didn't answer her. He felt the warmth of her glare on him, but she held her tongue and did not press the argument. Shortly after Kingberry, Parker turned off the state road onto the Hirts' private road and drove through a mile of woods to their destination, a glassy A-frame cottage, the kind that comes in a kit, situated at the edge of a lake—not a real lake, but rather a man-made ten-acre watering pond for Mr. Hirt's cattle, which were grazing on the pastures across the way. It must have seemed to Arthur that his hosts wanted to settle their dispute without him, for he wandered off to examine the heaped earth of the dam, leaving them to thrash out the law-enforcement issue as if the incident had not concerned him at all. As soon as he was out of earshot, Amsy said, "Are you going to call anyone?"

"Who do you want me to call? Sheriff Flood? He'd be pretty amused, wouldn't he?"

"What do you mean?"

"I mean when he saw you in that bathing suit. What do you suppose he'd think?"

"That I was going swimming."

"Oh, wonderful, Amsy. Good answer."

"What difference does it make what I'm wearing, anyway? They tried to run us off the road."

"No they didn't. They just tried to scare us. They wanted to remind us where we were."

"It's still reckless driving."

"But the sheriff wouldn't do anything about it if he knew you and Arthur were in the back seat, and that's the point."

"It's not either the point," Amsy protested, and her voice was raised. "You don't know what he would do. You're not going to call for some low-minded reasons of your own. That's what you're saying."

"It's not what I'm saying."

"That's how it sounds to me, as though you're embarrassed that you brought Arthur home and ashamed of me. I think you're a dope if you don't call and get those crackers off the road."

"Thanks for the advice. Are you done?"

She was. She stalked out of the house and busied herself with the chores. She and Dotty carried all the food into the house while Parker opened the sliding doors and windows. The place had been locked up for some time; the heat smelled of the cedar paneling, and the air was hot enough to scorch lungs. Parker was sweating after he'd set up the tables and umbrellas on the deck overlooking the pond, and he changed into bathing trunks and delivered himself to the water. On that particular morning the water was neither cool nor refreshing but especially sluggish and scummy, filmed with the tiny translucent bodies of drowned winged insects. Swimming out to the float in the middle of the pond, Parker kept getting mouthfuls of the water and the minute corpses, and when he stopped kicking and splashing, the hungry perch nibbled at his knees and toes. His swimming became a struggle and he flailed away at that element without succeeding in churning it up; it had a consistency almost of mud, and the second he abated his squirming it closed round him again with its dull, indifferent pressure. When he got near the float he felt like screaming and he dived down to do it, but the cries he directed at the muddy bottom did not penetrate more than a few inches before they turned to bubbles and squirted back into his face, and those that missed him merely rose to the surface, where they hissed like butter in a hot pan and promptly expired.

Nevertheless, Parker was calmer when he left the water, and he felt that he had vented the most urgent of the morning's frustrations. He accepted that black Dodge as conclusive, a submission that was more strenuous than any he had yet made. He believed that he'd confronted most of his own enormities, but he wanted to be wrong about his native place. He had not brought Arthur Kin home to solicit danger, violence, or bloodshed; he had wanted Ewell, his family, his people, to be better than he thought them capable of being, more peaceful, more generous, more just. He had hoped that he might, if his worst idea of them could be proved wrong, learn from them. But he wasn't wrong—except maybe about Amsy, whose mettle seemed to him more like the verve of a pom-pom girl than like virtue—and the arrival of his oldest friends, now metamorphosed into fraternity brothers and sorority sisters, only hardened his opinions.

Parker felt entirely collected and heartless as he watched them arrive. They made a lot of noise getting from their cars to the deck, and they popped open cans of beer with an enthusiasm that seemed excessive. They continued to make noise as they chose places beneath the umbrellas or stretched out to offer themselves to the rays of that unbecoming sun. Their banalities and preoccupations, their transistor radios and accents inspired Parker with detachment and contempt. Well Pah-kuh ole boy how does it feel to be back from the wars? See a lot of combat ovuh theah in Germany? Why Pah-kuh that mustache makes you look so mah-chure and day-ring, you devil you.

But the real devil, it was clear to Parker, was Arthur Kin.

He was wearing a small yellow sling of a bathing suit which revealed more black skin than the good young people of Ewell were accustomed to seeing and they didn't seem to like what they saw. They asked the questions that Parker had already heard from Amsy and his mother, but his answers didn't seem to make Arthur any easier to adjust to. Parker found it impossible, however, to take any satisfaction from the discomfort of his old friends. As for Arthur, he deflected most of the talk aimed at him, and the cumbersome solemnity of Arthur's questioners reminded Parker of the attitude of children carrying their little plaster sheep and donkeys to the manger in the Christmas procession— with mischievous levity or just plain silliness. He played constantly to Amsy, who he must have felt was his only ally in that crowd, and she kept herself close to him. After the topic of the Army and the trip home was set aside, Amsy gave a brittle summary of the friction on the highway, which was greeted by vague, sympathetic murmurs.

"Really! You'd think that sort of thing had ended."

"It's hard to believe."

"Sessions? I know that guy—a real greaser."

"Did they try to run you off the road?"

"Parker says they didn't," Amsy said. "They were just playing, he thinks."

"It was a lot of fun," Arthur added, "real exciting. It gave me a big charge."

"Did you report them?"

"Parker didn't recommend it," Amsy said.

"I didn't see the use of it," Parker defended himself.

"Well, it's a shame that it had to happen."

"I wouldn't have believed it could."

"I don't mind," Arthur said. "It made me feel right important to get all that attention."

And by a process of association that was perhaps natural, the discussion glided toward the subject of the recent convention in Chicago. The sudsy opinions on the deck were evenly divided; some approved the head-knocking and some did not; those who approved, Parker thought, were a bit inhibited by the presence among them of Arthur Kin. His view of those Democratic events was solicited, but he refused to take a moral position. He said that he would prefer to be on the side with the tear gas.

"You ever get that stuff on you when you were at basic?" he asked Parker. "I did, and it like to killed me. They made us take off the masks in this little shack where it was some tear gas burning like one of those pots on the highway— you didn't ever have to do that? We was sposed to stand there till the sergeant said put the masks back on, but I notice he never took his off to start with. My nose got to running like a faucet, and I wasn't thinking about putting on no mask, I was thinking about getting out of there. Cept I couldn't see the door with that stuff in my eyes. You ought to heard me banging on the wall of that shack, like playing a drum. The side to be on is the one with the tear gas."

"Come on," Amsy said. "You're not in favor of what the police did."

"Did I say I was? I'm talking about gas."

"What do you think of the mayor?"

"He's just like a mean old drill sergeant, see, and he's got these draftees that all of a sudden figure out how he's got hold of them—by the family jewels, that's where he's got um. So they get to carrying on and hollering lemme out, like me in the gas shack, and it's so many of um hollering all at once that the sergeant, he starts throwing gas everywhere, till it's inside and out. Then he opens the door for um."

Arthur chuckled, but no one seemed to get the parable, if that's what it was. Parker did understand, however, that Arthur was toying with his audience, and that his whimsy was attaching Amsy to him. When lunch was brought, those two had a mock combat with the skewers they were roasting wieners on, and they sat together under one of the umbrellas to eat from those weapons. The day was turning out to be a boiler, and the beer was rapidly converted to sweat; there was a steady drip, drip, drip as it slipped over cultivated Coppertone tans and fell to the deck. Because of the heat, all warnings about cramps were disregarded, and people took to the water immediately following lunch. The boat was cranked up, water-skiing got under way, and after a few showy performances on the boards by the experts in the group, Arthur was invited to have a try.

"I never been on those things," he said, but he was pressed by Amsy, among others, to give it a whirl. Making noises and gestures of reluctance, he allowed himself to be led into the water and he took hold of the rope. "Don't snatch too hard," he called to Tom Finlay, at the wheel of the boat, "I don't want to lose my specs." Amsy told him he might as well take off the sunglasses before he started, but he didn't have time to argue with her; the boat was off with a roar, and to the general disappointment of the spectators, Arthur kept the skis under him. A little wobbly at first, he picked up enough confidence after a turn or two around the small pond to venture a leap back and forth across the wake, and by the fourth circuit he was cocky enough to wave and bow as he sped past the deck and the little pier. Tommy decided to add to the amusement by testing Arthur, putting him through a few tight circles and then, with Arthur spinning like a stone in a sling, straightening out and giving him yards of slack before jerking him up again, but he couldn't dump him or even knock off those shades. The contest seemed to grow grim, and there was an end to bowing and waving; Arthur was just trying to stay upright. Tom ran the boat hard toward the dam and took a hairpin turn so that Arthur, clipping along at a colossal rate, skimmed around outside the wake and only a few yards from the shore. When he came into the shallow shelf at the corner of the pond, the roostertail changed from a clear spray to an arc of mud, the fins of the skis bit into the shelf like plows, and Arthur took a tumble. He skidded over the muck like a goose coming in for a landing, and there was a good deal of hilarity under the fringed umbrellas. Arthur was cross. He left the skis in the pond—his glasses were still, remarkably, perched on his nose—and walked back to the pier, where he shook off the mud in wet, heavy glops. "Right shallow over there in that corner," he said. "Guess ole Tom didn't know that."

For the rest of the afternoon Arthur stayed near Amsy, and she took upon herself the responsibility of entertaining him. The two of them spent hours on the pedalboat splashing and whooping in the middle of the pond. They played interminable games of Alligator and Marco Polo, and in her apparent desire to illustrate to them all how shabbily they'd treated a visitor, Amsy went farther than she should have. She dug her fingers into his wet hair and ducked him and their bodies slipped against each other in the deepest parts of the pond and Arthur, his head agleam with the drops that stayed in his hair, came up sputtering and spouting. The spectators on the pier and deck did not approve, and Parker knew exactly what they were thinking because he was thinking it himself.

During the course of the afternoon most of the guests, disgruntled and burping, returned to Ewell, and by the time Amsy and Arthur rigged up fishing lines and set out in the canoe to try for the bass rising on the far shore, the last of them had departed. Their terse farewells upset Dotty, who maintained a sullen silence as she and Parker gathered up the paper plates and beer cans. The sun, mercifully, was disappearing over the horizon of pines, and in the tawdry pink of its descent, its only display of the day, the fishermen gave up and paddled the canoe slowly back to the pier. "Guide this thing, Arthur. We're going in a great big circle." "You guide it your own self. I ain't no Indian." Amsy's blade swooped and smacked the water and sent a spray over Arthur. The canoe wobbled and their laughter spread over the smooth black pond. "Amsy certainly is having a good time with your friend," Dotty said.

They stayed at the cottage for supper. That too had been planned, and it was a relief to Parker, after that eventful morning ride, to think that the drive home would be made in darkness. They all moved inside behind the screens, and while the women cooked hamburgers, Arthur and Parker began a sloppy game of gin rummy. The moon rose across the pond and its image, large and pale, seemed to open a shaft in the water. Moths battled the glass and screen, frogs croaked and fish splashed; the whole of a summer night descended and surrounded the lighted cottage.

Amsy came over and sat down beside Arthur on the long window seat. She was rubbing lotion into her wrinkled hands and Arthur reached his own palm back for a squirt of the stuff, but Amsy said, "You'll get the cards all greasy," and promptly whacked a handful of it into the middle of his back. Arthur sat up straight: "Feels like I been attacked by ice cream." Amsy laughed and rubbed the lotion in, then fetched a tube of sunburn cream. She started a couple of inches of it on her shoulders and sat on the floor below

Arthur, her head forward and her hair pulled aside to reveal her nape. She asked Arthur to return the favor of an application. "Careful, Arthur," she said, "don't—" But he had already found out for himself that she was ticklish, and Amsy rose up and went for him with the tube; he grabbed her and Amsy squirmed and smeared a dab of the lotion onto his chest, and both went down wriggling on the mats of the floor.

That's when they started shooting, and Parker wasn't even surprised. *Boom, ka-boom*—it sounded like the cannon on the Big Bam, and it echoed grandly over the water. Parker couldn't tell where it had come from because of the way sound and echo diffused themselves; it seemed as impersonal as a demonstration of weather. Yet there was no doubt that it was shooting, and Arthur and Amsy quit their wriggling and playful lubrications. Their bodies, which now seemed pitifully exposed, became still and tense, and Parker was tempted to say, You see? Do you believe me now? You don't get away with anything here. Another shot was fired and the amount of light diminished; Parker realized that the globe on the pole outside the house had been shattered, and he had also seen the flame from the rifle's muzzle. "Those bastards are back," Amsy said, but looking toward the darkness, Parker saw only his own reflection in the glass.

Arthur pushed himself up and leaped toward the light switch on the wall. All the interior lights were on the same panel, and he darkened the house with one sweep of his hand. A single light remained on the deck in front of the house; there was another shot, another little leap of fire, and the light burst. The bullet passed through the windows above the beams at the rear and front of the house, and despite the noise of the shot, the expansive *boooom,* Parker heard the bits of glass break out of the large panes and ring upon the floor. The noise was strangely delicate and distinct, and before it ceased, without any interval of silence, Dotty was crying. Parker hadn't heard her begin. Already her sobs, measured, steady, soft, sounded as though they had continued for hours. "I knew it, I knew it, I knew it," she said, and so, he thought, should they all have known it, did all know it: the deepest, most certain knowledge, the surest dread. Those men had to be out there; they were always out there. Hidden among the thick pines, on the clean needled floor under the pines, they were as inevitable as the night itself, as much in solution in that air as moonlight or echo. From inside the house they couldn't see them, but they didn't need to; as their vision adjusted to the darkness, as Dotty wept, they could make out the silvery grass and the front silvery row of pines, beyond them the unassuaged blackness spreading up the slope behind the house.

"We didn't shoot to hurt nobody," a voice called. They heard it plainly enough, though it seemed to drift down the hill slowly, and the words gathered, stood, faded.

"Not that time," added another.

"Won't no harm come to the white ones if you send the nigger out."

"He can come out running if he wants to."

They chuckled and muttered to each other. They seemed pleased with their sportsmanship. They sounded drunk, but it was, Parker recalled, Saturday night in Manspile County.

"You stinking cowards!" Amsy shouted at the woods. "You awful, sorry cowards!"

"Aw, missy, do you love him so much?"

"You won't have no trouble finding another."

"It ain't no shortage of dark meat."

The gunners chuckled again and talked to each other and inside the house they lay still on the floor. The moon was so bright that Parker could make out the shine of Arthur's body even though he was flattened in the shadow of a counter. "You think they'll leave?" Amsy whispered, but Parker didn't answer her. "Hush, Dotty," she whispered, "they won't hurt us. They'll just go away after a while. They only want to scare us."

"We want that nigger and we're getting kinda impatient," called the voice, and Parker saw Arthur begin to slide toward the door. "Tell you what: we'll give you two minutes to turn him out, and I'm starting to keep the time as of this second."

Arthur was crawling toward the glass doors of the deck. "Don't do it," Amsy said. "If they see you out there, they'll kill you." Arthur didn't answer, didn't turn, didn't stop. "Listen, Arthur, they can't shoot in here. They won't risk hitting us. They'll go away if we just stay here and be quiet. Arthur, Arthur, stop!"

She couldn't hold him. He opened the screen door carefully and crawled across the deck. He went down the steps and Parker expected to hear at any moment fire from the slope. None came. "Why didn't you stop him?" Amsy hissed. "They're going to shoot him."

"Let's get in the kitchen," he said. "We'll be safer in there."

They moved across the floor. The kitchen wall which faced the slope was solid, no glass, and the stove and refrigerator were also on that wall. They sat with their backs against the appliances, and Dotty interrupted her sobbing to wail that the hamburgers had been forgotten. Amsy reached up and turned off the burner and took the frying pan off the coil and put her fingers on Dotty's lips. "Hush now. Hush."

"Time's up," the voice said. "We've waited just about as long as we're minded to."

"He's not here!" Amsy shouted. "He's already gone back to town!" She knew, as Parker did, that they'd seen Arthur inside, but she evidently thought that if she talked to them she could gain time for Arthur.

"Forget that story, missy. We seen him in the house with you. We know he's in there."

"He's not. He's already gone."

Several shots were fired in a burst, so close together that they couldn't have been counted. Parker didn't know where those shots were aimed—not at Arthur anyway, because they hadn't seen him yet. There was another chapter of echoes, but somebody on the slope objected. Parker heard him say, "Careful, goddamnit. He ain't the only one in there."

Then the spotlight flooded the house with such a rush of light that it seemed to have created it. The furniture and mats sprang into view, along with the scattered cards on the table and the crimped tube of sunburn cream dropped on the floor. The edge of the light was not a yard away from Parker.

"Aw, ain't this fun. They're hiding on us."

"I done asked for the last time. Now lemme see that nigger. Lemme see his black ass now."

From the woods two more shots were fired, both of them through the upper windows just below the roof. Parker could see the enormous webs that set instantly in the big panes of glass, for the light caught in every line. He couldn't see the glass at all, only the webs that appeared in it, as though there was nothing left between him and those armed men but a screen of cracks fixed in the light, a membrane of destruction. "Stop it, stop it, stop!" he screamed, and he stepped into the light.

They did stop. They waited. He looked directly up the hill into the source of light and he walked toward it, through the door and out of the house. "You ain't him," one of them said, "and we are through fucking around here. Where is he at?"

The question surprised him. In those few steps he'd forgotten himself and what he was doing there, and now something as unthinking as his blood responded for him. He lifted his arm and pointed: "Down by the pond. There." Though the light shone on the length of his arm, Parker hardly knew it as his own. The way his thumb was raised, his finger pointed—his hand imitated a pistol. His thumb the cocked hammer, index finger the barrel, his hand was as fatal as any weapon they possessed in the woods. The light remained on him for several seconds; he didn't move. Then the eye of the beam turned and the cone of light glided from him. They had the sign they wanted.

They scanned the shore deliberately, without hurry, until the beam reached the shallow corner where earlier Arthur had fallen in the mud. Sighting down the arm which he did not lower, Parker saw all that happened. There, exactly where he pointed, Arthur lay behind a tiny cedar, the only bush on that bank, and it divided him. The bush wasn't much bigger than a top hat; the line of Arthur's bunched shoulders appeared on one side of it, the backs of his thighs on the other. On the slope they laughed when the light centered on him, and it did seem funny that a man running for his life would hide so poorly. Arthur got up slowly, facing the light, and for an absurd instant Parker thought that it was all over, a contest that ended with a simple act of finding. Then a rifle bolt was slammed home, and Arthur was running; Parker could not see him precisely, not his shape, only the flash of the yellow bathing trunks and shifting gleams on his arms, flanks, and legs. They were firing, but still Parker did not believe that he could be killed, did not believe that a bullet shot into that insubstantial motion of light, into the glowing arcs that seemed to linger in the air after Arthur had passed, could kill him. There was a gaudy beauty in his flight as he ran toward the nearest point of trees; the swirling, luminous nebulae generated by his passage left a message in the air like a child's sparkler.

Then the roar of the guns ceased altogether. If there were echoes over the pond, Parker didn't hear them. In the same instant, clarity returned, and the air contained only Arthur Kin. His head was bent back as if on a hinge, the leg coming forward stopped, and his arms streamed behind his body. He looked as if he were already dead, soaring, not touching the earth at all, but he fell to it with the terrible, final thump of a bird downed in a field. His full, falling weight, the smack of matter, a single slight bounce as his shoulders lifted and his body skidded forward on the damp grass, and then he lay still. The spotlight was extinguished after a due pause, for they had concluded that they would not have to shoot again. They did not speak, did not make any sound—no footsteps, no banging of weapons, no snapping of twigs—that Parker could hear. Darkness, silence: the woods were empty and black behind the first moonlit paling of trees, as if no one had been there at all. When Parker lowered his hand, the frogs and crickets resumed, a fish jumped and rocked the reflection of the moon on the placid water.

The disturbances all ended so absolutely, and the night resumed so casually, that for a moment Parker came near believing that he had imagined everything. He had not pointed, they had not shot—it was just another muggy summer night that belonged to the frogs, the fish, and the moon, and another black man was slain. He did not doubt that even when he doubted the rest of it. Blinded by the glare that had now been removed, he started walking toward the spot where the body had fallen, and when his sight came back to him he made out a human form in the wet clover. Arthur lay on his front, his arms stretched uselessly at his sides, palms up. His legs were spread apart, the soles of his feet were also up; he seemed to have landed comfortably in the deep, dewed clover. Parker knelt beside him.

"Act like I'm dead," Arthur whispered.

"Arthur!"

"Shut up."

Parker's heart was beating like a sparrow's. It was as if he were the one resurrected, not Arthur, and he felt not just his heart but the air invading his lungs, breath flying past his face, the racing of his senses. To have breath, and to see it equaled on Arthur's rising back—that was more of life, and love, than he had ever seen before.

And he knew exactly what had happened. Arthur was not injured, but had launched his body in that deathlike fall in order to escape. Living, he had been a target, but his imitation of death had delivered him. Ancient cunning, playing possum. Parker wanted to hoot, it was such a consuming hoax. Arthur cautioned him again, above the grassy murmur of his breath, to keep silent so that he would not give him away before the men with the guns had departed.

"Parker? Parker?" Amsy began to call, from the house at first, an urgent cry that carried to him along the shore. He didn't answer. Her voice rose, a door slid, and she began to walk toward them.

"Parker? Where's Arthur?"

She was close enough to see him. She advanced slowly. She stopped when she was within ten paces of her brother. "He's dead, isn't he?"

"Guess again," Arthur said, and he rolled onto his back and sat up facing her. He chuckled, *tee hee.*

Amsy groaned and covered her face with her hands. She sobbed, coming forward to look at Arthur and to touch him. "Hush," Arthur said, helping her to her feet. "No crying, and no hollering until we let those dogs clear out of the woods."

They made their way back along the water to the house, Parker following them. Their whispers, trembling with joyous excitement, seemed as much a part of that restored night as the noises of other creatures. *I'm here, I'm here—* that's all they could have been saying to each other. Trailing along behind them, Parker realized that his trip home was completed. He had returned to Alabama, to that night, to those people, and he could not conceive how to make amends to them, how to unite himself with them, how to say, as they were saying, *I'm here.*

2

Four

He had chosen the small, orderly room at the back of the house. The only table was placed before a window; seated there, he looked over the yard and down into the lattice of brick walks which contained his mother's flowerbeds. The air was alive with birds. Sparrows and warblers dipped and darted, ascended and plummeted, agitated by the abundance of that feeding ground. Cardinals splashed a profusion of sunflower seeds onto the brick, and the downy and red-bellied woodpeckers alighted with momentary nerve on the balls of suet. Yet, for all their activity, the birds were entirely silent; they neither sang nor chirped, and there was nothing for him to hear through the open window. The sounds he made—scrape of the chair on the wooden floor, crepitation of paper—seemed to strike abusively the aroused ganglia of his spine and neck. He strove to make his preparations without sound and he sat forward with exaggerated care, but he succeeded only in hearing more acutely the creak of the wood, the brush of his hand on the paper, his own laborious breathing. For a time he did not move, as if perfect stillness might accommodate his presence to that cool and dustless room.

There were no ghosts in that crisp air, no spirits lingering about the high walnut bed, the chest of drawers, the two straight chairs, the table. That was the extent of the furniture; the room was plain, practical, even austere. But the room had been occupied by Parker's father, whose clothes still hung in the closet and whose silver brushes stood upon the bureau as if his return were daily expected. His shirts were stacked in the drawers, pressed to the thinness of paper by years of their own weight. Faded sachets were tucked in among the shirts, and the drawers had been so seldom opened that a spicy fragrance persisted in them. All this Parker knew from previous inventories. This room is not a shrine, he told himself, and if he had been asked why he came there to work, he would have replied querulously that it was the place in the house where he was least likely to be disturbed. The room was tucked off in a corner, separated from the upstairs hall by a larger room which had been a nursery and a playroom for the children. And unlike his own room, this small chamber was neat and tidy, for his mother looked after it herself, dusted the furniture and kept the door and windows open so that the air renewed itself. Her pretext was that Iva had enough to occupy her without bothering about the unused rooms in the house, but Parker believed that her motives were to keep the room and its contents disinfected and to take the weekly specific against poisonous memory. For this was not only the room in which his father had lived but also the room in which he had taken his life, and Mrs. Livingston's fidelity was scrupulous: she had replaced the original white figured bedspread with its duplicate, and she had never removed Philip Livingston's pistol from the single shallow drawer of the table at which Parker now sat.

Parker knew what the pistol looked like, and for as long as he could remember he had known that it was kept in that drawer. His father had shown it to him, fumbled with it, got the cylinder stuck, dropped it to the floor. "To keep off marauders," his father had said, and Parker had never forgotten the words or his father's abashed grin as he groped for the weapon he had dropped. He seemed too embarrassed to take his eyes off his son, and Parker ended by picking up the revolver and returning it to his father's hands. "We better hope no marauders get after us," his father winked, "and, Parker, don't you let on that you know where the gun is. This is between men." Parker must have nodded solemnly. He wondered how old he could have been then; he was eleven when his father killed himself, and his own life was dated by that event, so that memories which included his father seemed to belong to the remotest childhood.

He pulled open the drawer. The dry wood jammed, he jerked, the pistol and holster lurched into his view and struck the front of the drawer. The four loose cartridges rattled against the wood. The racket seemed to violate the very air, but even that noise failed in the ominous silence, and instead of penetrating into the place, Parker had only reminded himself, again, of his intrusive presence.

Nevertheless, he left the drawer open and stared at the family pistol. The butt of the thing stuck out of the thick leather holster, and the bulk, the shape of it—lobe of leather, blunt lobe of metal and horn—made him think of a human heart. Resting upon the thin, grainy boards of the drawer bottom, it appeared potent and immense, an indestructible liver-colored heart. He slid the drawer to as quietly as he could and leaned forward to begin his work, but he imagined that he heard that heart, its pulse. Seated, his body curled around the pistol, he heard of course only his own heart, a humming tissue which seemed to imitate the pistol not twenty inches from it.

He held the pen above the paper, but before he could form his first words his mother appeared in the yard below him. She called cheerfully to the birds, which fluttered but did not seem frightened by her. She scolded the cardinals for scattering the seed and hung a new ball of suet for the woodpeckers. From behind the peach tree, she glanced up at the window where he sat, and he suspected that she had heard him and come out to see whether he was in the room.

"Yes, I'm here," he called.

She looked about as though she did not know where the voice came from. "Was that you, Parker?"

"I'm up here."

"Oh, there you are." She smiled. "You shouldn't stay indoors on such a pretty morning. Did you see the tanager?"

He did not answer, and she did not seem to expect him to. She whistled once for the benefit of the quail, then cocked her head; a response came almost at once from the stand of pines at the back of the yard. She smiled once more at the window before going inside, and then he began.

The Deposition of Parker Livingston

Write the facts, you said. Write down what happened, what you saw and heard, everything you can think of that seems to bear on the case—and you sounded as if you were still talking about the facts. Everything I can think of, every-

74

thing I know, does bear on the case. The facts are easy. I am a free white American, 21 years old. I was born and continue to reside in Ewell, Manspile County, Alabama. Arthur Aerial Kin is male, black, aged 24, and he comes from Biloxi, Miss. On the night of September 7th, 1968, he was shot at. The incident occurred following a water-skiing picnic on the farm of Mr. Theodore Hirt, near Kingberry, Manspile County. Mr. Kin was wearing bathing trunks. The moon was tremendous. His assailants—is that the word, Booth? or is that a presumption too?—were concealed in the pine trees. There was considerable shooting as Mr. Kin ran along the shore of the lake, but he was not injured. Authorities arrived on the scene to investigate the mischief.

There are some facts for you. What is this: The only good nigger is a dead nigger. A fact? Proverb? Motto? Campaign promise? What if they say it on the courthouse steps when they discuss this crime? Is their trial going to be any different from the trial inside the courtroom? Is their trial going to be the only trial? Maybe they will try the case at the barbershop too, and the poolroom, and at selected cafés. Hear them: Sessions must not of had his rifle sighted in yet to miss a target like that, running or no. Got to keep them in their place, especially ones like that. Two white girls out there and he wasn't wearing nothing but a little yellow swim suit, one of them European jobs, fit him just about like a glove. Any white boy that would set by while a nigger fooled around with his sister. Brought the nigger to his house and was in the car with em going out there.

Is that testimony? Judgment? Is it admissible? But you know better than I do what they're saying, Booth—and you *do* know, don't you? You work at the courthouse, Mr. State Attorney. You hear them every day. The only good nigger is a dead nigger.

Facts. What's needed here is truth, not facts.

Because we all know the essential facts. Arthur Aerial Kin —and ain't that Aerial just a *typical* name?—attracted attention because he was seen in the company of white women. Sessions, Fuqua, and Bates conceived it to be their plain duty to enforce the social and moral standards of the state of Alabama. Therefore they took up their weapons and fired at him—I won't say attempted to kill him, since that offends you. I won't say it, but I'm the last person in Ewell that anyone would talk to about this, and even I know that Sessions' own version is that he missed. He jokes about his marksmanship. Would it matter to you, Booth, if he'd hit and killed Arthur? Would you try the case then? I know the precedents and justice of such a case, I know what the verdict would be, but would you have prosecuted? You say that it's difficult for you to mount a prosecution without Arthur's full cooperation—would his death constitute cooperation? Would that make him a satisfactory and reliable witness? Or just a good nigger?

About this word *nigger.* I don't say it myself and never have. It wasn't permitted at home when I was a boy and even at Ewell Elementary School it was forbidden. You got your mouth washed out with that gritty powdered soap for saying it there. But if this is a legal document, and I am trying to tell the truth, isn't nigger the right word? Isn't that the true name for them here? Isn't that the reason the case won't come to trial? Suppose that a man has even heard the word—could he then prosecute or judge the case? Would he be a fit juror? The law is designed for the protection of society, right? And don't we all need protection from persons so named? Isn't that what you think, Booth? Isn't nigger the right word?

And isn't niggerlover the right word for me? I brought

Arthur here, he was a guest at my house, he was seen with my sister. If he is the menace, then I am his accomplice— we're the ones being tried in Ewell's various courts. Well, Booth, I want you to appreciate how I've had to work to become one. I had all the opportunities and experiences of a childhood right here in Ewell. When I was sick with the mumps, Queen Iva—there's another typical name for you, and it embarrasses me so much now that I call her plain Iva —insisted on rubbing sardine oil on my scrotum. To keep my little nuts from dropping, she said. Sonny Stallworth, who sometimes helped Mama in the yard, bought me the first Jax premium beer I ever drank because I was too young to buy it for myself, and he made me pay him two extra dollars—one for buying the beer, one for not saying anything about it. Waldron, the greenskeeper at the country club, once kindly shared his lunch with me, hog jowls and chittlins, but I couldn't choke it down. Sara B, our cook for a while, had three sons of three different colors, and she quit working for us when her man threatened her—he didn't want her in the house with my father. And I saw numerous others of the colored race in their now legendary poses—the women hoeing cotton, the half-naked children playing in the dusty streets, the young men cut open in the Cosmos billiard parlor, the old men in town on Saturday on their mule wagons.

So I know they are different from me; I know they are superstitious, lascivious, and prone to razor violence. I know more than that too, heard more, just as you did, Booth, you or any other white child in Ewell—their heads are harder, their brains smaller, their members larger. They are just crazy about moon pies, they breed like rabbits, and they all live on welfare. Though they're poor, they're happy, and they wouldn't know how to live without dependence on the white man. Oh yes, I heard all the lore, couldn't help hearing it, and I can't remember now where I heard it, or from whom, or on what occasion. I can't even remember if I believed it then—that available information, those *facts,* ha! I simply knew them, breathed them in with the air, and until I left Ewell I did not realize what a doom my education was.

Let me tell you what happened to me in the Army, and this *does* bear on the case. I was at Fort Dix, PORing—processing for overseas replacement, and, as the sergeant said, you know over which seas. But my orders were for Germany—out of an advanced training class of forty men, I was the only one not assigned to Vietnam. The inscrutable Army. Well, I confess that I was grateful, and I didn't mind the delay at Fort Dix, my embarkation point, while I was waiting for a flight to Frankfurt. It seemed to me that I had been spared, but I didn't have to go to a war in Asia to learn about the dark races. I found out the price of citizenship right here at home, in New Jersey, on an acre of pavement in front of the Fort Dix mess hall.

I was on my way, alone, to supper. It was just getting dark, and even at Fort Dix the dusk is a peaceful time of day. On the far side of the big paved area, coming out of the mess hall, I saw two black troopers. The uniform, those dingy green fatigues, ought to make everyone look the same—it's designed to daunt and chill the spirit. But these two characters, like so many of the spades, had a way of wearing it insolently. Yes, *insolently*—I thought that. Their caps were pushed back on their heads, the creases in their shirts and trousers stood out like blades, and lights shone in their boots and belt buckles. Their shoulders were back, chins high, arms swinging. Insolent, hostile, sassy, uppity —that's the description I gave to myself, based on the evidence at fifty yards. Why didn't I think instead that they were two resourceful men who managed to survive the uniform, two individuals vigorous enough to energize even fatigues? I just didn't. I saw two mean spades making straight for me. One of them was picking his teeth, and the other lifted his cap and pulled out that black comb they all carry, stout enough to curry a mule, and forced it through his hair. They did not move an inch to avoid me.

And so I attributed malice to them. They wanted me to step aside for them. I imagined they had identified me as the enemy—me, in baggy greens and dull boots, cap drooping down over my eyes, back slouched. I admit that I wanted at that moment to look as meek and inoffensive as possible. And though I hated to step aside, I did so—oh, it was bitter! I felt I had betrayed my heritage, those centuries of the doctrine of superiority. I did not want to give way to those two, and I excused myself because they were two and I was alone. I stepped aside, whistling, pretending to wander. I didn't want to seem to back down, didn't want them to have that satisfaction. And then they moved, changed course, bore down on me. The arrogance! I was convinced of it. They wouldn't even let me save face. I began to wonder what help I could expect from the mess hall if I was attacked. At such moments the mind of the semi-educated Southerner is truly lucid. I strayed even farther from my original direction, and still they approached, finally blocked me. I stopped. They stopped in front of me.

"Man, you got a dime?"

"He needs to make a phone call."

"Yeah," I said, but I didn't reach for my pocket. Isn't that ridiculous? Here in Ewell they say a nigger has an instinct like a dog's; if so, the fear I was giving off should have been dense enough to knock them down. However, I stood my ground like a man, didn't give up my self-respect, didn't trade my pride for a dime. Ewell would have been proud of me.

"How bout lending me a dime? I need to make a phone call *bad*."

Then I reached. I brought up a handful of change and sorted out two dimes. "Here. I'll treat you both to a call."

I dropped the coins into a waiting palm. They were bounced. "You know what?" said the holder of the coins, talking no longer to me but to his buddy. "I don't believe I want this white mother's money." You know the story, Booth: the little colored baby said *mothuh*, and his happy daddy exclaimed, "Ain't dat boy smart? He done learnt half a word." And the coins fell at my feet.

Well, any true son of Alabama can recognize an insult from a member of the Negro race. My training did not fail me there. I was standing on the pavement while those two sassy bastards cruised away, wondering whether or not I ought to pick up the dimes, and I was not angry, I was mortified. Better to have charged through them, or taken a swing when they stopped me, better even now to scoop up the coins and throw them at their backs. But your average racist is always terrified, and almost never acts alone, and I did nothing. I told myself that I'd seen one more proof of the intractability of the Modern Negro, and I was sure that these two were militants, not the southern darkies I'd been raised with. I left the dimes where they were. If they didn't want them, I didn't either. I was having nothing to do with their leavings.

But suppose I'd given them the dime. Suppose I'd just walked toward them, and when we met, I'd dug in my pocket, said "Sure, buddy," and handed over ten cents. It seems possible that I invented their malice, that they simply wanted a coin to make a call. The only phones in that barracks area were pay phones, and you couldn't get change without walking half a mile to the PX. Maybe they looked on me as a fellow private soldier, another dude in uniform—a dime isn't much to ask for. Maybe if I'd given it right away and freely, we'd have talked, bitched about the Army, ended up drinking a beer together or shooting a game of pool. As often as I've thought of those two, I can't remember that they menaced me in any way until I begrudged them the dime. Insolent, truculent, surly—I created the opportunity for them to be. I didn't know how to give them any other opportunity.

Humiliation, or violence, is all that can come of what I know of the black man.

Let this episode prove to you that I feel outrage as deep as any Alabaman when the jigaboos act bad. I don't take a shine to every black man that crosses my path, don't feel obliged to lead him directly to the nearest white woman—for that is the drift of local talk, isn't it? I am the guiltiest party in Manspile County right now. I'm depraved, got to be—right? I do suffer confusions in living out my identity as one of the white elect of Alabama, but who doesn't? Is it more confused to shelter a black man under your roof than it is to shoot at him? More confused to want his attackers to be punished than to leave them at large? That's my question for you, legal wizard. What are you going to do about Sessions and Fuqua and Bates?

I recognize the delicacy of the situation. This is still Alabama, you told me, your very words. Indeed it is—do you think I could fail to appreciate the weight of that? And you probably would never become governor of this still sovereign state or even get yourself reelected State Attorney if you prosecuted the case. I realize that. Your friends would quit asking you to their barbecues, but what else have you got to lose? A lot, I know—I *do* know, and I apologize for carrying on as I have. But when you tell me you don't know what charge to bring, give me a dime's worth of legal mumbo-jumbo—what are all those tomes in your office for anyway? Weren't you elected because you were supposed to know how to use them? Furthermore, I didn't enjoy getting turned out of your office, although you did it diplomatically. Let's not discuss this until it's all down on paper, you said—and that got rid of me. But do you really think I am dumb enough to believe that this deposition is an important legal document? That it's going to help you decide, once you have your facts, how to handle the case? Dream on, Booth, dream on. I'll leave you alone for a while, and you will get the deposition you asked for. Maybe you don't plan to read it, but I am going to write the truth if I can.

He stopped there and laid the pen across the paper. He opened and closed his hand; he had written almost all morning with scarcely a pause and his fingers were stiff, forearm cramped. When he sat back in the chair, he became aware that his shirt was damp with sweat. Almost noon, the room was hotter. The crisp morning had dissipated and the air seemed now to have mass and substance. In the yard below, a few sparrows continued to feed, but the other birds had vanished till evening. The trees in his view were mimosa, holly, peach, and magnolia; he did not catalogue them, but he thought, *they can't move.* The air pressed downward upon them, and although he saw in their branches and motionless leaves the plainly delineated proof of patient growth, although he could remember an earlier view from this same window when the trees were smaller, he almost believed that they had swelled to their fullness that morning as he was writing, creations of the humid, monstrous air. He thought again, *they can't move,* and he sympathized with them in their exposure, but on the whole the fancy tickled him, it was so odd. *Trees, if you take my advice, you'll beat it out of this town.*

His own voice startled him, for he hadn't meant to whisper or even to speak aloud. He was surprised too that the voice was animated with the tremor of a laugh, for he had written out of anger and exasperation, and his last lines, with their combative assertions, had delivered him to his doubts. He really did not know whether Booth Lovelace would read his deposition—what he'd written was more petulant and irrational than anything he had said to Booth, and his intention when he sat down was to argue, reason, and persuade, to make his appeal in Booth's own tongue. He had rather hoped and even expected that he would be able to frame his account in a language with the authority and certainty of the law, but he'd managed only to be rancorous.

"This is getting us exactly nowhere," Booth had said to him, and he would likely repeat the phrase when he read the deposition. Parker's interviews with the lawyer had all led to that same frustration, even the first interviews, at which Arthur Kin was also present. At Booth's request Arthur had remained in Ewell for two days after the shooting, but Arthur was not inclined to volunteer much to any representative of law and order. Though Booth's questioning was considerate, even deferential, Arthur maintained a composed reticence. When the lawyer explained that charges would have to be brought by the state, Arthur muttered, "It didn't seem to me like it was Alabama they was shooting at," but that was the only time he betrayed any trace of indignation. Parker didn't see how he could urge Arthur to be more cooperative; he suffered through the interrogations, noting both Arthur's desire to be gone and Booth's willingness to let him go. And he was infuriated when he dealt with Booth alone, for the lawyer's treatment of him was not cordial but pained and official. In a voice much too declamatory for a small office, Booth explained the niceties of aggravated assault and attempted murder as well as the procedures of arraignment and indictment. Parker listened attentively, but his chief impression was that the State Attorney was multiplying the complications, even though he believed that Booth deplored—the lawyer's own word—the breach of peace and that he desired justice.

"If you really want to help, if you want Fuqua and Sessions and Bates to stand trial for what they did, write me a deposition."

Booth wasn't even looking at Parker. His chair was turned toward the window of the office and he held a silver letter opener, its point in the whorl of his index finger.

"What do I write in it?"

"Names, places, the facts, everything that seems germane to the case. Get it down on paper. Be as specific as you can. Try to remember the exact language of what was said to you."

"I've told you all that already."

"Well, write it down."

"It will be the same as what I've told you."

"You might remember more if you make yourself write it out."

"I remember it now."

The lawyer revolved abruptly in his chair. "Would you mind doing me a favor? Would you undertake the writing of a deposition? And when you write it, you can leave out the allegations, if you kindly would. Confine your remarks to what happened. They're responsible only for their actions, you know."

Booth punctuated his address with the smack of the letter opener on the blotter. Parker knew that Booth was waiting for him to rise, but he didn't want this visit, their third private meeting, to end as the first two had, without understandings or agreements of any kind, without at least a forthright statement of the antagonism which had so far impinged upon them, and he remained in his chair. The air-conditioner hummed behind a vibrating plastic grille, and Booth sat back from the desk and folded his arms across his chest, the posture of a chieftain, announcement that council was over. It was the sort of display Parker had come to expect from him. Booth's heavy arms and solid neck protruded from his short-sleeved shirt, his blue eyes hardly blinked. He was just old enough so that Parker had not been quite sure whether to call him Booth or Mr. Lovelace, but Booth had insisted, with a friendliness that struck Parker as the instinct of a cornball politician, that they get on a first-name basis.

"I didn't come here to pick a quarrel with you, Booth."

"I know that. I never suspected you did."

Another pause. The reddish hair, neatly barbered and brushed, the broad black frames of the spectacles, cheeks in which ruddiness was overcoming the freckles, chin still firm—Parker waited, but the lawyer did not relent his gesture. "This deposition—is it a legal document? Will you use it?"

"I wouldn't ask you for it if I didn't expect to use it. But I don't anticipate having it notarized or introducing it as evidence in court. Normally, I wouldn't request a deposition from a witness I can talk to, but, frankly, you and I still need a place to start from. So you go on home, avail your-self of pencil and paper, and write down the unvarnished facts. Tell me why Arthur came here, what happened on the road that Saturday, what happened that night. Terseness and cogency would be appreciated."

Parker stood up quickly in the midst of these instruc-tions. "I understand," he said. "I'll write it." And he turned away. That final explanation had punctured a final mem-brane in his ear, penetrated directly as the sound of Booth's authentic voice, a single, uninflected pitch as abrasive as the stuck horn of an automobile. It drove him from the office and down the slanting corridor, down the worn rub-ber runner of the long staircase. He noticed, as he always did, as he had reason to notice, the old-fashioned caution at the bottom stair: a gloved hand, forefinger extended, pointed at him like a pistol from the dim wall. The legend on the sleeve: WATCH YOUR STEP.

He had been too cross to begin the deposition at once; he gave himself several days to calm down. Apparently the delay was not long enough, for he couldn't explain the virulence of what he had just written or even why he had written at all. The explanation he offered—that he wrote to tell the needed truth—was, he knew, the most groundless and also most wishful of all his claims. He couldn't even say what he meant by truth, except that his version of it was different from Booth's, different from the town's. How to write his version so as to compel belief? And if believed, what action was required to fulfill the truth, not just for Booth and the town, but for himself?

He did not know, but still he was maliciously pleased with the pages he had filled. He counted and numbered each of them, made a neat stack of the morning's work. He stood, preparing to leave, and decided that he did not want the deposition left on the table where his mother would surely find it. But he did not want to take it from the room either, and after hesitating, he opened the table's single drawer, shoved the pistol and cartridges to the rear of the drawer, and placed the thin pile of the deposition at the front. The stack of clean paper and the yellow pen were still upon the table, but otherwise he left the room as he had found it.

Five

The deposition became a habit and Parker became a species of writer. He experienced the heats of composition, grew anxious about punctuation, fumed when he could not fashion utterance to his intention, despaired his lack of a sense of form. The deposition was a Hydra and grew two heads for every one he lopped off; it was a bloody business and he was not Hercules. The document was getting the best of him as it heaved its way toward autobiography. The tone of it remained belligerent, of course, as that seemed the easiest way of keeping it from biting him, and Parker often succeeded in believing that the belligerence was directed at Booth. Yet he was unable to conceal from himself the number of confessions stipulated by the deposition. They proliferated like heads, or like Booth's explanations; they were a bit stunted and deformed, and there was no apparent end to them. To explain why he had brought Arthur home, why he had betrayed him, why he now sought the recourse of law seemed to require nothing less than an audit of his life. He was defending himself, he knew, and even though confession was not the tactic he would have preferred, he could not imagine how else to proceed.

In any case he adopted what he took to be the routine of a writer. He slept late, dressed in jeans and T-shirt, breakfasted frugally, and with a cup of coffee in his hand and sand in his eyes he repaired to his table, his father's table. The cup of coffee was the first of several he drank each day; he speeded on the stuff and compounded the affront to his constitution by smoking heaps of Camels. He was fussy about his paper—Blue Horse looseleaf filler, five-holed— and could write only with a BIC fine point, black, of which he laid in a supply. He spent a good deal of time gnawing at the black stoppers atop the yellow shafts of these pens, but as soon as he had unseated one he became disgusted with the pen and threw it away. His penmanship, which had always been excellent, was a gratification, and he made a fetish of clean, legible, meticulous presentation, as if neatness might substitute for coherence. Rather than strike out a line, he would copy over an entire page in his angular, upright hand. Despite these conditions, the stack of finished work in the drawer of the table did increase, page by labored page. If he wasn't getting it right, he was at least getting it down, and the top joint of his middle finger where he held the pen was dented as it hadn't been since the third grade. He often wished that his pace were less glacial, but when he reflected that the deposition was the last plea for justice, he found patience to grind forward a word at a time.

His was, he reminded himself, the only continuing voice, and Booth seemed to need the provocation of voices. He was gathering evidence, he told Parker, but he did not specify what evidence and he seemed to be taking his own sweet time to decide whether the state had been offended. What the lawyer called the "property aspect" of the case had already been settled out of court; Mr. Hirt had been paid for the broken windows and lights, and he did not, to Parker's knowledge, have any interest in pursuing the matter further. He was extremely sensitive to the damage done to his own and his daughter's reputations. Arthur, of course, had returned to Biloxi, and Amsy, the ally Parker wanted most, had also deserted Ewell in order to reach Virginia in time to register for the fall semester at Hollins. They hadn't spoken much during those few days between the shooting and her departure, but when Parker had implied that she was turning her back on a duty, she retorted that his appetite for justice was ravenous because it was created by guilt: "You just want to get it all off your conscience." He acknowledged the accuracy of her charge, but her tone hurt him past replying, and one of his hopes for the deposition was that it would prove to her that he honestly sought justice, not merely justification. Booth was the named reader of his deposition; Amsy was its nominated reader.

Once he'd got well started on the deposition and the pages in the drawer began to accumulate, the task became obsessive enough to reconcile him to his abandonment in Ewell. He rose, he wrote, he retired—it became as repetitive as the conjugation of a Latin verb. And in spite of his routine he wasn't able to spend more than four or five hours at the table—after that length of time his fussiness was exacerbated and every word seemed the wrong one— so that he did have afternoons and evenings to fill. He decided to repaint his bedroom and get rid of the pennants, the lamps with cowboy-and-Indian motifs on the shades, the rug upon which beef were being driven across the plains to a siding at Dodge City. He emptied the cabinets and closet of old games, toys, football gear, model airplanes, baseball cards, and magazines. He occasionally ventured into Ewell to buy paint and materials for his redecoration, and though he was always prepared for malice at Lutrell's Hardware, none was forthcoming. He was recognized and asked in the usual way how he was getting on; his townspeople were capable of stunning blandness. They seemed bent on demonstrating that life could go on in the agreeable, loquacious way it always had, if only he would let it. Well, he wouldn't let it; he wasn't going to be undone by civilities. He did, however, shave his mustache—to deprive people of the comfort of dismissing him too easily as a freak. He was one of them, and he didn't want them to forget it.

At home, Iva and Mrs. Livingston observed the same silence about what had happened at the lake. Mrs. Livingston took an interest in the progress of his painting; she approved of the project and envied his ruthlessness in disposing of things. "You'll have to help me clean out the garage storeroom some Saturday morning," she said. "I always find it so difficult to throw things out." "It's easier to throw them out than to keep them," Parker said. Queen Iva picked over the boxes of stuff and took home nearly half of it, to distribute not among her own children, who were grown, but among the children of neighbors. Those two women, Iva and his mother, dusted, vacuumed, ironed, washed, and gardened; they did, in short, what they had always done, and kept that house as spotless and unencumbered as if it were a soul about to be translated to heaven. Their silence sometimes addled Parker and made him want to pinch himself to make sure that he, lumpish, defiled, and loud, existed where it reigned. And his ears were not entirely trustworthy; he occasionally believed, while in conversation with his mother or Iva, that he heard his deposition bellowing from the drawer, and when he wrote certain passages he was certain that the women, at their chores beneath him in the house, must hear the words as he formed them on the paper.

It's wonderful to be home, all right, just great to be back in Alabama where everybody looks and acts the way they're supposed to act, where men are men and niggers are niggers, and always will be, I guess. It's a whole lot less confusing here. I knew right off, and so did Arthur, and so would anybody, which one was Sheriff Flood when the posse came out to the lake. He was the big meaty one in the cowboy hat and whipcord britches; his white nylon shirt was sweaty under the arms and he was, natch, chewing a big plug of tobacco; he looked like he came to us straight from the lot of M-G-M or 20th Century-Fox. And when he went through the rigamarole with the lights and guns, and deployed his men for a firefight—only an hour or so after Sessions and his pals had cleared out, but, as he said, "it's no point taking chances"—and finally got around to asking us what had happened, he clapped his eyes on Arthur and said, "A knee-grow." He's quite advanced; he probably reads the liberal press, at least since Selma and Birmingham, when he got the idea that an Alabama law officer might become a national figure, and he doesn't say *nigger* any more. But he knew, as soon as he said *knee-grow*, just what had transpired. He was confident that the others had played their parts as reliably as he played his. He pushed back his hat and scratched his noggin, and he worked on his chew; he looked at Amsy in her bathing suit and Arthur in his; his quick-working bear-trap mind banged shut.

Alabama expects each man to do his duty. There was the sheriff doing his; Sessions and Fuqua and Bates had just left after doing theirs. They saw Arthur and Amsy down on the floor of the cottage, squirming and squealing, and they were under arms and hidden in the woods—and that wasn't just duty, it was zeal—just as the textbook requires. The sin was heinous, the response prompt. They shot; they became part of a long tradition; they were three good students of history who knew that our biggest mistake was losing the war, and they certainly didn't want the mistake to be repeated because they were remiss. And Arthur too did his duty, or a facsimile thereof; he played dead and he did it well enough to convince the custodians of order in Manspile County that he really was.

So maybe this is the New South after all, and maybe we have not observed in vain the centennial of Gettysburg and Shiloh. A hundred years and things have changed so that you don't have to slay a nigger; you can fulfill your obligation by making him look dead. It's not so much an affair of blood as an affair of honor. They do get to eat with the white folks now—I saw some at the counter of Ho-Jo's in Athens—and some of them go to school at Ewell Elementary. The Supreme Court decision keeps on percolating, and maybe we will all be coffee-colored someday, but not yet, not by a long sight. There's still the grounds, and there's still the cream, and you don't have to be any smarter than Sessions or Fuqua to know which is which. If you keep your weapon handy and stay on the lookout, if you remember that certain lines are drawn as permanent as the equator—which you might sail right over if you didn't know it was there—then you too may be drafted by your state, by Alabama, called upon to do your bit and your duty.

You, I keep saying, but I'm thinking of me, me, me. It seems as though my duty should be complicated, right? I'm the one with a brother the color of coffee with cream, the one whose father wasn't satisfied until he had produced a beige son as well as a white one. I'm not the unregenerate type of Southerner, I'm the guilty type. My role is every bit as essential and historic as Sessions' or the sheriff's or Arthur's, but let me tell you, it's no joy to be a character in such a worn-out plot. This story is so familiar that it's not even melodrama. It's the story everybody, including me, has long since tired of—but it's still my story, and it doesn't stop just because I want it to. It goes right on playing through the years, and when the lights came up I knew my part well enough. That's what you should notice: that, after all, my duty wasn't so different from Sessions'. I might have arrived at it differently, but I too was summoned to point in *a suggestive and threatening manner*—I underline that phrase because I think it has a nice legal ring—at Arthur Kin. He was my visitor, my guest, my kin, if you'll allow it, and, like Sessions, I was only interested in exterminating a pretender.

Pretender. He didn't get the pun until the word had stared at him from the page for a few seconds, and when he did get it he didn't much like it. That, like percolate, was the sort of accident the deposition produced. The events he chronicled seemed to call for hapless irony, and he discovered that most of his language lent itself to dismal jokes. Some he resisted, others he wrote out—why not? The deposition, he had come to believe, was being shaped by the same sullen, aberrant, malicious prejudices that had brought about an armed incident at a cattle pond, and by letting his own prejudices riot as they would on the page, Parker meant to throw light on the prejudices of Sessions and Fuqua and Bates. He assumed that they all operated in much the same way he did. He did not, or at least not often, suppose that they had entered the woods with a deliberate plan to murder Arthur Kin. He believed that they were victims of their own idle capacity to imagine hatred and violence; if they *knew* anything before they started shooting, they probably knew that they didn't want to kill anyone. But they had guns and they did shoot as the occasion required, they couldn't *not* shoot after they'd got Arthur running.

They might deny, with some honesty, that they'd intended to murder Arthur, and in a case like this one, Booth had explained, intention was everything. He had also cited the many difficulties of establishing intention to the satisfaction of a court. Parker, as he wrote, was becoming more and more certain that intention could be apprehended, that his own intention, at least, was leaking out in language the way vital gore drips from a wounded beast.

He wrote: How I Made the Acquaintance of the Aforementioned Arthur Aerial Kin

And thought: Livingston, if you expect anybody to read this, you had better keep a civil tongue in your head.

Wrote: A few nights after the mess-hall episode I've already described, I boarded a military flight to Frankfurt, and the next night, after a train ride and a trip in a motorpool sedan, I arrived in Badstein, headquarters of the Ninth Infantry Division. In the Headquarters Company orderly room I woke up the Charge of Quarters, a fat buck sergeant asleep in a swivel chair with a copy of *Gent* folded over his belly. He examined my orders and signed me in on the company roster. He told me that I was replacing a person called the Hawk who had volunteered for a tour in Vietnam so that en route he could get some leave time in the States to see his girl, that I would work for the Adjutant General, that the only trouble with Headquarters Company was a sadistic First Sergeant. Then the CQ unlocked supply to give me my bedding and we walked the long corridor to my billet. The barracks gave me the creeps; it was an old Wehrmacht building lit by naked bulbs, the halls were dim and chilly, the echo of our footsteps on the tiles banged along behind us. The halls were wider, the ceilings higher, the place altogether more ample and substantial than any American barracks I'd been in. They certainly knew how to build. Achtung! Achtung! Wouldn't you know that this story would begin in a Nazi kaserne? I'm not even making it up; this is the way it happened. At least the place had rooms and doors; it wasn't just a big open bay crammed with bunks like the barracks I'd lived in at Forts Polk and Dix.

"They all smell the same, don't they?" asked the sergeant.

He had opened the door to my room, and his freckled nose was wrinkled up. I thought he meant the barracks, the standard Army odor of floor wax and shoe polish and stopped-up crapper. But he had poked his face into the darkness of the room and he was referring to some fragrance there, so I stepped forward to take a whiff myself. Yes, they do all smell pretty much the same, a sort of compound of peanut hulls, quilts, bacon grease, burlap, tobacco, wood smoke, horse corn, and sawdust. And those are merely the elements that come to mind immediately.

The CQ sniffed again delicately. "Don't it stink, though?"

And he whispered to me that there weren't many of them at the headquarters, that the Fighting Cocks were selective, that I would probably be able to get into another room after I'd been there a few weeks. Then he switched on the light in the room. Kin, Arthur Aerial, Pvt E-3, according to the tag wired on the iron rail of the cot. His knees were drawn up and his hand, his pale-palmed nigger hand with its deep black love- and life-lines, dangled over the edge of the mattress. "Cut off that fucking light," he said, and I don't believe he was even awake.

"New man," said the CQ. "Got to square him away."

Arthur Kin peeked at me. He tilted his head up until the blanket was beneath his eyes, across the bridge of his nose. Then he grunted: one more honky. And he went under again, pulled the blanket over his head, and that was the extent of his appraisal.

And you know what I was thinking: That man is a nigger. I am going to share a room with a nigger. There was a fact to reckon with. I had lived with black men in the communal barracks at basic training, but this was different. Integration was official Army policy, but I never expected it to happen to me. Now that I'd had time to sort out the various smells coming off Arthur Kin, and time enough to absorb the warning of the fastidious CQ, I was rather shocked. I felt the way I did the first time I saw Negroes in a restaurant, Mama and Papa and two little girls with braided pigtails and the hair on the top of their heads scraped into a maze of parts. The way I felt when I first saw one on the street—in Washington, D.C., not in Ewell, where I have yet to see it, barring of course Arthur and Amsy—with his arm around a white girl. I approve of equality, but it takes getting used to. Ain't democracy terrific?

Despite his attempt to make his prose jocular and saucy, Parker found that this particular confession smarted like a sty. As he wrote it he remembered with pungent clarity the smell of houses he had eaten and slept in, the dwellings of black families which he had entered as an invited guest, a boy—how could he refuse to remember it or to recognize it elsewhere? He had once stayed the night with Commando Brown; they'd played together all day and Commando's mother made a pallet on the floor, gave the white guest her son's bed; Parker got down off the bed and slept beside Commando on the quilts and blankets, and it was like sleeping on the surface of the earth itself, smelled of the beaten earth beneath the house. When, how did he learn that the odor of that night was the characteristic and offensive odor of a race? When did the CQ learn? As soon as that barracks door was opened, the two of them had understood each other. A bond, pact, secret order—even there, four thousand miles from home, Parker was linked with a man he'd met minutes before, plunged into conspiracy with him. And he thought *nigger,* as if the loving past had never existed. That was what he had to confess, but it did not seem to him that confession had the power to expunge that word.

The other occupants of my room were Davy Gentile, a goofy, nervous Portuguese Catholic from Providence, R.I., whose footlocker was so stuffed with holy pictures and statues that it looked like an altar, and Spec 5 Wade Strickland. He was the ranking man in the room and therefore the Room Commander, and he was just the sort of grim, pimpled, ignorant redneck who would take a title like that seriously. Strickland came from somewhere in Texas, where, according to him, he owned a ranch and a Sting Ray and left peckertracks a mile long. When he wasn't in uniform he dressed up in cheap red-and-blue cowboy boots and string ties and he spent a lot of time in the EM Club losing money to the slots and getting drunk on cut-rate beer. He scowled constantly and tried to talk tough; he owned a pearl-handled switchblade which, of course, he called his nigger-sticker; he liked to show off his cool hand at that idiot's pastime in which the fingers are spread and a knife's point quickly punched in and out of the spaces between them. His fingers were gouged and there were bloodstains all over the table in our room.

Strickland was always after me and Gentile to wax the floors and shine the windows and dust the radiator pipes —the usual GI drill. Poor Gentile, who was afraid of rank and hierarchy and whose worst fear was getting reported to the First Sergeant for slacking, did everything Strickland asked, even used Brasso to polish his spray cans of shaving cream and deodorant. He was the ideal slave, but it wasn't Davy that Strickland was trying to master, it was Arthur. Most of our Room Commander's schemes were designed to harass Arthur and put him to some dirty work, but Arthur always had an excuse and Davy and I ended up with the fatigue. Arthur worked for a full bird colonel in G3, and the colonel always got him relieved from company duty. Arthur slept till the last possible moment every morning, then made his bunk and scooted over to the mess hall and went straight from there to his office, while Gentile and I got the room ready for inspection. That colonel wanted Arthur to open the office before he arrived there, to brew him some coffee and fill his in-basket, and Strickland couldn't do a thing about it. So Strickland scheduled some GI parties in the afternoon, after duty hours, thinking that he would catch Arthur that way. Arthur never showed up. Strickland stood around supervising Davy and me and sucking on his lip in his habitual way. He finally complained to First Sergeant Boyles, who relayed the complaint to the colonel, but the colonel took Arthur's part and Boyles chewed out Strickland, who couldn't believe that Arthur Kin was getting the best of him, day in and day out. Arthur hadn't been a nigger all his life for nothing.

I took Arthur's side against Strickland too, even though Arthur and I never had much to do with each other during the year and a half that we shared that room. Arthur wasn't talkative; he did his work over at the Staff Building and afterwards, if he didn't go to basketball practice—he was a deadly outside shooter on the headquarters team—he came back to the room and changed his clothes and signed out on pass. He'd already been in Badstein for a year when I arrived there, and he wasn't looking to make friends, not with me anyway. Strickland informed me about Arthur's activities in Badstein; he asked me if I'd ever heard the saying "once you go black, you never come back," and told me that in Arthur's case it was the reverse. That was one of the reasons that I didn't know how to approach Arthur to begin a conversation. The others were that he was reserved, self-possessed, and evidently intelligent. How are you supposed to talk to a nigger like that? When I act equal I do so magnanimously, and I expect gratitude for it.

He was interrupted there by a bitter memory—nearly all of his most urgent memories were of failures and humiliations—of a black soldier raking leaves beneath the trees at the edge of the parade ground. It was a cold fall morning, and when he left the office for coffee—he didn't really have to go out—he walked straight to him. His intention was simple and, he thought, magnanimous: offer the man, who wore no insignia but the white armband of the guardhouse, a cigarette and take his order for a hot drink from the snack bar. When he drew near Parker saw that the man was short and so black that he was almost purple, that a fresh, raised scar ran from his ear to the corner of his mouth. He had stopped working and leaned on the handle of his rake, blowing steady plumes of breath in the cold air.

"You need a smoke?" Parker extended a pack of cigarettes.

"I 'preciate it," the prisoner said.

"I saw you from where I work. Right chilly morning to be out in. Need a light?" He struck a match and the black man bent his head down to his cupped hands. "Keep the pack if you can use it."

"I sholy can."

"What'd you do that they put your ass under the jail?"

The stubby scar-faced prisoner smiled. "I cut a guy pooty bad."

Parker stared at the scar on his cheek. The prisoner said, "Yeah. You got it right. He caught me too." He ran his gloved fingers over the mark. "I didn't hardly feel it, though."

Parker had difficulty answering. "Keep the cigarettes," he repeated, and he departed hastily as the black man pocketed them. This man was as foreign to him as Arthur had ever been, his expression as sealed, his voice as closed—but he'd expected that. It was Parker's own voice, his own expression, even his own aim which dismayed him. The cigarettes—in the act of offering them he remembered that he'd seen his father throw packs of cigarettes out of the car as they drove past men working on the road in chain gangs, all black men, and seen them scramble for the cigarettes. But worst of all was his voice—a broad false Alabama drawl, the thickest dialect, an imitation of a Negro voice, as if to put the prisoner at his ease, to show him that the generosity of the white man need not be forbidding. The mime was involuntary, the false accent beyond his control—but he might as well have been in blackface. The self-deception seemed pitiable and abject: how could he have imagined that he had resources for kindness, charity, mercy?

I'll bet it sounds to you as though Arthur, because he was black, could do no wrong in my eyes. As though I, guilty and paranoid because I happen to be white and southern, took his side against Strickland just as I take it now against Sessions and Fuqua and Bates. It makes an open-and-shut case. But I didn't admire Arthur for his Badstein exploits, as I've already said, and I didn't like the way he left his share of the work in that room to me and Gentile. I withheld judgment on Arthur Kin, but I admit that I thought I could learn something from him about the condition of the black man, and I thought I was prepared to learn. Being in the Army, in Germany, away from Ewell—I believed that I could change, and I wanted to. I knew that there was danger I would make too much of Arthur; I was tempted to confide in him my awareness of bigotry and injustice, and I wanted that reserved black man to declare that I was different from the others. I tried to resist that temptation. And no matter what you may think, I didn't dislike Strickland because he expressed all my prejudices for me, because he was one of the others I wanted to be different from. It sometimes did seem to me that I'd been stuck in that room with him so that I'd have to listen to my own worst voice, but I disliked Strickland because he was vicious and mean-spirited, and I wanted to talk to Arthur because he seemed to know where he was in the world, and I still believe that I can change in any way that my intelligence can conceive and my will command.

That was a mouthful. He wrote it down quickly, after

working on that section of the deposition very slowly, extracting it like a crumbling, rotting tooth. He didn't want to look at it again and he gathered up the pages, stacked them, opened the drawer of the table, and put them at the bottom of the pile, out of sight. He didn't know whether that final outburst solved anything—he doubted it—and he felt that he probably ought to take the paper out of the drawer and excise the last page altogether.

He didn't. He removed the pistol instead. He'd been conscious of it all morning, the monitor of his palpitating heart, and he pretended to himself that his curiosity was mechanical. Did the thing still work? The fastener on the holster was stiff and creaking, but it turned, the gun slid easily from its case. One of the handle plates of checkered brown horn was loose, but the cylinder revolved, the hammer spring was still tight. Just so, he thought, his father must have tested the pistol; Parker believed that the first of the two shots his father had fired had been a trial to make sure the gun would kill. The bullet went through the wall beside the window, and even under the new paint the patch on the plaster showed. The sheriff, trying to make the suicide more tolerable, speculated that Philip Livingston, drunk, might have been fiddling with the gun. An accident. Parker knew better even then, even after having seen his father's clumsiness with the weapon. His father had simply not wanted to put an impotent weapon to his head, pull a trigger on an expired cartridge. He had decided death and he wanted assurances—the blast, flying plaster, hole in the wall. Smelling the acrid powder, examining the smoking muzzle, his father must have felt after that first shot that he'd already witnessed his own death, the essential physical proof of it. Because the second time he saw, heard, smelled nothing; the last thing he would have known was the tightening of his finger on the trigger.

Those two shots, as far as Parker knew, were the only two his father ever fired. No marauders had come, but the pistol had found its purpose after all. In an access of bitterness Parker thought, *He didn't have to do it.* He replaced the gun in the holster and removed the four cartridges from the drawer, intending, before he heard his mother, to take them from the room, to get that murderous equipment out of the table he'd chosen to work at. But she was at the top of the stairs, and she called him. "Parker? Parker? Iva's been keeping your lunch warm for you. Are you coming down soon?"

"In just a minute." It wouldn't do to have her find him with the gun in his hands. He returned it to its place, put the deposition in front of it, closed the drawer as noiselessly as he could.

He heard her walk through the hall and the room that had once been the nursery. She opened the door cautiously. "You ought to leave this door open when you're in here. This room gets so stuffy."

"There's not any breeze today."

She advanced into the middle of the room, glanced at the paper and pen on the table, but she did not ask any questions. "It is peaceful back here. I wish I could think what to do with this room." She looked around at the contents of the room—bed, table, chairs, her husband's things—and at her son, who was making them his own.

"Well," she said, "shall we eat now before Iva gives up on us?"

He followed her from the room and through the dim nursery.

Six

They'd worked for an hour, and already a small patch of lawn was littered with lame furniture, mildewed trunks, crusty paint cans, broken or outgrown toys and tools, festering debris which for years had been undisturbed in the storeroom at the back of the garage. In the damp storeroom, massed and piled to the ceiling, among the competing odors of decomposing upholstery and toxic paint and seized engines, the cast-off possessions had seemed a material album of Livingston history, a museum of artifacts pressed, impacted, and preserved like plant sprays in a Bible. Both Parker and his mother had expected minor adventures of recovery, but what they had so far pried loose and dragged out into the light and air wasn't worth saving. The squashed ottoman was lumpy as a cauliflower, and Parker's first record player, minus both tone arm and turntable, was now a cube of fermented cardboard. Nothing had improved with age, nothing worked or had all its parts or stood up by itself. On the grass, in the clear sunlight, with the peeling, corrosion, and other decay all too visible, the claim of the familiar objects was altogether canceled—just junk, after all. Parker didn't find a thing that he wanted to revive, and his mother was no more sentimental than he.

They worked together considerately and efficiently, without much chatter. Occasionally she asked him to lift down something she couldn't reach or to carry something too heavy for her, but the job was dirtier than she had imagined and her face was set in a decisively sour expression. She was wearing jeans and gloves, a scarf over her hair, an old cardigan because the morning had not warmed at all—the air was sharp enough to pierce, the first day in which autumn was tangible. Her birds seemed to feel the change and jabbered constantly as they fed, and they irritated Parker. Their noise thickened audibly each time he emerged from the storeroom door, and they hopped a few feet in the direction of safety, returned to posts nearer the activity each time his back was turned. He tried to ignore them, but their vigilant wings threw feathery reflections of the sun at him, and their noise swelled to a defiant cackle.

"Why don't those birds squawk at you?" he asked his mother. "That chirp chirp chirp is driving me batty."

"I'm sure it's nothing personal," his mother said, and he couldn't tell whether she was serious or not. "They're not used to you yet."

Even as she spoke, Parker was rummaging through a group of objects leaning against a wall—rakes, golf clubs, scraps of molding—toward a providential discovery. He managed to extract from the bottom of the heap his BB gun. The barrel was scrawled with rust, and the handle which once had cocked it hung loosely, unsprung. When he tilted the gun, a couple of BBs rolled somewhere in its interior.

"It's still loaded," he said.

"Where did you find that thing?"

"Right there—and I wonder how it got there. Did you hide it from me? I seem to remember that one day I had my trusty Daisy and the next day it was gone, never to be found again."

"I couldn't stand thinking you were out shooting birds with it."

"I didn't shoot any birds. Lots of bottles and cans, but no birds. You can tell me now, Mama—did you hide it down here? I'm old enough to stand the truth."

She didn't share his amusement and made only a tacit admission. "You shot at least one warbler. I thought you were too young to have a BB gun."

"It's broken now," he said. "All the little freeloaders are safe."

But he walked to the door and put the gun to his shoulder, laid his cheek against the plastic stock, and aimed at a blue jay. *"Ping.* You wouldn't mind if I shot just the blue jays, would you?"

"That's not funny. Throw that gun out."

But Parker, standing in the doorway, aimed again and repeated his *ping.* Some of the birds seemed to recognize the danger and they evacuated. Parker laughed.

"Put it away, will you, please?"

"The exercise will do them good," he said, but he complied and leaned the child's weapon against the outside wall. "These birds are too fat. What's the point of feeding them at this time of year? There's plenty of natural food."

"I like having them around."

"You're going to spoil them. When the winter sets in, they'll be too logy to look after themselves."

"Isn't it touching that you're so concerned for them."

The acerbity, unusual for her, rather abashed her and she

turned back to work to terminate the conversation. She had cultivated patience since Parker had returned, but the fits of spite which interrupted his habitual lugubrious solemnity often provoked her despite her desire to remain equable. She took it as her maternal duty to be gentle, placid, and forbearing while her son was embattled, and so she had refrained from discussing with him any matters related to Arthur Kin (and anyway Amsy, before leaving for school, had told her all she wanted to know). But Parker could be maddening—that BB-gun business was puerile goading—and she sometimes couldn't prevent herself from being a bit sharp with him. He deserved it.

And yet she wished that she'd minded her speech. She hated to be catty, especially with her children, especially with Parker. She had a fearful respect for his emotions, and she had come to think of herself as too shallow to plumb her son's necessities, just as she blamed herself for having failed to diagnose the killing extent and depth of her husband's unhappiness. Blamed herself, but the measure of blame was the indisputable proof of her shallowness—she had never felt all that guilty, and in fact she had grieved far less for her husband, and for herself, than she believed she should. The parallel between Philip Livingston and Parker had occurred to her more than once, and not just recently; her husband and her son were brooders and long-nurturers of misery. She imagined that they were able to read her frivolous and forgetful heart as easily as God detected sin, and that was another reason she regretted the lapse of her tongue—she'd only given Parker a further demonstration of her incapacity.

She therefore interpreted the finding of the snakeskin as swift and merited punishment. She had reached up for a baby-carrier, a criblike affair which had been used in the back of the automobile when Parker and Amsy were infants, and upon its cover she touched the skin. Because of her gloves, she did not identify it until she had pulled the tail over the edge, and even when she saw the black tip she was slow to name it. She withdrew several inches of it before she realized she was fast to a snake, conceived and discarded in the same instant of panic the notion that it was a live snake. It was merely a dry, empty skin, and she shuddered and exclaimed, emitted a distinct *Ugh.* She tugged the whole length of it off the carrier, holding it gingerly between her fingers. It reached almost to the floor.

"Look at this damned thing, Parker. It's vile."

"Where'd you find that?"

"It's all there, even the head. Isn't that disgusting?"

"It's enormous."

"What kind is it, can you tell?"

"It must be a blacksnake."

"There aren't any markings."

"That's why it has to be a blacksnake."

She carried it to the door to have a better look at it in the light. She held it by the tail, her arm stretched straight out from the shoulder. "It was lying up there on top of your old car crib, just as if the snake had crawled right out of it. I thought they had to rub the skin off. Have you ever seen one whole like this?"

"No."

"It doesn't look very old, does it? When do they cast their skins?"

"In the spring, I think."

"This skin can't be that old. It looks as though it was fresh this morning." Then, in a tremor of revulsion, she drew back her hand and dropped the skin to the threshold. "God, I loathe snakes."

Parker couldn't keep himself from smiling at her outburst. "A blacksnake keeps the mice down. It can't hurt you."

"Those things live off the birds."

Parker picked up the skin by the tail, holding it as his mother had. "This snake is long gone, Mama. It's not going to bother your precious birds."

"I've seen those things curled up around nests with chicks in them," she said. "There was one up in the big cedar tree last year wrapped around a waxwing nest. The parents kept flying back with food, but they couldn't get it to the chicks. I couldn't get to the nest because it was so high up in the tree, and even if I had got a ladder up there, the snake was coiled around the nest so tight that I wouldn't have been able to kill it without knocking the whole thing down. Don't wave that skin at me. Get rid of it."

She turned away abruptly, and Parker found himself holding the skin to her back as though he'd been tormenting her with it. He left the storeroom and crossed the yard, entered the stand of thick pines and flung the skin away. When he returned, his mother was standing outside, among the things they had removed. Her arms were folded, shoulders hunched, as if she'd had a chill.

"Done," he said.

"That was silly of me," she said. "I don't know why that should have upset me, but, really, I couldn't bear to look at that horrible skin."

Parker smiled again, not to reassure her, and he had to smother a small malevolent laugh, a cruel snort of amusement at her discomfort and confession of weakness. He caught it in time; it expired silently in his throat. A laugh would have been brutal, especially since the smile she faced him with was her brave one—lips pressed together upward, eyebrows raised.

"I should have had someone come and empty the place out," she said. "There's no point in picking over this junk. There aren't going to be any discoveries."

"I don't mind doing it," Parker said. "I'll finish dragging the stuff out so that it can be hauled away. There must be something in there that we want."

Her smile deepened in affection and thanks, and as it did, her face was transformed: scores of fine, tiny lines, like the marks of razor or scalpel in the subcutaneous membrane, suddenly appeared beneath the covering of her lovely skin. It was like seeing a school of fish rise up from the depths in water that had seemed entirely transparent, without depths. At rest her face was almost preternaturally youthful and smooth, her complexion girlish, but when she smiled as she did now or when she was shaken by emotion, the erosions of age were apparent enough, shocking. For Parker, those deep, delicate scars were the tracery of a past that had always been concealed from him. Even as he watched, his mother's face restored itself, the lines vanished, sank out of sight, and she became again what he was accustomed to: a woman whose trim figure gave the impression of vigor and fitness, whose face was strangely empty and untroubled. He acknowledged, as he looked at her miraculous face, the truth of what he'd often heard— she looked hardly older than he did. And in spite of the eerily unruffled spaces of cheek and brow, she was an attractive woman who could surely have had another life if she'd wanted it.

"Mama, why did you stay here in Ewell?" He blurted out the question—not the question, if he had to choose only one, that he would have asked, but it would do. The other, more urgent inquiries were joined to it like a running line, coiled for years, to a harpoon. And this question, launched, would draw the others in its train.

His mother considered. She betrayed no surprise, no alarm that the subject closed for years was opened now as she stood in a plot of waste, junk up to her knees, a flood of useless things spread over her ordinarily impeccable yard. She said, "Why don't we sit down?"

Parker placed two peeling wooden lawn chairs so that they faced each other, and when they sat, they were almost knee to knee in the midst of the morning's refuse, surrounded by it. With a whole lawn and clear October air to choose from, they'd settled there, and they were so near that they seemed to have but a single lap between them.

"Why did you stay in Ewell, Mama?" Parker repeated. "Why here?"

"Nowhere else to go," she said simply. "Your father left me this house and an income here—the rents—just enough to take care of you and Amsy. I'd have to sell the house and all the other property to raise money to leave. I've thought of doing it."

She selected her words deliberately, for despite her outward calm she was conscious of striving to convey to her son an impression of thoughtfulness. She didn't entirely understand how they'd fallen so promptly into this conversation, and though she foresaw its awful possibilities, she couldn't think how to avoid continuing.

"Why didn't you? Did you want to stay here?"

"I've always lived in a small town. I was afraid to move, to sell the house. And what would I have done somewhere else? I've hardly even been anywhere, except on the wedding trip I made with your father. I couldn't just pick up and leave."

"You could have gone to Montgomery, or Birmingham, or Atlanta."

She smiled. "I was thinking of California. Does that sound silly? Everything seems to grow out there, and they have very exotic birds."

She surprised herself with that gentle self-deprecation, the fond taunt at Parker, but his response was peremptory. "Why here? Any place would have been better."

"I've never really considered marrying again," she said, answering the question he hadn't been able to ask. "I suppose I would have had better chances nearly anywhere else. But, Parker," she enunciated distinctly, "I did not want another husband."

She decided she had better conceal something from him, and she watched him narrowly: her full-grown son, hands on his knees, eyes on his hands, embarrassed, cross with himself for being so. Full-grown, but he seemed to her, for all his depth and mystery, painfully young and naïve. She was rather pleased that she had secrets from him. She had managed her affairs and passions discreetly, and it seemed wisdom to have done so.

He didn't ask about them. Instead, he stammered noticeably as he phrased his question. "Is it because of the way" —he halted, choosing between *Daddy* and *my father*— "Daddy died, because of that you didn't want to marry again? It must have been terrible for you."

His sympathy, clumsy but genuine—to make the intrusion bearable. That was, of course, the question she should have expected, but she'd been distracted by her self-congratulations, and she studied the averted face of her son to find out what secrets he was keeping back, how he was trying to spare her. "That's not what held me. It was terrible after he died," and she didn't say *killed himself*, didn't even say *your father*. She found herself on the verge of confessing her inability, or refusal, to be overwhelmed by grief, outrage, pity. She didn't require his sympathy. What had been terrible was not her own plight but the willingness of her neighbors and family to abuse her deceased husband. They seemed to have been waiting for his death, and the manner of it confirmed all their smug judgments. It was Philip who needed sympathy, not she.

She said, "He wasn't a monster, Parker. You know that."

"And you stayed here because of him?"

His insistence brought her his vision of her: romantic, sacrificing, faithful to the memory of the husband who was never faithful to her. It was distressing. "No, not because of him. It's hard to explain—once he was dead, I had things to do, you and Amsy to look after, the estate had to be settled. I didn't have an idea about money. I'd never done anything but write checks. So I was busy, and by the time I felt safe, by the time I felt I could take care of things by myself, I already had a sort of routine. I didn't want to give it up."

She had been determined not to give it up. Independence had seemed the only way of answering the ugly, prying attentions of her neighbors, and a means of demonstrating her forgiveness of Philip. She interested herself in his business affairs (he had a law degree but a minuscule practice; most of his income was from real estate), kept his downtown office, drank coffee in the male preserve of the Elite Cafe, refused to comport herself as a widow—and gave no one, neither her mother nor Philip's, the right to say a word about it. She supposed that she had hastened her mother to her grave—she believed, despite her own appearance, that emotion ravaged the body as well as the spirit—and she knew that she was implicated in Mrs. Livingston's flight to New Mexico, where she'd become Mrs. York, taken up pottery, and except at Christmas ignored her daughter-in-law and grandchildren. She regretted that, but it had seemed necessary. And she was proud of successes in managing the business and providing for the children, proud also of the way she had filled her own life. She played bridge and golf, and of course she had the garden and the birds, and in the late fall and winter the horses and the hunt. She didn't mind admitting to herself that she was a small-town girl, raised in one Alabama county seat and married into another. She had sufficient pastimes in Ewell, and she had more than that: she had passions. It wasn't just routine which sustained her; it was freedom, so novel and so ravishing that she'd never got accustomed to it. It didn't matter that it was hedged round on all sides, for she was not wanton. She was steadied by the children, the house, the business; she was delighted by flowers and birds; she was elated when she rode to hounds and by the possibility of love—yes, she would call it that—in her life. So she remained in Ewell: choice, not duty, not blind fate, no matter how it looked to others.

"What *was* Daddy like?" Parker asked, and shook his head, impatient with himself. He looked at his mother and revised the question, apparently nerved to ask for once what he intended. "But I can remember him well enough. I suppose I mean, why did he kill himself? I know it's ridiculous to expect an answer to that, but you must have an idea." He waited a moment, continued when she didn't speak. "I know you can't say exactly why, can't explain it. But, Mama, you must have thought about it. You must have guessed." He paused again, then said all he could, asserted his right to ask. "I know he had other women. I know he had been at Esther's that night. I know he had been drinking. Please, Mama."

"I'm not trying to protect him, Parker," and she told the truth. "I do have a foolish sort of theory about it—but I didn't know that you'd heard all that."

"About Esther?"

"Who told you?"

"Some kids at school."

"How did they know?"

"From their parents, I guess."

"What did they say?"

"That Daddy had a black woman."

"What else?"

"That he had a black son."

"Did you know about this before he died? Or after?"

"Both."

"Did you believe it?"

Parker hesitated. "I asked Iva. She told me it was true."

"Why did you ask her, not me?"

"I wasn't sure you knew," he said. He didn't add, *And I didn't want to be the one to tell you.* He asked, "How did you know about it?"

"Mrs. Purlis came and asked me for money. Did you know about her too? She was before Esther. Your father had been taking care of her two children. Maybe they were his, maybe not. She wanted him to think so. But I knew before that. He didn't make a secret of it."

"Daddy told you?"

"When I asked him." She watched her son carefully, and this time she anticipated the next question. She was prepared for it.

"Why did you stay with him if you knew? Didn't you—"

"Try to stop him, keep him at home? Yes, but I couldn't. I think he loved them—Esther, and even that Mrs. Purlis. I think he wanted to be married to us all. He didn't want to be just our lover, he wanted to be our husband."

"Didn't you mind that?"

"Not as much as I would have if he'd cheated like other men do. Like other husbands here—Parker, you wouldn't believe me if I named the men in Ewell who've pawed at me. But your father wasn't like that. If it had been just sex —some secretary or receptionist or telephone operator— that would have been worse. But he wanted a house, wanted to sit down to supper with a family around him, wanted to play with his children. He took them all little presents, just as he brought things to you and Amsy. He even borrowed my maternity clothes for Esther to use."

Her voice was indulgent, not bitter. She didn't seem able to foster a grudge against Philip Livingston, living or dead. He'd been a timid, rather awkward, wonderfully droll, gentle man who, as anyone could see, was dying a mile a minute. At the age of thirty-eight, despite his perpetual smile and his bright eyes, he'd lived as long as he was able to. His hair was half gone and his face was as skewed and scored as an old boot. Whatever was consuming him gave him no peace at all, and though he never seemed mean-tempered or wretched, he was often so drunk or exhausted or both that he appeared to exist on the energy of his nerves alone. She wished that she'd known how to go about saving him. There were signs of him around her where she sat—his golf clubs, purchased in the flush of one of his occasional vows to reform himself, to pursue a more placid life, to enjoy common recreations, used not more than three times—but nothing which caused hard feelings after all these years. She didn't have to remind herself that it was Philip who had suffered most, not she. And when she looked at the tense, drawn face of her son opposite her, her own mild emotions warming her as pleasantly as the October sun overhead, she was overcome by one wild pang of dread. Parker looked like her if he looked like anyone—none of Philip's children, lawful or otherwise, resembled him in the least—but, as different from his father as he was, as still and near as he sat, he seemed to be as alien and remote as Philip had been. Of all judgments, that would be the sorest—to fail to reach either of the men bound to her by family.

"I'm sorry," she said. "I haven't explained anything, have I?"

"Don't stop. I've never heard this. I'd always thought Daddy's affairs were— I thought you'd feel differently about them."

"They weren't affairs, not for him. That's my theory, if you can call it that. He killed himself because he couldn't look after us all. I don't think he was guilty about Esther. I don't think he regretted that. There just wasn't enough time or money, wasn't enough of him. It happened to be me that he let down—he didn't get to the hospital when I needed him—but it might as well have been Esther. Does that seem too simple-minded to you?"

"No. It seems . . . generous."

He evidently offered that word as praise, but to her the voice was chilling. Generous? What did he mean? She'd given him, somehow, the wrong impression; she did not want to be pitied by him. At once she wanted to reveal all that she'd held back, the details of her passion and appetite, to make claims for her life.

"I think it's been harder on you and Amsy than it ever was on me," she said. "I probably should have told you everything before. I don't know why I didn't. You shouldn't have had to learn about your father at school and from Iva."

Had she failed them? Her voice was not apologetic; it was not Philip she wanted to talk about; it was herself. And she felt angry resentment that Philip, ten years dead, should stand so between her and Parker. "What have you been doing in your father's room?" she asked suddenly. "What are you writing in there?"

He evaded her eyes. "A deposition. It's something Booth asked for."

"What is it?"

"He asked me to write down what happened when Arthur was here."

"Doesn't he know? Why can't you tell him? Why are you writing it?"

"That's what he asked me to do. He wants to make sure we get things straight."

"Why are you writing it in your father's room?"

"No particular reason. It's quiet there."

She stood up and looked at the clutter on the lawn. "I don't think I can face this mess. This lawn looks like a dumping ground. I'm going to call someone to haul everything off."

"I'll finish cleaning the storeroom."

"Don't. It's a filthy job. I'll get Leroy to do it the next time he comes."

"There's no need for that."

"Leave it for him. That's what I pay him for."

She surveyed the garden-sized patch of detritus. As she turned to leave, she noticed a pair of frantic martins which shrilled from the peach tree toward the storeroom wall and back again. She walked around the shrubs and found their nest neatly cemented to the wall and the top of the window frame. But why the uproar? There couldn't be chicks in the nest this late in the year. She almost didn't see the snake —it was stretched full length on top of the window frame, its head not three inches from the nest, but she'd taken it at first for a clear bar of shadow. She probably wouldn't have found it at all if it hadn't turned its head to look at her.

"Bring me a hoe, Parker. Hurry."

Ten steps and he was beside her. "What is it?"

"Give it to me."

The snake had begun to move, but on her first swing she caught it cleanly behind the head with the blade. Blood smeared the wall, and the snake fell to the ground. She hit it twice more, as if that settled everything. When she lifted it up on the hoe, the head remained attached to the body by a thread of gristle, and the body itself was motionless.

"That's the one," she said. "That was his skin we found."

"New skin, same snake," Parker said. "No more birds for this one."

"Get rid of it." She handed him the hoe. "I don't want its mate around here looking for it."

His mother braced her shoulders and walked up the gentle slope to the house. The martins stayed in the peach tree, were still there when Parker came out of the pines, too frightened to return to the nest at once.

Seven

Parker gave himself a rest on the next day, the Sabbath, but on Monday morning he was at the table early. His mother had already cleaned the room; the table had been dusted, his stack of paper squared in the middle of it, the pen laid across the paper like a hyphen. Had she read the deposition? It didn't seem to have been disturbed. Parker took it from the drawer—no, she wouldn't look at it until it was thrust into her hands with instructions, *Read this.* If she'd left the pistol there—and he believed she'd known it was there before it was used, not just after—she wouldn't remove a stack of paper.

Before he began, Parker completed the intention which she had interrupted days earlier. He moved the pistol and cartridges from the table to a drawer of the dresser. He didn't conceal them, but left them in plain sight on a pile of shirts where, if she opened the drawer, she would find them at once. A trap—he wanted to see if she would replace them, if her scrupulous arrangement with the past would require that of her. He had believed her on Saturday, accepted her account—as *hers*, the version which preserved her. She hadn't tampered with her husband's memory, hadn't, if Parker heard her right, meddled in his life. Her curiosity about the deposition sounded to him like anxiety; she wasn't concerned that he was writing a deposition, only that he was writing it in a room which she did not want violated. Well, he had made the violation unmistakable.

He forced himself to read over the last pages he had written. He heard his mother leave the house—one of her business mornings. She crossed the lawn beneath his window, but did not look up or wave. The office she went to, his father's old office, as unchanged as his room, was only two buildings from Booth's. Would she ask Booth about the deposition? No, not that either—but what would Booth say if she did? Probably that Parker wasn't able to be *realistic,* and he would expect her to understand. Parker read no further, but began to write.

I had my first insight into Arthur Kin, and into justice, on Exercise Deep Hole. This was a command-post exercise, and all the headquarters troops, but no field troops, took up their battle stations when the alert sounded. It sounded, of course, in the middle of the night, but we climbed out of bed and loaded all our office gear onto trucks and by six a.m. we were operating at Burrow, an overheated and badly lit bunker bequeathed to us by the Third Reich.

Gentile and I were runners for the Adjutant General Communications Center, and our job was easy enough. We took the documents as they came through on the AG wire, and we trotted through that underground maze to deliver them to the staff sections. We carried pink receipt slips because all the messages were classified, most of them *Secret* or *Cosmic Top Secret. Cosmic,* you hear—this Deep Hole may have been fiction, but it was no joke. Gentile was normally a draftsman and he wasn't used to handling classified stuff. He was so confused by the amount of paper—we left the Comm Center with twenty or so messages and the same number of receipt forms—and so muddled by the message numbers and so frightened that he would lose or misplace one, and thus be jailed for a security violation, that he never managed to learn the subterranean layout of Burrow. Down there in the bowels of Germany he was lost and frantic, kept wheezing and said he couldn't breathe. I remember watching him speed down a corridor in his stiff military walk and perform, when he reached the end of it, a series of facing movements with utterly no idea of which direction to take. Left face, right face, about face, and he ended up coming back the same corridor. Somehow he always scrambled the messages and receipts, and his hands were so damp with sweat that he smudged everything he touched. And on that first day he steadily licked the point of his ballpoint pen to keep the ink flowing, and he got ink all over his tongue and chin and cheeks and nose.

Davy was upset, as anybody would have been, by the Deep Hole scenario, as it was called, which he was able to gather from the messages he carried. It seemed that the Warsaw Pact nations, staging maneuvers on the far side of the Iron Curtain, began to feel territorial. They sacked Berlin, gassed Munich, bombarded Hamburg. They dispensed death on a generous scale. In the G3 War Room, where Arthur Kin hammered away steadily at his typewriter, the officers were in a hubbub as they moved their significant pins all over the wall maps. The maps were solid with black pins from Danzig to Budapest—and black represented the enemy. What other color is there for menace and evil? The citizens of the free countries of Europe were in a state of panic; evacuations were under way from all major cities, and the Autobahns and railways were jammed. The enemy was everywhere, and it wasn't always easy to remember that out of our own heads we had invented their attack and their malice. Talk about paranoia—you get a dose of it in the military.

One of the most distasteful parts of the exercise was dealing with Strickland. He was the G4 message clerk, the man Gentile and I had to negotiate with. With his complexion and demeanor, he seemed to belong to that festering bunker. I say festering because by midday the dampness above ground was clogging the ducts and ventilators, and various moldy stenches, particularly near the kitchen and the crappers, took hold. I associate Strickland with that cloacal Deep Hole stink. I had lived with him, and I am here to tell you that niggers are not the only persons with a distinctive aroma. Strickland smelled bad, sitting there in his dandruffy and ripe woolen GI shirt, and he stared balefully at the messages Davy and I brought him, checking the message number and description on the receipt against the message itself. There was no need for this thoroughness; Strickland was just tediously, perversely slow in order to make every transaction an ordeal for Davy and me. The delays Strickland caused Davy were a real grievance, for he was always behind and anxious to be off on his other deliveries. Aware of this, Strickland detained him as long as he could, trying to confuse and further unhinge him.

Well, the day raged on, and just before we were due to go off shift, Davy ran a message down to G4. It contained information about an ordnance convoy stuck in evacuation traffic, and the G4 colonel was the action addressee, the man who had to figure out how to get that ammo to the troops at the front. Davy knew that the message was a particularly important one, since the AG himself, Lieutenant Colonel Saunders, hopped up and down until he was sure that he had communicated a sense of urgency. He succeeded in terrifying Davy, who carried the message under the heel of his sweaty palm. The ink was damp to begin with, and when Davy reached G4, Strickland took one look at the bleary message and sent Davy back for another copy. Davy ran back to the Comm Center, almost in tears; I helped him set up the master on the duplicating machine to run a clean copy; in the meantime Strickland's colonel discovered the delay when an officer from G3, who'd already received an information copy, stepped over to ask when the ordnance was likely to reach his men. The G4 colonel stormed into the Comm Center; Saunders entered the fracas; threats, curses, crimson faces; I showed them the message Strickland had refused; "Hey hey hey," Davy yelped when the colonel took God's name in vain. There was a consensus that the original message was legible and we all marched in a delegation down to G4, where stinking Strickland got properly reamed. It was one of the most remarkable and wide-ranging orations I ever heard from an officer of the U.S. Army, and I was gratified to be present. Davy wasn't; he said to me later that it wasn't entirely Strickland's fault, the message really was sort of hard to make out. I tried to make him see the larger issue, but he didn't feel any triumph.

That night back at barracks—we left Burrow and returned to our peacetime quarters to sleep—Strickland was nursing a heavy grudge. He was scowling and he kept his most lethal wall-eyed glare on Davy and me, all the while making his little sucking sound with the side of his mouth to let us know that he was brooding on revenge. He put on his boots and the rest of his cowboy suit and went over to the EM Club to drown his sorrows. He woke us all up when he staggered back in at midnight. He was still muttering and sucking as he crashed around in the dark, and it was Arthur Kin who volunteered. "Strickland, when you gone to learn to keep your sorry mouth shut and act right?"

The effect was magnificent—Strickland shut up. He must have been as stunned as I was to hear Arthur's voice. He did keep making that nasty sound with his lip and he banged his locker door more often and more loudly than he had to, but for a few minutes as we listened to him a comradely feeling seemed to exist in the room. There was Arthur in his bunk, and Davy in his, and I in mine, and we were all thinking the same thing, we were all pleasantly half asleep, we felt united. Davy said, "Hey, Arthur, thanks for that," and Arthur said, "The pleasure was mine."

That was the first day and night of Deep Hole, and by the morning it seemed to have been forgotten. Arthur slept late, as usual, his elbows and knees poking up as though the ticky Army blanket covered a chair or a machine and not a man at all. Strickland looked at him and announced that he must have inherited that way of sleeping from his ancestors the jungle bunnies, who slept in trees. So things were back to normal, more or less, and Arthur was as taciturn as ever when he did roll out onto his feet. We went out to Burrow again and we kept on playing war games; we got used to the twelve-hour exercise shifts, the underground life, the make-believe carnage. I wasn't appalled, not until I found that I was among the survivors of the first nuclear spray. That meant that I had to continue the game, proceed to the secondary headquarters, named Neversink, while the victims returned to the surface and resumed their regular lives.

I was transported to Neversink, an old Nazi bunker in a

piny hillside, in the back of a soggy truck in the pouring rain. There were a few crumbling huts and tables scattered among the dripping trees, as though the place might once have been the scene of pastoral Third Reich outings, but a stout, square concrete maw lined with iron opened into the flank of the hill. A shaft led deep underground to a vault divided by a few flimsy partitions. This was the new War Room. Over the years patches of cement had fallen from the ceiling, and there, where the subsoil was exposed, the water that came through the hill gathered in those swagging, bellied, upside-down puddles. Black electric lines were festooned from the ceiling and generators hummed. The war maps were unfurled and tacked on the partitions and sprinkled with silver umbrella symbols denoting atomic blasts.

Though only a hundred or so troops were still among the living, all my roommates were there at Neversink, not only Gentile and Strickland but also Arthur. I was disappointed in him that he hadn't found a way to get himself on the casualty list, he was such a practiced shirker—they're supposed to be expert at it. Arthur was disappointed in himself, it appeared, for he sat like a lump on a footlocker, harnessed in his field rig, head in his hands. He wasn't bothering to pretend to play soldier. Somehow he was beyond reproach; if Gentile or Strickland or I had collapsed like that, you may rest assured that we would quickly have found a boot applied to our rectum, as First Sergeant Boyles liked to say. But no one, and the First Sergeant was there, spoke a word to Arthur, and I soon noticed that he had disappeared.

The commander at Neversink was a colonel, the general and other high brass having perished at Burrow, and he considered this his moment to shine. He kept everyone at duty stations, enlisted men and officers alike. No matter that there was no duty—very few messages trickled over the wire, for no one was left to send them. We were the last free men in the world. The colonel had us decorating the place, sweeping and swabbing and moving the tables and partitions around, just to keep us busy. He seemed to believe, and the rest of us hoped, that we would soon take a direct hit—get *bummed,* as he said—and we would all be able to go home. But no message to that effect came, and toward midnight the colonel made a command decision to send some of us to bed. If Neversink held out, he wanted fresh replacements in the morning. Gentile and I were in the detachment for sleep, but Strickland was kept on in the War Room—he was a Spec 5, and the colonel wanted some senior clerks on hand.

The colonel granted us six hours of sleep and we heaved our packs onto our shoulders and marched out of Neversink in the rain. The military lamps, one above the concrete entrance to the bunker and the other above the latrine, were the only beacons in that filthy night, but we steered by them to the nearest hut. It was a tarpaper cylinder with single windows protruding on either side like the eyes of a mule. Inside we found a few soaking canvas cots and two inches of water on the earthen floor. What else did we find? Arthur Kin, tightly zipped into his mummy sleeping bag. Above his cot he had built a sort of tepee with other cots. The whole construction was covered with his shelter half, for there was no square yard of that hut where the water did not drip. "Cut off that mothuhfucking light," said Arthur, but I don't think that the man who had switched on a flashlight and shined it in Arthur's face intended any malice. He was just admiring the accomplishment. Arthur was snug and dry and comfortable, had been for hours. We all tried to imitate him, but the best I could do in that leaking shelter was arrange myself so that I had a single drip upon the knees. I was asleep before it could bother me.

A light awoke me. As soon as my eyes opened, I was conscious of aches: I was cold, wet, shriveled, and stiff. The rain had stopped, I noticed, but it was still black outside. I knew it couldn't be 0600 yet, and I knew also, though I can't tell you how—smell maybe—that this intruder with the light must be Strickland. He was looking for someone and poked his beam into a few faces near me. I surmised that I had been wakened by his sticking it in my face. The light stopped when it hit Gentile, the big whopping Portuguese chin with sprouting nocturnal whiskers. Gentile had the heaviest beard in the whole unit. Davy blinked and rolled his head, but Strickland kept the goddam beam right in his eyes, about a foot from his face. Davy quit trying to escape it and sat up, struggling to get his arms free from the mummy bag.

"Hey hey hey. What's this? What's going on here? What's the meaning of this?"

"Shut up," said Strickland.

"Shut up! What? Who's that? What's this?"

By then Davy was almost awake, still blinking but coming to. He stopped fighting the soaked bag and sat there trussed up, helpless, thinking. He tried to obey Strickland, to whisper. "Is that you, Specialist Strickland? Is it six o'clock yet? Is it time to go back on duty?"

"Yeah," said Strickland. "It's duty time. It's 0300 and I'm going on sick call. They need a replacement for me. I'm sending you."

"Oh. Me, huh? I see. Right now? You mean I'm supposed to go now?"

"Right now. Get your ass out of that sleeping bag."

Gentile started to squirm again, looking for the zipper. The light stayed on his face, where it had been throughout the exchange, but it swung toward me when I croaked in the dark, "Strickland, what sort of a crock is this?"

"Is that you, Livingston?"

"It's me. What are you trying to pull?"

"What's it got to do with you? This is between me and Gentile."

"Don't get up, Davy. Go back to sleep. There's no sick call out here. And, Strickland, you get that fucking light out of my face."

He did, but he put it right back on Gentile. "Up," he said to Davy, "and that's an order."

"Hey, are you really sick?" Gentile asked. "What's wrong with you anyway?"

Stiff and aching as I was, I was beginning to enjoy this visit. I was tickled. I'd never heard Gentile challenge anyone before. "You heard me," Strickland said. "I'm ordering you to the bunker."

"Tell him to kiss your can, Davy."

Gentile was trying to look past the light at me, to see if I was to be trusted. He was weighing my advice. Then he tried to locate Strickland, to look him in the eye. "Okay. I think I will tell him that. Specialist Strickland, why don't you kiss my can?"

I laughed, and so did Gentile at his own temerity, and we were joined by a chuckle from the tepee. Sneaky Arthur was eavesdropping. "You tell him, Gentile," said Arthur. "Give him the good word."

Strickland's light bounced around to find this new source of disrespect. "So. You too, Kin, you too."

"Yeah. Me too, Strickland, me too." Arthur mimicked the grimness in Strickland's command voice. "And if you don't cut off that light I am going to get up from here and take it away from you and shove it where the moon don't shine."

I never claimed that Arthur was an angel. He could be very ugly when he wanted to be. Strickland took heed of his words and dipped the light and went to work on Gentile again. "All right, Gentile. This is it. I'm ordering you for the last time. Get over to that bunker or you go on report."

I could tell that he alarmed Gentile. And so, to thwart Strickland and take Davy off the hook, I interrupted again. "Order *me,* Strickland. Try to send *me* over there."

"Gentile, are you going?"

"Davy, he's picking on you. Can't you see? He won't order me to go. He wants to scare you into it. *He's* supposed to be there, not you. He can't do a thing if you refuse."

Davy deliberated again. "Yeah. I see. I think I can figure this out. Hey, Strickland, are you going to order Livingston or what?"

And Strickland was so angry that he did. "Livingston, I'm ordering you right now to replace me at the bunker. Are you going to do it or do I put you on report?"

"Strickland, you moron, why don't you just go away?"

He wouldn't. After I refused, I heard him sucking on his lip. I knew he had the evil eye on me—much good it did him in the dark behind the beam. He decided to complete his failure, to go zero for three, and he ordered Arthur to replace him at the bunker.

"Get out of here," Arthur told him. "This shit is getting old."

And then Strickland did leave. What else could he do? But as soon as he left, Davy began to worry, and Arthur and some of the other sleepers, who woke just at the end of

Strickland's visit, told me to pipe down. I was trying to cheer Davy up, but soon our friendly hut settled and slumbered again.

What happened next is this: scarcely had I closed my eyes and dozed again when somebody else with a flashlight barged into the place. This person apparently did not mind rousing everybody. "Livingston! Kin! Gentile! On your feet, and I mean now!" I knew that voice well enough—First Sergeant Boyles. In a few seconds I was standing in my stocking feet in the water and mud of the floor. Arthur was standing too, and the First Sergeant himself unzipped Gentile because Davy didn't move fast enough to suit him. By chance the flashlight discovered Davy with an erection in his longjohns, and the First Sergeant kept the beam on it during our lecture.

"I get it now! You wanted to stay here and pound your pud!" And so on. What he said doesn't bear repeating. After he was satisfied that he had shamed Gentile, publicly accused him of mortal sin when Davy was merely dreaming, he began a routine of threats. He promised to lay Article 15s on us, to peel off our stripes, to get the maximum. Like Strickland, the First Sergeant directed most of his comments to Davy rather than to me or Arthur. He could keep up this kind of harangue indefinitely, as we all knew.

I spoke up. "You're not going to Article 15 anybody."

He whirled. He stuck the light inches from my face, and I could feel his own face inches behind that. "What'd you say? What was that, Livingston? Let me hear that one more time."

"I said you're not going to Article 15 anybody."

"You'll change your mind about that when the stripe comes off your arm."

"If you take off that stripe, I'll be in the Judge Advocate's office so fast you won't believe it."

"What Judge Advocate's office?"

"The Seventh Army Judge Advocate's. You don't have the authority to give out an Article 15."

"You're telling me I can't lay an Article 15 on you?"

"I'm telling you what's in the Uniform Code of Military Justice. I saw a movie on it at basic training."

Then I had a surprise. "Knowing that," said Arthur Kin. "Seems to me I remember that movie too. Got to be the captain that gives out the Article 15. Yes indeed, I recall that now, First Sergeant."

Which was in fact the case, as the First Sergeant was well aware. He'd evidently forgotten in his passion. Now that Arthur had added his opinion to mine, the First Sergeant had the short side of the argument. He realized it, but didn't like it. "All right, you two wise asses, we'll just see how much difference it makes whether it comes from me or the captain."

"It makes a world of difference," Arthur said.

Niggers have a genius for insubordination. Arthur put no special tone in his voice, but the First Sergeant's rage was intensified—it had been routine before, all in a night's work, but now the light shook in his hand and he bit out his final words. "I got better things to do than stand here and argue with a couple of guardhouse legal experts. If all three of you aren't in that bunker in five minutes, it'll be worse than an Article 15. I'll have your ass under the jail."

Well, the long and short of this affair is that we did get Article 15ed. We slogged back to the bunker, where we were not urgently needed, and sat around there until Neversink finally did get bummed. Hot damn. We closed the place up in minutes and boarded the trucks to return to headquarters, and as soon as I arrived I was summoned to the captain's presence. Arthur and Davy joined me and we all three took our medicine together. The charge was refusal to obey a direct order and we were fined $50 each. Not even Davy minded that, and as for Arthur—the spades are used to it. And it was a victory after all, for Strickland was moved to another room when he came back from the hospital. I don't know how he got himself admitted, but he was taken there in a staff car from Neversink and he persuaded them to let him in. I was sure that he had faked it.

So there it is, my one firsthand experience of justice. Justice? Yes, there was a measure of justice performed during that exercise, but it had nothing to do with military law. Justice was done when Arthur and Gentile and I looked into Strickland's light and made him clear off. The three of us were—may I say it?—united by principle, not just by a desire to oppose Strickland. And the law, of course, punished us. I wonder: is the law any closer to justice here in Alabama than it was in the Army?

And for the moment he left it at that. It was Friday afternoon and he'd spent one working week producing the annals of Deep Hole. He'd sat for hours above each page and the pen had been propelled only by small fits of exasperation. Neatness had suffered; words and sentences were lined out, and the margins were crowded with fierce doodles which had left impressions on the pad half a dozen pages deep. Parker didn't care for the way the deposition kept turning into story, with dialogue and quotation marks, but that had been the only way to proceed, since he knew what had happened but no longer why. The last paragraph had come with particular reluctance; there were enough differences between Deep Hole and the Hirts' pond to keep him from pressing comparisons. Furthermore, his nerve in standing up to the First Sergeant seemed no occasion for vanity—here he was again, braving legal action, but he hadn't been so ready to defy Sessions. Even though he imagined that real dangers might attend a prosecution of Sessions and the others, he couldn't convince himself that they would be equal to the dangers which had done him in at the pond. The law was safe, and he didn't have an elevated opinion of his crusade to bring Sessions to trial.

Days at the table, and he'd produced a few pages of choppy script which he was tempted to chuck out altogether. The paper itself, when he gathered it up, made a swollen and wavy stack, for the pages had wrinkled under the heel of his humid hand. He was as sweaty as Gentile. But he kept that increment of the deposition; he expected that Booth would be mighty curious to know what Deep Hole had to do with Sessions and the 7th of September. The prospect of the lawyer's impatience rather pleased him as he opened the drawer of the table and tucked the new pages under the rest of the deposition.

The drawer was empty except for the paper. Though his mother had passed several times through the room on her cleaning missions, she had not yet discovered the missing pistol, or at least she had not mentioned it. Parker always rose after she did, and each morning she preceded him into his father's room to empty the ashtray and wastebasket and remove the coffee cups. He left the brimming ashtray and coagulating cups as deliberate affronts to her sense of order, evidence of his continuing intrusion, hints of more serious upheavals, but she was not provoked. She did not press her inquiry about the deposition, nor did she refer to their conversation on the lawn.

All that week she had obeyed faithfully her own schedule of work and garden and sport, but she was home each night to share with Parker the meal that Iva left warming in the oven. Together they watched the evening news on the television and they ate immediately afterward. Their usual topics of conversation were the news, the coming election, the Livingston properties. When Mrs. Livingston described their administration, the intricate details of renting a couple of dirt farms, a few stores and offices, a dozen rundown houses, she induced in Parker a boredom he couldn't conceal. She did not linger after dinner; she had two weekly bridge games and she drove as far as Montgomery to play duplicate. She was gone, Parker thought, more frequently than her bridge meetings required, but she had mentioned that plans for the season's hunt were under way and she was negotiating for a new mount. He did not ask for further explanation. Left alone in the house, he watched more television, read, or puttered about in his room, which he had nearly finished painting a clinical white.

He seemed always to find himself at the television for one of the late talk shows, usually Cavett. He was tired but not tired enough to sleep; it had become difficult for him to distinguish between honest weariness and depletion. His mother invariably returned sometime during the program; she stood at the door for a moment as though she might be interested by what was on the screen, but she never was. After she went upstairs, he watched until Cavett signed off and the evening prayer was intoned. By then he was able to sleep; he conked out as soon as his head touched the pillow, but he expected to wake again in a few hours. His insomnia was merely dilatory. At three or four o'clock his eyes opened, and in the darkness dreams raged through his conscious mind. He thought of them, anyway, as dreams. They had the convincing detail of dreams (the hair of his drowning sister spreading on the water of a pond; an empty pitcher on the podium as he addressed a crowd, throat so parched that he produced only a dry static, as a beetle might) as well as dreamlike inevitability. Even awake, he couldn't stop them. They reeled on in a space in his head; he knew their physiological location, actually felt that his mind was a bright cubicle which refused to shut down, a sort of all-night diner which attracted strays and waifs. He submitted to the dreams, for he knew that he wouldn't sleep again until first light.

That wretched deposition was taking over his life. He stood up and angrily slammed the chair under the table; he grabbed for it at once to hold himself upright. The blood drained out of his head, he felt dizzy, he saw points of light all around him. He swooned, he swayed, he managed to keep his feet and quaking legs under him. When his head cleared, he decided he'd better go downstairs and find sustenance.

Eight

Queen Iva was installed in an upholstered chair and tuned in to *Love Is a Many Splendored Thing* on the kitchen Sony. Both the television and the chair were concessions only recently won. Iva had been obliged for years to take what comfort she could on a high and wobbly stool, and the only time she'd been able to see television was when she took the ironing into the library. Mrs. Livingston was not a taskmaster and she was devoted to Iva, but she believed that relations with help were most satisfactory when certain clear standards were maintained on both sides. She had yielded, finally, to the improvements only when Iva delivered an ultimatum: "I'm too big and too old and got too much blood pressure to sit where my feet won't reach the floor, and I'm alone in this house too much to be without company." After the chair and the television were allowed, Iva took it upon herself to relax other regulations; she exchanged her starched gray uniforms for white nylon drip-dry outfits which were convenient and waitressy, and she replaced the prescribed oxford shoes with cloth slippers. "I'm sorry, Miss Eleanor," she told Parker's mother, "but I don't want you to say nothing about it. The corns are on *my* feet, not yours." Mrs. Livingston didn't care for the tone of the remark and charged it to Iva's age, but she was willing to condone much in the case of the woman who had been her first servant and who was still a decent cook, a good housekeeper, and a loyal dependent.

"Bout time," Iva said to Parker when he entered the kitchen. She got to her feet and flicked off the tube. "Waiting on you has got me watching this trash."

"You didn't have to wait for me, Iva."

"I made some egg salad. How many sandwiches you want?"

"Just one. I can get it. I'm capable of making a sandwich for myself."

"You set down."

"Iva, there's no reason for you to make it."

She disdained argument. She pointed out the place already set for him at the breakfast table, and Parker reluctantly seated himself. No use protesting—her manner announced loudly that reckoning was at hand. Parker, who'd done his best to avoid it since he came home, was stuck. He was wedged into the breakfast nook, his mother's birding station and plant sanctuary, greenhouse and observation post. Once a pantry, the nook was now a glassy corner; the windows took in most of the lawn, and the bird guides and binoculars were always handy on the table. Beneath the windows, tiers of ferns and philodendra were arranged to catch the sun. Ornamental tubs of feathery climbers and trailers were hung on the walls. Parker could never remember their names. Cyclamen, asparagus fern, flame pea, lantana, begonia—it was all chlorophyll to him. The place smelled of humus and nitrogen, and it was lush and tropical and a fatal temptation to the birds. As Parker sat there, as Iva got his lunch, a sparrow sailed into the glass at top speed, folded its wings, and fell to the flowerbed below.

Iva heard the thump. "That's the second one today."

"You think it's dead?"

"Might be. Out cold anyhow. Some of them lie there under the window an hour or more before they get up and fly off again."

"Mama ought to put up a sign on the window."

He expected Iva to chuckle—her disapproval of his mother's bird and plant programs was historic and good-natured—but she said, "I suppose you the one going to teach them to read. You got the time for it."

She brought him his food, too much of it on too many plates. It took her three trips from the counter to spread it all before him. The bread for the sandwich was toasted, the crust trimmed, and there were separate plates for a bean salad, cottage cheese, peaches. She was wheezing as if she'd just climbed flights of stairs, and Parker squirmed. He didn't want to be waited on, not by her, not so elaborately, not so doggedly. Her attention had become a kind of reproach: she hadn't changed even if he had, and she was not going to be put off.

"Eat," she said, and lowered herself into a chair. He was blocked, and he knew he wasn't going to get away from the table until she'd had her say.

"I wish you wouldn't go to so much trouble."

"Seeing that you eat ain't no trouble." She supervised a few mouthfuls as she settled herself in her chair.

"Mighty good egg salad," he said.

"Your mama is worried about you," Iva said.

"Worried? Why?"

"She wonder what you going to do. It don't seem natural

for you just to sit around the house like you been doing, never go out, never see nobody."

Parker knew at once that these were not his mother's worries, they were Iva's own. If his mother had talked to Iva about him, she would have regretted the interruption of his education and discussed his plans to resume it. Only Iva would point out what was natural for him.

"None of my friends are in town now, Iva. They're all at school. That's why I'm underfoot all the time."

"Why ain't *you* at school?"

"I'll probably go back after Christmas."

"That's three months off. What you going to do till then? Keep haunting this place like you been doing?"

Her voice was impatient, but he put off the explanation she was after. He tried to win a smile. "Haunting? Do I look like a ghost to you?"

"You up there in your father's room all morning long—what you doing up there anyway?"

"I'm trying to write something for Mr. Lovelace."

"Write what?"

"What happened when Arthur was here."

"What for? Is any of that going to court?"

"I don't know yet."

She considered for a moment, only a moment, before dismissing the law. That wasn't what concerned her. "That boy Arthur didn't have no business coming here," she said. "He ought to have had better sense than that."

"I asked him to come."

"You gave him a ride here. You was helping him out. Didn't nobody *make* him stay and go out to that lake the next day."

"There was nothing wrong with that. Nobody had any reason to bother him."

She refused to discuss the others. "That boy was on his way home. What'd he want to stay here for? What'd he expect but trouble?"

Parker didn't try to reason with her. Of course she'd blame Arthur, expect him to know what she'd been learning for a lifetime. The rules for her and her people—rules and the penalties for violating them—must have seemed as clear and immutable as the commandments carved in the tablets of stone. How could he tell her that they didn't bind Arthur, didn't even have to bind her?

"And look what he done for you. Look at the mess he got you in."

"If I'm in a mess, I got myself in it."

"You here when you ought to be at school. You not working, not studying, not talking to nobody but a lawyer. About what? About Arthur, and I notice that Arthur is long gone. Just left all the trouble in your lap. He wasn't about to stay around here for no trial—he had that much sense. This is your home and you got to live here, but he's gone back to Mississippi. Now you tell me why you got to do anything for him."

Her voice sounded familiar. It took him a few seconds to identify the tone as exactly the tone his mother might have used in correcting Iva. Frustrated because her good advice was being wasted, she still felt it her duty to utter the advice. Iva spoke to him as if he were wayward and improvident; not equal to the most common daily necessities, such as eating, he wasn't very likely to show wisdom in larger matters.

"I stayed home because I wanted to, not just because of Arthur."

"Look at you. You not eating enough to keep a bird alive. You getting thin and puny. You need to shave and cut your hair. You been mooning around here for a month now, not looking after yourself—because you want to?"

Parker picked at his food, as if to convince her he could do something right. Iva had spoiled him from the cradle; she expected him still to need the same careful ministering. But he was no longer, wouldn't pretend to be, the child she had bathed and dressed, hugged and fondled. He believed that he'd outgrown her, and he pitied her because she wanted him to remain that child.

"Iva," he enunciated slowly, "I'm here in Ewell, and not at school, because I'm trying to do what I think has got to be done. Arthur Kin was shot at. I don't think that should have happened. I think the men who did it should stand trial."

"You believe that's going to keep it from happening again? That once they get in the courtroom they going to feel sorry all of a sudden for what they done? They going to see how wrong they been?"

"Maybe they won't. But they broke the law all the same. Don't you think they ought to be punished?"

"They white men. Nothing going to happen to them."

"Even if nothing does happen to them, maybe some other white men would learn from a trial."

"What you learning from all this, that's what I care about. Something eating you up. Don't tell me you like the way you been acting. I known you too long to believe that. You keep off to yourself, don't talk to nobody white or colored, not to your mama or me either one. Is that what you been learning?"

She leaned forward across the table. Disheveled, formidable, she seemed to gather the force of her presence to save him. Her broad face pressed against the space between them until it was not a foot from him.

143

"Please don't get upset," he said. "I've tried to do what I thought was right."

"What you call right?" she asked, and she offered her face as if it were the ledger and exhibit of love, the mortal field of justice, a claim too powerful to be defended against.

"What do you think I should do?"

"Look first to your family and those that care for you," she said. Her hand touched his arm gently. "We always here."

And then, quite brusquely, she withdrew her presence. Parker heard but even more felt her leave, as if the air she'd forced before her into the breakfast nook now rushed out through the space she vacated. She removed his half-eaten lunch, grunted several unflattering remarks about his appetite, scraped and rinsed the plates. Apparently she was content with the interview, for she was bent on chattering and her voice again entered its normal register, sailed effortlessly from her—plain lively talk. "Your mama called the house around noon, gave me a message for you."

"She didn't want to talk to me?"

"She said don't disturb you. I said if it was me up there, I'd pay to have somebody disturb me. But she said no, she didn't want to bother you. Told me to tell you that Mr. Minny—that ain't his name—was coming to eat supper tonight and she want you to meet him."

"Mr. Minny?"

"That ain't his name. Minny, McMinny, McNaminy—something like that. I never have got it right."

"Who is he?"

"Her new friend. Nice-looking man. He comes from Montgomery. She ain't told you about him?"

"Not a word."

Iva smiled, but did not at once volunteer any information

about Mr. Minny. She continued to tidy up the kitchen; it occurred to Parker that no preparations for a meal were evident. "Are you going to stay to fix dinner?"

"Uh-uh, no, not when Mr. Minny comes. He brings his own food with him, cooks it all himself. Makes a big mess too. I bet you a nickel it ain't one clean pot or pan in this kitchen tomorrow morning."

"What kind of food does he bring?"

"He says French. Onions is the main thing with him. Got to have onions frying, he says, else it don't smell like a kitchen. Oh yes, I know Mr. Minny."

"Does Mama like this man?"

"What you think? Sho she likes him. She's the one asked him to come. But if you mean how much does she like him —he's still doing the cooking."

Iva laughed, much amused by the thought of Mr. Minny at the stove. "He wears an apron too, and your mama sets there at the table and talks to him while he cooks. 'Umm-umm,' Mr. Minny says, 'taste this,' and he trots over with a spoonful of something to give her a lick of it. No, child, I was here the first time he came, but I'm not needed when Mr. Minny comes for supper."

Parker noticed that "child," old endearment, and was grateful for it.

"Your mama says clean up tonight to make a good impression on Mr. Minny. I say the same. Your razor and comb ain't overworked. I say make a good impression on your mama."

More serious advice. Iva had come to a halt in the middle of the kitchen, and she gave him a steady look. "I think she bringing him here because she don't want to hide nothing from you. She more worried what you think of her than what he think of you."

"I'll be so clean she won't recognize me."

"You would be if I washed you." She looked at the clock. "I got to fly," she said. "Got to catch my ride down the street." She stepped into her shoes, fetched her coat and a black hat of Napoleonic size and shape from the closet. She jammed the hat onto her head. He followed her to the door, and she stopped for parting words at the threshold. "You remember what I told you, you hear?"

"I'll try to."

"You grown up now, but you still somebody's son."

"I'll behave."

"Tell your mama I'll be here in the morning."

"I will."

"Bye, then. Don't forget."

And as soon as she'd gone he carried out her most practical instructions. He showered and shaved, even trimmed the ends of the hairs that lapped over his ears. No drastic barbering, just a narcissistic flutter. And contemplating his image in the mirror, he wondered about his mother and Mr. Minny. After Iva's parting counsel and her less-than-recommendation, he had no idea what sort of evening to expect. If Mr. Minny was witless as a fish, why did his mother put up with him? And why did she produce him now for examination? Why such short notice? Why relay through Iva the message that he was to scrub himself? Parker could answer none of the questions he invented, but he suspected his mother of having designs. To himself he phrased it nastily: *It didn't take her long once the subject of marriage was mentioned.* He admitted, to keep things fair, that the suitor might represent the impossibility of marriage rather than its imminence. In any case, Iva's rendering of Mr. Minny had inspired neither dread nor anxiety, only a conscious wish and resolution to gratify his mother.

When he concluded his pampering and dressed himself in fresh corduroys and clean shirt, he endured an onset of loneliness. He contemplated a letter to Erika, the German girl whose ardent communications he had not once replied to. But he wanted to write about Iva, and Erika was not the appropriate correspondent. He cleared his desk of the brushes and cans of paint, got a head-clearing whiff of turpentine, rummaged about in his drawer until he found a piece of stationery and a trusty BIC. He would write, of course, to Amsy, the sharer of his past, who might understand when he wrote that for Iva inequality was the very condition of love. Iva had served, wrapped her years around his, and she expected love not as a right or privilege of servitude but as its consequence. Parker was going to explain to his sister that unless Iva were allowed to dote, as soon as she was deprived of the forms and gestures of servitude, once she was no longer permitted to spoil him, she would feel he had cast her off. He believed that Iva, and others like her, saw acquiescence as their lot and burden; they seemed to accept it not so much to protect themselves as to protect white people, to keep them from knowing what they might be accountable for. He believed that Iva had put herself in the way of destroying knowledge—and she had, but not to shield him. He had intended to complain that he was compelled to suffer the supererogatory ministrations of a hobbled black woman who was too old to change her ways. It didn't occur to him that Iva's long, exacting scrutiny was like the gaze of any other lover, that what seemed to him her abasement was no more than necessary forgiveness. He didn't know that as she had numbered the teeth which broke his gums and estimated with her hands every inch and pound of his growth, she'd already realized that love had better be humble as long as time continues. The white baby ticked with its own life; it converted love to its purposes as easily as it consumed air, milk, cereal.

He didn't know that, but he knew enough to abandon the letter before he began it, and he crushed the blank sheet of paper in his hand. He'd been about to make an appeal he did not feel entitled to, a presumption of intimacy that he had denied himself. For Amsy had been a passenger in the Impala with Arthur, she had shared the day at the pond, and she had been left behind when he stepped into Sessions' light. Since leaving for school she had written to their mother but not to Parker, as if she understood what was needed to restore the intimacy implied by family.

Parker tossed the paper away and left his room to stalk energetically about the house. He entered the library first, but he did not care to read there, and then went to the back porch, but he certainly did not intend to witness the hectic dusk activity of the birds. He came inside and experienced such oppressive discomfort that he couldn't bring himself to sit down. The pillows and chairs were sleekly plumped, the ashtrays were cleaned and geometrically aligned on their tables, and the music books on the piano in the living room might have been set out with a carpenter's rule. All clutter had been banished, and yet a rebellion seemed to lurk; chairs, tables, lamps, all the objects in the filled and familiar rooms retained their places with the barely mastered ferocity of beasts under a whip, coiled to spring the moment his mother's will relaxed a notch. For Parker knew that his mother, and not Iva, was the author of this order. And since he wished to please her, he decided he ought to remove himself. Despite his spanking and cleansed enclosure of skin, hair, and corduroy, he felt uncontrollably riotous in that ruled environment.

And so he was once again driven upstairs to his own room, where the degree of messiness suited him better. Socks on the floor, paint cans on the desk, record jackets everywhere, the room was turbulent but not squalid, and it answered his own discomposure. But he was no less lonely after he switched on the record player—the Grateful Dead —and stretched out across the bed, carefully, so as not to rumple his clothes. Simple ordinary horniness might have been at the bottom of his mood, for he had kept himself chaste as a Jesuit since he'd been home. Now, groomed and scented with Lilac Vegetal, he had nowhere to go but downstairs when his mother came home with her Mr. Minny. He was mildly curious about his mother's passions; he wondered if her habitual discipline was threatened by impulses as imperative as his own. He knew that she was capable of a kind of violent, consuming ecstasy, for he had seen her once, years ago, put a wild chestnut mare over a series of jumps. It must have been summer; the horse was lathered and each blow of its hooves lifted a feather of dust from the packed earth of the ring. Those particles speckled his mother's damp face and arms and spotted her moist blouse. Her body repeated the curve of the flexed shaft of the mare's neck, and when she poured language into the stiff ear in front of her—when he could hear her voice, when it wasn't lost in the reverberation of the horse's drumming—she damned the beast. Plunging, foaming, the mare finally took every gate and fence it was put at, lifted, it seemed to Parker, by the tension of his mother's knees and thighs on the laboring pads of muscle. She appeared almost to float above the saddle, but the reins were drawn like blades and the heels of her boots were spaded into the mare's flanks. It wasn't the danger that frightened Parker, the mass and power of the beast or its cutting hooves, it was the change that had come over his mother. Watching through the rungs of a fence—he wasn't tall enough to see over it—he was tugged by a fear that the woman he knew had been usurped by this one who cursed and grunted while engaging an animal in a hot field. This woman seemed no more conscious of him, her observing son, than she was of the time or the temperature. Her present was the force she was astride, the lovely motion she commanded and received.

Of course his mother had become herself again, at least the self he was familiar with, when she dismounted, and he had never again seen her on horseback. That was the only time he had accompanied her to the club stables, which were nearer Montgomery than Ewell. He'd been there for various functions, for drinks and dances, but his mother had discouraged him and Amsy from riding. To keep that part of her life apart from them? To conceal her passion from her children? She needn't have discouraged him, not after that one sight of her. He abominated horses, and the memory sufficed to put a stop to the erotic stirrings he'd felt when he entered the room. He felt vaguely profane; he sat up on his bed; he began with a rush of energy to tidy up the room, but the energy quickly waned; he really couldn't face the chore just then; he reached for his book.

Nine

Parker read a few plethoric pages of Faulkner. The book, inscribed with his father's name, was oddly sedative and reassuring; on the whole, Parker preferred his Alabama to Christmas's Mississippi. The door was closed behind him, the Grateful Dead still spun—third time through—and he heard neither his mother's car in the driveway nor her step in the hall. Her sharp rap on the door surprised him. He hid the book under his bedspread, a guilty reflex which irritated him, and lowered the volume of the record player before he opened the door. She'd evidently come directly to his room, still wearing her light coat and scarf and carrying her briefcase.

"Did you get the message I left with Iva? About Mr. McKemeny?"

"She told me. What's his name? Iva didn't seem to have it exactly."

"Frank McKemeny." She pronounced it carefully. "Iva knows his name perfectly well."

"She had some trouble with it."

His mother did not comment on Iva's difficulty. "He's bringing supper with him. We hoped that you'd be able to eat with us."

"Iva told me. I'd like to."

Mrs. Livingston gave no indication of relief or pleasure. "He'll be here in a minute and I've got to change." But she lingered at the door. "You look very nice tonight," she said finally. "That's thoughtful of you."

She asked him to let McKemeny in if she wasn't downstairs in time. He accepted the assignment, and though he wanted more information about the guest, he didn't try to detain his mother. She was in an obvious hurry to shed her office get-up, and when she went to her own room Parker uncovered his book, put away the record, and descended to meet Mr. Minny, a name which he found decidedly superior to McKemeny. Who was the gentleman and why was he being presented on that particular evening? He was convinced that there was deviousness afoot. His mother, despite the efficiency of her manner, had been on edge. There was no reason for her to repeat the invitation which Iva had already conveyed, and Parker's neatness should have alerted her that he'd accepted. After thirty consecutive evenings at home, did she think that he was going to sally forth that night on social errands? Parker took a very dour view of his mother's intentions, but, remembering Iva, he renewed his resolution to be fair and amiable.

He did not have to greet McKemeny, for his mother changed swiftly and joined him before the visitor arrived. The velocity of her transformation, however, made it more overwhelming; the garb and countenance of the woman of commerce had been discarded and this new apparition was bathed in the vapors of the boudoir. Parker was literally speechless. His mother wore pants and top of some downy cream-colored material, an outfit he had never seen her in, and though the clothing was neither tight nor fitted, it clung to her like a pelt of exotic fur. Her short hair seemed twice as deep and luxuriant as it had minutes before, and her face was somehow blurred—the effect of makeup probably—like the face of a woman who had just come from strenuous transports. Of course she hadn't; she had merely changed clothes, but that made no difference to Parker. The outlines of her face and body were diffuse, and her eyes were unfocused; it was as if the air and light no longer enclosed a defined physical being, as if his mother had become instead an emanation of her own lust. For Parker the vision was brief—maybe five steps as she passed through the broad arched entrance of the living room—but it sufficed. The illusion of his mother's carnal glow conveyed all he wanted to know about the evening ahead.

"Frank's not here yet?" she asked, and her voice was still businesslike.

"No sign of him."

"He probably had trouble getting away. He hadn't shopped yet when I talked to him this morning. He was going to pick up the food on the way here."

"Iva told me he was quite a cook."

She frowned slightly. "She seems to have told you a good deal about him."

"She didn't really. I'd like to know more before he comes."

His mother informed him that Frank McKemeny was a real-estate developer whom she had met at a professional convention. He was divorced, the father of four children, and, naturally, a horseman. She declared that he was intelligent and well read, but Parker's principal impression was that she was describing a man who had possessed her.

153

"How long have you been seeing him?"

"About a year now." She mentioned that Frank was involved in an attractive scheme for a planned community of townhouses and Parker heard her talking about mansard roofs and recreational zones, but he was not interested in McKemeny's career and would have preferred less discretion. He craved revelations—what lusts, appetites, emotions tied his mother to this man? But he didn't ask and she didn't offer, and McKemeny himself arrived.

His mother answered the door (at least McKemeny rang the bell; Parker noted that he didn't have the run of the house, immediately modified that satisfaction by guessing that special orders obtained for the night because he was present). He carried a bag of groceries under each arm and so merely bent his head forward to claim a kiss. Mrs. Livingston planted a domestic peck on his cheek. McKemeny at once looked round for Parker. He deposited the bags on the hall table and advanced with hand outstretched. "Frank McKemeny," he was saying, "your mother's told me a lot about you, including the fact that you were a bit hirsute." The voice was hearty, the criticism jovially intended, the handshake grinding.

"You should have seen me before I shaved my mustache."

"Heugh heugh," brayed McKemeny.

The handshake was unabated. McKemeny's grinning face, the face of an athletic meat-eater, loomed steadily in Parker's view. "El, I'm glad you finally gave me a look at this son of yours." Parker's mother appeared at McKemeny's shoulder. Her name was Eleanor, and Parker had never heard anyone make free with it. That proprietary *El* confirmed all suspicions.

"Well," McKemeny said, at last releasing his hand, "this

is an occasion. Shall we imbibe?" He dwelt on *imbibe* as he had on *hirsute*, apparently expecting Parker to admire his vocabulary as much as he himself did. Parker's opinion was that he was grossly affected and that his accent was about as elegant as LBJ's.

"I'll put the things in the kitchen. Martini for you, Parker? It's less hard on the palate than whiskey."

"Sure."

McKemeny retrieved the groceries and Eleanor followed him—tagged along behind him, Parker would have said—to give the guest, he supposed, a last-minute briefing in the kitchen. Parker flexed his hand as soon as he was alone. The hand wasn't numb, but he needed some gesture to make visible to himself his disapproval of this stranger who had all the charm of a Dale Carnegie honor graduate. Parker was confident of his instantaneous judgment that McKemeny was an ebullient bore and an oaf of magnitude, and he'd conceived an equally sudden distaste for McKemeny's person. One glance had been enough to take in the full-time care the body received (the flat belly, razor-cut hair, manicure, firm jaw and cheeks) as well as the studied raiment. Flush, ruddy, done up like a dandy, McKemeny gave off sensual energy like a secretion.

When he returned with the drinks he was stripped down to his Pierre Cardin shirt and his sleeves were rolled back, exposing heavy wrists and forearms packed with muscle. He wanted to drink to their first meeting, and as soon as the glasses had been lifted, he suggested that they sit in the library. "I'm not parlor company in this house," he said, and he swept Parker and Eleanor before him into the room.

McKemeny commenced at once to praise the library. He liked the shape and proportions of the room, but he had particular admiration for the paneling of curly pine, which he found unusual and exquisite and which, he knew for a fact, could not be duplicated at any price. He pointed out the fineness of joining and grain and when he had finished his pitch he turned upon Parker with a look which both dared him to disagree and called upon him to applaud the connoisseurship.

"I'm not thinking of buying the house," Parker said. "I already live here."

"Heugh heugh. I'm afraid I do sound as if I'm trying to sell it. It's a bad habit." McKemeny took a sip of his martini, but the small thrust seemed to have nettled him. "El tells me you're going back to school this winter."

"I expect to."

"You're very fortunate. Washington and Lee is a fine school."

"I guess so."

"You'll have some catching up to do when you get back."

"I've been away for a long time," Parker agreed, and he wondered if this was a topic his mother had primed McKemeny to discuss, if she'd enlisted her stud to persuade her son of the value of higher education.

"You shouldn't have any trouble, not if you know what you want. I was at Tuscaloosa after the war when the place was full of vets, but they were all in a rush to get their degrees and go out and make a bundle. Take advantage of college while you can—I was as bad as the vets, I couldn't wait to get out of school and go to work. I didn't want all of them to get a head start on me, but now I wish I'd spent more time at the university."

Parker winced and McKemeny caught it. "I know how corny this sounds, Parker, but I'm serious. Every now and then I read a good book—"

"You read all the time," Mrs. Livingston interrupted.

"Not as much as I'd like to. But when I do read a good book—I'm not talking about novels, I mean history or economics—I always regret that I didn't have more time and that I didn't use better the time that I did have. You take that book there—" He pointed, and then he stood up and he did take it, the first volume of *Lee's Lieutenants.* He went right to it, knew its exact location on the shelf, and that book, like the others in the library, had belonged to Parker's father.

"I think I learned something from this book. This is a history of what was best about the South."

"I'll have to try it," Parker said.

"You could do worse," McKemeny said, and he continued to extol the book, but Parker wasn't listening. He was simply staring at the book in the realtor's meaty hands. Most of the books in the room were Civil War history, and there was a Lincoln collection—all his father's. Even the objects in the room, from the leather chair that Parker sat in to the horseshoe nailed above the central bay of the shelf, had been selected and placed by his father. In spite of determined housekeeping and in spite of the glassy eye of the new color television, the room still bore the impress of Philip Livingston, and McKemeny's presence in it, handling those books and dispensing bogus paternal advice, entertaining Parker for the sake of the woman he called *El* and whom he confidently expected to screw that night, was objectionable and obscene. Parker looked at his mother to see if McKemeny had the same effect on her, but when she met his eyes her face was more complacent than ever: *Your father was not the only man in the world. I'm getting along just fine, kiddo.*

All Parker wanted then was to get out of the room and away from those two people, but he stayed where he was.

He did manage to divert McKemeny to the subject of his work—the "people business," McKemeny called it—and thereafter he displayed his sentiments by sinking into a monosyllabic torpor. No one seemed to notice, and McKemeny soon announced the urgency of his appetite. They all repaired to the kitchen, and there Iva's words became flesh: McKemeny assumed an apron and peeled two onions. "Dear God, what a root the onion is," he said, with tears drooling from his lashes. He made neat work of freeing the two oversized onions from their skins and he hefted them for the benefit of his audience. He cut them up and put them in a skillet to sauté. He ate several coils raw. "The onion-lover is your true eater," he told Parker. "The raw onion is the test of the gourmet. It's one of the most volatile flavors you can taste. But if you can't get down an onion—well, you're deprived, that's all. Disadvantaged, I believe the word is now."

Parker listened with his mother from a leafy seat at the breakfast table. It was some relief, but not much, to be out of the library. McKemeny, as he said himself, was in his element in the kitchen, and he evidently supposed that the spectacle he provided was plenty edifying. He gave them a blow-by-blow account of the meal to follow—a simple repast: a coquille, steak with béarnaise sauce, two vegetable dishes, and a chocolate soufflé. He was assured, absorbed, and seemed to require no participation from his gallery. As long as the chef was so sublimely content with himself, Parker felt at liberty to sulk as he pleased and he thought they might lurch through the evening without conflict.

He was wrong. McKemeny asked him: "What's this El's told me about the Negro you brought home with you? She says it's been bothering you."

McKemeny was leaning casually against the counter,

drink in one hand and spatula in the other, as blasé and oblivious as if he'd asked Parker's date of birth or his Social Security number. Parker was stupefied not just by what he said but by the fact that his mother had ratted on him. She'd never uttered a word to Parker about Arthur Kin, and for her to have confided in McKemeny amounted to perfidy.

"El's told me pretty much what happened," McKemeny continued. "You all went out to a lake, went swimming, drank some beer, and then a couple of rednecks turned up with guns and took a few pot shots."

"They didn't take pot shots," Parker said. "They shot out a light and they shot into the house and then they shot at Arthur."

"This Arthur is the Negro, right? You really believe they shot at him? If they could hit a light, they wouldn't have had any problem hitting a man."

"How come they all fired when he was outside the house, then? What would you say they were shooting at?"

"They were probably shooting up in the air a hundred yards over his head."

"Listen. They hollered for him to come out of the house, and they waited for him. They didn't shoot until they saw him."

"That doesn't necessarily mean anything. They just wanted to give him a good scare."

"They did that."

"Don't misunderstand me. I'm not defending them. I think that sort of business is reprehensible, but unfortunately there are still a few throwbacks around who think that's the way to handle a Negro when he steps out of line."

"Arthur didn't step out of line," Parker said, "and there are more than a few."

"How many were out there? Two? Three?"

"Three."

"And three is just about all you'd find in this town who are capable of that kind of trashiness. You ask the people here in Ewell and you'll find out that they're just sick about the whole thing."

"That's ridiculous. They think those three did the right thing. They think it's a laugh."

"You're wrong, Parker. I think you're mistaken about these people."

"If the people here are sick about it, they're staying quiet. There hasn't been what you'd call a public outcry for justice. Sessions and Fuqua and Bates had to pay for the light and the windows they shot out, but they haven't even been charged with anything else."

"What's there to charge them with? Firing a few rounds in the general vicinity of a Negro? Disturbance of the peace? Illegal use of firearms? Be practical about it. There's no point in hauling them into court for some petty charge."

"They ought to be tried for attempted murder."

"That's crazy," McKemeny said. "You don't seriously believe that?"

"Yes, I do."

"They couldn't possibly be convicted."

"Not in this state, maybe."

"Not in this state or anywhere else. It wouldn't even be a trial, there'd be so many reporters and lawyers and demonstrators down at the courthouse. Do you know what would happen the minute they were indicted for something like that? This town would be overrun with mobs of people who didn't know the first thing about the case or about Ewell—but that wouldn't keep them from making a lot of noise about it."

"So to keep Ewell peaceful we ought to forget the whole thing?"

"Unless you want to get everything so distorted and blown out of proportion that somebody really does get shot."

"And that would solve everything. Why not tell anybody that wants to that he can take his gun and blast away—the law won't touch him as long as his target is black."

"That's not going to happen and you know it."

"What's going to keep it from happening?"

"The fact that nobody wants it to."

"Only those three, huh?"

"They're not heroes, not even to themselves. I bet if you asked them how they felt now, and if they told the truth, they'd tell you they felt as low as dirt, and just as common."

"What a lot of shit."

McKemeny laughed, *heugh heugh.*

"Please don't argue," Mrs. Livingston said. "Isn't dinner almost ready?"

"An argument stimulates the appetite."

"Please, Frank. There's no point in quarreling."

"I like to get my teeth into an argument," he said, and he grinned, as if to show the disputatious incisors, before turning back to the stove with a nasal chuckle. "But I don't believe in fussing over good food, and we're about to eat. I declare a moratorium."

Parker had to hold on to his seat just to keep himself at the table. The food might have been good, but he could hardly taste it for the anger which rose like bile in his throat. McKemeny really was a miscreant, but he had fulfilled his intention: Parker was provoked. McKemeny knew it and he ignored him, devoting most of his attention to his El, plying her with choice morsels from his own coquille. He fed her from his fork and dabbed the corners of her mouth with his napkin, and Parker masticated his way through the meal feeling like a voyeur at the foreplay. He didn't last until the soufflé. The lights had been dimmed by then, and McKemeny announced that the soufflé was ready, needed only to be popped into the hot oven and it would rise like the full moon. Parker bolted.

"I'm going out for a while," he said. "I think I'll try to catch part of the football game."

"Don't rush off," McKemeny said. "Dessert is still to come."

"I'm stuffed already."

"Do you really want to go to the football game?" his mother asked. "Hasn't it already started?"

"We can save him some of the soufflé."

"It really is superb," Mrs. Livingston said. "It's best to get it hot. It's not the same later."

"I couldn't get down a single mouthful more," Parker said.

"See you later, then," McKemeny said, and shoved back his chair to make way.

"Right," Parker said. "Excuse me."

He had announced the football game as his destination only because he'd heard the noise. The cheers and the swells of the band had carried on the still air of an October night and reached him, a mile away from the field, as he sat at the wine. Once outside the house, the cheers were louder and the band's bursts were identifiable as tunes. From the backyard Parker could see the dome of light above the field, and he thought that as long as he'd said he was going there, he might as well.

He drove his Volkswagen, but the nearest parking place was two blocks from the gate. Halftime—the band was on the field and crowds swarmed toward the concession stands. Parker bought a ticket from a man wearing a Shriner's fez emblazoned with a tinsel *Kazam*. Inside the gate, he was still a hundred yards from the playing field in a dim parking lot, and he hadn't taken twenty steps before he sensed that the two figures approaching him in a corridor of fenders had designs upon him. He walked on, more surprised by his own calm than by the spontaneous antagonism inspired by his public appearance. The band, he noticed, was playing a lugubrious version of "The Battle Hymn of the Republic," and his enemies, the outline of their heads and shoulders framed against the illuminated crowd buying Cokes and hot dogs, marched toward him with the stiff spread-legged stride of movie gunfighters. Because it amused him, Parker converted his own pace to a meaningful stomp in time with the dirgelike beat of the music.

The two, he realized, could see him more clearly than he could see them, for the light at their back was in his face. They were within ten yards of him before he could distinguish their features—a pair of plain young goons, maybe nineteen or twenty years old. They stopped, and one of them hooked his thumbs over his belt. Parker recognized the face of this one, but couldn't name it. The other he had never seen before, but both were so familiar that he immediately attached biographies to them: they were a year or two out of high school (graduated or "quituated," as they would have said); they were making what they considered good money at their first back-breaking jobs; they believed that their labor and income made them forces to contend with, and they'd consumed a bottle of whiskey at the football game to dramatize their new status; they were the owners of jacked-up, deafening automobiles; and they were spoiling for trouble. When he was near enough to get a powerful noseful of booze, Parker stopped and confronted them.

"We're looking for a nigger," the biggest one said. "Maybe you can tell us where to find one. You seem to hang around with em."

"Try the Cosmos pool hall," Parker said. "You'll find plenty of them there. They'd be glad to see you too."

Parker knew that he was calm, but he hadn't expected his voice to be so prompt and ringing. Neither had the goons; they weren't prepared for resistance, and the speaker repeated lamely, "We thought you'd know where one was even if you didn't have one with you."

"I told you where more than one was."

"Those aren't the ones we mean."

"What's wrong with them? Too many of them?"

"We was looking for you to have one with you, like you had the night you met up with Sessions."

"I'm by myself, but if I did have one with me, that would make us even, wouldn't it? Two of us and two of you."

The big one didn't know what to say. Evidently he'd equipped himself with no more than an opening line. After a long pause, he managed, "You looking for a fight?"

It wasn't quite a question, nor was it a threat, and Parker actually laughed. "I'm going to the game," he said, "and you're between me and it. What I'm going to do is walk around you, and if you touch me, if you make one move, you'll find out whether I'm looking for a fight."

But before he took that step, the smaller of the two hissed like a snake and spat vehemently at his feet. "C'mon, Billy," he said to his partner. "I wouldn't touch this son of a bitch with a stick."

"Wait. I want to stay for this walking around. I'm getting interested in him now."

"C'mon," the small one said, and as he turned away he tugged his buddy's arm. The big one shook the arm loose. "Any time you want to try it, let me know," he said to Parker. But he left with the spitter; they both showed Parker their backs and returned the way they'd come.

And Parker, after a delay of only seconds, followed them toward the crowd. They'd confirmed that in Ewell he would henceforth be identified as niggerlover, and he wanted to be seen. His calm had not left him, and he plunged down through the throngs at the concession stands and exposed himself to view in front of the new brick-and-concrete bleachers, where thousands, literally thousands, of his townspeople were gathered. He didn't imagine that they were looking at him; they were watching the principal of the high school introduce the homecoming queen and her court. Five years before he had stood on that field on just that occasion, to escort Dotty Hirt, one of the queen's attendants; he'd stood and faced up into that hometown crowd, wearing a smile which pledged that he would in the future endeavor to justify the honor of being one of Ewell's favorite sons. That future was upon him, and he'd have a message for them now if he was given the microphone at the fifty-yard line.

Fellow citizens, you all recognize me, you have known me and my family since I was just a tot, you saw me perform on this very field as outside linebacker, wearing the scarlet and white and the helmet with the red devil painted above the earhole. Because of our long familiarity with one another, I am sure that you will not mind and that you will agree with me when I say that a good many of you here tonight are potential murderers. As a matter of fact, two young townspeople have just this evening performed a make-believe assassination so that when their real opportunity comes they will not let you down. I know that they will give a good account of themselves, as I myself have done, and that they will prove to be worthy of this outstanding little community.

Yes indeed, good people, I am the very Parker Livingston who once took part in the ritual celebration of white southern youth which is being reenacted here tonight, and I have culminated and fulfilled my education and my trust. It was easy. Ladies and gents, I was ready, I was prepared, I raised my hand against a black man. I was willing to take his life. That's all there was to it. I saw into my own heart, and that is why I confidently address you as killers all. Thanks for everything, folks.

But they weren't killers, and Parker knew it. As he drafted his speech, he stared into the stirring bleachers, and the crowd sent forth a girl named Paula. She was near the top of the stands, and she seemed to emerge from that host with the simple act of standing. She entered and entirely occupied Parker's vision. Paula had been the homecoming queen the year Parker was an escort, and she was now a mother; a three-year-old child clung to her hand as she came down through the crowd. And she would soon be a mother again. Her blue coat was buttoned over an enormous charge, precious cargo, but she seemed to float down from her place with the serene and lyric drift of a balloon. Beaming, unhurried, certain that the feet she couldn't see would find secure purchase beneath her, she smiled generally as she received the smiles of those about her. His classmate, a woman bearing lives, advancing toward him from the populous scene, from the height of his tiered neighbors poised against the sky, and he turned away, his shoulders trembling, his eyes stinging with tears.

His calm had left him, and he gripped the fence around the playing field. McKemeny was right; they *were* good people. They were members of families and members of a peaceful community, and the tribes of little boys who played near him were not practicing for violence. The cheerleaders whose wet hair stuck to their glazed and dazzling foreheads, the uniformed players in the end zone sucking quartered oranges, the solemn young girls on the field, half hidden by the bouquets they carried—this whole pageant was buoyed by immense and decent hope. Out there on the grass, the principal said, "Let's have a big hand now for these fine young people, the homecoming court," and the spectators responded, the band launched a lifting tune. The turf was as bathed in good will as it was in light and music. Sessions and Fuqua and Bates and those two in the parking lot were not the town's representatives—how could he have mistaken them so? He remained at the fence, looking out at the field as the band massed to leave, so that no one could see his face, and when a hand touched his shoulder, he had to rub his eyes before he could turn around.

"Parker? I thought it was you. Where have you been hiding yourself? I heard you were in town, but I hadn't laid eyes on you."

Parker steadied himself so that Dr. Price could look him over. The old man's greeting was brief and peppery, for the doctor seemed to diagnose symptoms of distress. They spoke for a moment, and by the time the healer moved on to his seat, Parker was braced enough to face the crowd.

Two other men returning from the concession stand stopped long enough to welcome him back from the Army; they seemed to think that he was going to school, home merely for the weekend. Parker didn't try to explain. He had started to mount the bleachers when he heard his name called and saw Booth Lovelace stand and wave at him. The wave constituted an invitation, and he made his way past a row of knees to sit in the midst of a family. Booth's two sons, freckled and red-haired, were paraphrases of their father. Jane Lovelace, smiling, sharp-featured, greeted him as old number 44.

"How do you remember that?"

"She's a keen student of the game," Booth said.

"It's the only chance I have to get out of the house," she said, but there was no rancor in her voice.

"This is the first game I've been to," Parker said. "Are we as good this year as we're supposed to be?"

"Better," Booth answered. "This is one of the best Ewell teams I've ever seen."

The players came back to the benches, and Booth was all football. The instructions he shouted when play resumed were particular—he knew the players by name and directed a linebacker to protect the outside, a guard to pull more aggressively, a tackle to keep his head up. His most frequent cheer was *Execute!* and from high in the stands he barked at the players as though he expected them to heed his counsel. Parker knew that Booth was one of Ewell's most celebrated linemen, a center who'd gone on to start for the Crimson Tide, and sitting beside him, ears full of Booth's critical enthusiasm, Parker was conscious mainly of how parsimonious his opinion of Booth had been. The explanatory prosecutor had a family, a past and future outside his office, an ongoing life in the small town he'd grown up in—domestic cares and joys, commitments to a profession and place. It had crossed Parker's mind for an instant when Booth beckoned that the lawyer wanted to talk business, but he didn't. He was a man with his wife and sons at a high-school football game, and when his eyes fell upon an acquaintance who appeared to be alone in that crowd, he extended the offer of company. It was that simple, and it made Parker, as he watched the Ewell Red Devils salt away a victory, wonder how he had managed such lamentable dislocations in his own life. He seemed to have no visible future, no present worth mentioning, nothing but an afflicting past, and he would have given much to be able to cheer as Booth cheered, to be able to laugh as easily as he did when Jane said, "Booth, it's not sportsmanlike to keep hollering when you're four touchdowns ahead."

Booth agreed with her, and he spent the rest of the game explaining the action to his sons. Parker spent it in meditation. He did not pity himself, for it was his own vain error that he confronted. He'd fallen through the embraces of family and spurned offers of plain kindness, all for the sake of a deluded righteousness. The yellow air above the playing field, with particles of victorious light suspended in it, enriched with the cries of his neighbors, came to him like a cleansing draft, the first nourishment in weeks he'd taken outside his house, outside himself.

At the final gun—an official reached over his head and fired a blank into the air—Parker parted amicably with the Lovelaces. Only then did Booth ask about the deposition; Parker said he was working on it. "Let me see it as soon as you're done," Booth said. Parker promised that he would, and he joined the flood of people leaving the stands. He felt contrite, and he resolved—the third time that night

—to make amends to his mother. He *would* get along with McKemeny. He expected to find the two of them still at the table, and he prepared himself to make efforts of affection.

He parked his VW in the garage. As he crossed the yard to the house, he noticed that a light was on in his father's room, and he began to trot. His immediate thought was that his mother or McKemeny, or both, had plundered his deposition. When he approached the back door and looked through the window at the deserted table, he was certain of it. He imagined them laughing at it, McKemeny reading aloud for the amusement of El, her head on his shoulder, his drawl the instrument of sarcasm and contempt.

Parker burst into the house. He did not stop in the littered kitchen, but ran down the hall and up the stairs. The door to his father's room was slightly ajar, and he shoved it open without knocking. His anger carried him two steps into the room before he halted, but he found only McKemeny. One shoe on and one shoe off, otherwise fully clothed, McKemeny was stretched upon the bedspread. His mouth was open and he emitted a long whistling snore. His hair was mussed and his shirt was twisted so that his belly gaped through the openings between the buttons, but the room did not seem to have been disturbed. Parker walked around the bed to the table and opened the drawer; the deposition had not been touched. He removed the stack of paper and closed the drawer, making no effort to be silent, but McKemeny did not stir. He seemed to have collapsed under the weight of his own vitality, and the sheets of muscle which had rippled under his clothing now bulged like strips of meat peeled from some other beast. Without animation, his face was merely a heel of flesh, his body a carcass.

When he left the room, his mother was waiting for him

in the hall. Parker ordered, "Get him out of there."

She was dressed as she had been when Parker left, and when she spoke her face was clouded with amazed sadness. "I was waiting for you—"

"Get him out of here."

"He had too much to drink. He—"

"What about you? Are you drunk too? Or did you tuck him in?"

She obviously wasn't drunk; the thickness in her voice was sorrow. "I told him to go to that room because it was out of the way."

"And he wouldn't be disturbed. How kind."

"What is it, Parker? What is wrong with you?"

"Why didn't you just take him to your own bed?"

"What are you saying?"

"I'm saying get him out of this house. I won't have him here."

"You won't . . . " But she couldn't continue. "This house—"

"I don't want to spoil anything. He came for the night. Maybe you can revive him later."

"You're so interested in your father," she said, and her face was transformed. Those buried lines appeared, pressing toward the surfaces of cheek, temple, and brow, as if in this present stress the past was cutting her face to pieces. "You'll never know what he was like."

"What does that mean?"

"He cared about other people. He knew what they felt. He was loving, not . . . "

She couldn't finish. She put her hands to her face as though lesions might be felt there, and she remained erect when she turned and walked to her own room. Parker, his deposition in his hands, watched her go.

Ten

"What happened here last night?" Iva asked as soon as he set foot in the kitchen. She was at the sink, in suds to her elbows, her back to Parker, and her voice, addressed to the wall in front of her, was pugnacious. *Boy, you better tell me what you know.*

Parker took in the kitchen, the pots and pans on the counters, the stiffening remains of sauces and hardened oozes of grease, the disorder which Iva had predicted the day before, but the tone of her voice signaled that she took no delight in the accuracy of her prophecy of Mr. Minny. "What do you mean, Iva? Mr. McKemeny came and cooked dinner here."

"Don't ask me what I mean. You know what I mean. Just you tell me how come your mama was all upset this morning and out of this house and on her way to Montgomery at eight o'clock."

As she spoke, the cookware beneath the suds rumbled against the sides of the sink and her hands churned the water like a ship's screw. "Saturday ain't her day to go to

Montgomery, it's her day to work in the yard, but she couldn't wait to be gone. So I know that whatever got her troubled happened last night"—she lifted her hands abruptly and shook the billows of detergent from them, turned and faced Parker with damp hands held away from her body—"and that you was here and know what it is. Don't tell me it ain't my business to ask, either."

"I just woke up," Parker protested. "I didn't know Mama was gone." It was true that he hadn't heard her leave the house. After he woke, he'd remained in his own room, listening for her and McKemeny before he came downstairs. Finally, after hearing nothing, he remembered that McKemeny had parked in the driveway and he went to a window at the back of the house to see if the car was still there. It wasn't, and when he peeked into his father's room he found that the bedspread had been smoothed, the window opened wide, all signs of McKemeny effaced. But he'd expected to meet his mother downstairs, and the information that she'd departed came as a reprieve.

"You fuss with her?" Iva asked. "She didn't run after that man to apologize for you, did she?"

"Was he still here this morning?"

"Did he stay the night here?"

"I don't know," Parker said. "He was asleep when I went to bed."

"Where was he sleeping?"

"In Daddy's old room."

"How'd he get up there?"

"I don't know, Iva. I went out to the football game for a while and he was up there when I got back."

"You went out and he fell asleep and this morning your mama was too sorrowful to look me in the face."

"I'm not trying to keep anything from you. Let me get

some coffee started and sit down and I'll tell you what happened."

"Coffee's done made," Iva said, and after she'd quickly dried her hands, she poured him a cup.

"You're not going to have any?"

"Bad for my blood pressure, the doctor says."

She brought his cup to the kitchen table and sat down with him. She was wearing a clean print dress and a gray sweater with the sleeves pushed up—street clothes, Parker knew. Iva worked only a half day on Saturday if she worked at all, and when she left the house at noon she went shopping. Her social apparel gave her the look of a visitor who'd stopped to call but, finding herself needed, willingly set aside her coat and hat to do what she could. Her gray hair was pulled back and gathered by a tortoise-shell barrette, a gift from Amsy; beneath the barrette a tuft of hair like a warrior's queue hung down over her collar. And on this Saturday, Parker had noticed, Iva even wore shoes, a pair of black pumps so turned over that she walked on the sides of them rather than on the beveled heels.

"You didn't get on with him?" she asked. She did not let McKemeny's elusive name become a distraction.

"Not very well, but we didn't really quarrel. I got angry with him."

"About what?"

"About the same thing you and I talked about—Arthur and that whole business."

"What he say about it?"

"It wasn't really a quarrel."

"Whose side your mama take?"

"She didn't take sides. If she was upset this morning, it wasn't because of what he said."

"You think she didn't see how he riled you? I see it now.

When you leave here? After that fuss?"

"I stayed and had dinner."

"And your mama had to take up for you after you left."

"Maybe she did, but when I came back he was asleep. That's when Mama and I—I said some things I shouldn't have."

"Why? Because he was up there in your father's room?"

"I have some things up there that I didn't want him to see, the things I've been writing. I lost my temper for a minute when I found him up there."

"He been in your things?"

"No."

"Well, then. Why you lose your temper?"

"Oh, Iva, I don't know why. The whole night was strange. I'd never seen Mama with another man—I knew she went out sometimes, but she never brought a man here, not while I was here, and I didn't like McKemeny. I didn't like having him in this house."

"You jealous of him."

Parker tried to laugh, but the noise emerged in a nervous little puff and did not succeed in disinfecting Iva's assertion. "Why should I be jealous of someone that Mama goes out with?"

"I don't mean jealous that way. I mean jealous for your daddy, keeping your mama for him like he was going to walk back through that door this morning."

"That's silly," Parker said, but his eyes followed Iva's gesture toward the door.

"It ain't silly," she said, and she continued as though she'd reached at last the heart of the matter. "Your daddy has been in his grave these ten years. It don't matter now, not any more, what he did or what he didn't do. Your mama is still a young woman and she hasn't lost none of her looks.

The men are going to find her even if she don't go out of this house. They'll learn where she's at and they'll study ways to get to her. You old enough to know that."

"I do know it," Parker said. "I don't expect her to lock herself in."

"She hatn't forgot him," Iva persisted. "I say she thinks on him too much, just like you do. How come a woman like that don't have a husband? All she got is a big empty house with his things still in it. You and Amsy stay gone now and your mama got nothing but me and some flowers and some birds. What kind of life you call that?"

"Iva, I don't want her to be alone either."

"But you don't approve of this one that was here last night. What'd you say to your mama anyway?"

"It doesn't matter. I'm sorry I said it, and I'll tell her I am."

"Time for you to get over your daddy," she said, and she had the air of a prosecutor summing up. "It's no disrespect to him now for you to get out from under him. He never wanted you all to suffer for him anyway. Why you think he killed himself? So he'd be gone and you'd be shut of him, not so you'd still be dreaming about him ten years later."

This mention of his father, and the energetic, simple explanation of his motive, did not offend Parker. Iva's advice seemed appropriate for that morning, the blast he deserved. Her voice was the voice of the place, the voice which belonged to the house, and she could claim to be the arbiter of what went on under that roof.

"You want some breakfast?" she asked.

"I'll get myself some toast."

Iva raised herself up from the table and rolled back the sleeves which had inched down. "I got to finish cleaning. What you gone to do today?"

176

"I have to write more on the deposition."

"You do it in your own room," she ordered. "Give your mama that relief anyway."

"I was going to," Parker said.

But when he returned to his room and spread the rescued pages in front of him, he encountered the allegory of Deep Hole and his concluding barren reflections on justice and law. He remembered them well enough—only one night had elapsed since he wrote those words, but the sentences intended to rile Booth now seemed pitiable. What did he know about justice? He refrained, however, from striking them out, and he began on a fresh page, determined to write that morning something that would restore him to Iva, to the Booth he'd seen last night, to his mother and Amsy. He wrote, but the lines he cast on the page would not enclose the sentiments he wished them to enclose.

That was our night of solidarity, but to tell you the truth it didn't last. I thought that it should have, that Arthur and I should have been tight buddies after Deep Hole because we had Shared An Experience. We had met the oppressor and we had been oppressed, together. It seemed to me that our common punishment should have welded a bond, but it didn't. I sat with Arthur at meals and teased him about his late nights in Badstein, I reminded him of Deep Hole whenever I had a chance, but he was not inclined to reminisce and he wasn't interested in my repeated overtures. He became as taciturn as ever, or perhaps he only seemed so because I expected more from him. None of his habits was altered; he continued to sleep late and leave his corner of the room for Davy to tidy. His aloofness puzzled and hurt me, for I believed that we had satisfied the preliminary conditions of friendship.

I see now that the only way a friendship could have developed would have been for us to get Article 15ed every day. The fines the captain gave us weren't preliminary to anything; they were conclusions. Our understanding was over when we saluted and walked out of his office. Maybe it was over even before that, when the First Sergeant walked out of our hut, but in any case we depended—*I* depended—on some hostile external force, on Strickland or Boyles, to join us. We *had* shared certain feelings of anger, sleepiness, irritation, and even moral indignation when Strickland woke us up and Boyles shot off his mouth, but those feelings never passed directly from me to Arthur or from Arthur to me. They had to bounce off somebody else first. You could say that we were like two moons which, when the phases were right, happened to catch the light of the same sun. The phases weren't often right.

And speaking of illumination, I found out when that beam came on at the Hirts' pond that a change in the source of light revealed how separate we were and what spaces had always divided us. We weren't soldiers then, we weren't in Germany, we didn't have those temporary, narrow, military identities that we had had in the hut at Neversink. We were at home, or I was at home and Arthur was on his way, and we were two individuals, one white and one black. That's what we'd always been, and it was a primary fact for both of us, but it was the last fact I wanted to reckon with. I had trusted that once my social, political, and legal beliefs were aligned with Arthur's, more personal and more essential agreements would follow. They didn't, and I don't know if they ever can. Men are not principles or propositions, and if justice is ever to be done, men have to be loved.

I apologize for introducing that word, but I don't know of another one that will do. All I mean by it is that if I had valued Arthur Kin's life, I wouldn't have done what I did. I wouldn't have brought him here, and I wouldn't have given him away—and there wouldn't be any need for law in that case, because Sessions would never have had his chance. Maybe there's no need for law anyway, since it can't replace love or create it where it never existed. It seems to me that real justice, if it is an ideal of harmony among men, has nothing to do with the courts. Justice might have occurred when Arthur Kin spoke out in the dark in Germany, but I don't see how it can occur in a courtroom in Ewell, Alabama.

There's some judgment for you, and I already know how wrong it is. I know, for example, that laws are not merely restraints; that they can change behavior, and by changing behavior they change attitudes. Maybe if Sessions and I had grown up where the present laws were enforced, we wouldn't have met as we did at that pond. Maybe, and I hope it will be so, we're the last ones who will be driven to act as we did. Maybe the law will improve us—we need it.

Parker halted there. The morning sitting had gone on long enough, and he knew that he was no more capable of writing that word *love* another time than he was of feeling it. Its absence he could feel and had felt all morning; in that absence his proclamations about it were no more meaningful than howls. And yet, now that the point of the BIC had been forced from *l* to *e*, he thought he had named his failure. Amsy, Iva, his mother—it was the same mistake over and over again. The only way to correct it was—he couldn't even bring himself to think that word, but its absence was a pang that demanded assuaging.

He bleakly anticipated a televised football game, Alabama vs. Ole Miss. He knew that his mother hadn't returned (and wondered if she really had pursued McKemeny, as Iva guessed, or whether she'd left the house to avoid him), and he knew that Iva was still on the premises. The phone had rung several times in the last hour, and she'd dialed calls of her own; the mechanical sounds reached him plainly, but her voice traveled through the structure of the house as a tremulous impulse. It actually seemed to climb out of the floor and up the legs of the chair so that its curved back became a delicately vibrating register and he heard through his spine, not his ears.

Parker put off going downstairs for fear that she lay in wait for him with a four-plate young-master's lunch. He needn't have worried; he heard the phone dropped in its cradle, heard Iva toiling up the stairs, heard his name called. She thumped on the door—thumped, not knocked; it sounded as if she gave the door a swat with her hip—and let herself in. She was breathing hard, and her whole frame shook as her heart drove the rods of blood through the stiff passages. She sat down on Parker's bed before she spoke.

"That's Esther been calling on the phone all morning long," she said. "Her boy Andrew running around loose with a shotgun and say he gone to use it."

Too much information; Parker's receiver jammed. "The Esther I know?"

"That's right, that Esther, your daddy's Esther." She didn't have to explain that the armed Andrew was Parker's mulatto half-brother. "She tried to stop him when he was home to get the gun, but he pointed it at her, his own mama, and told her get out of his way."

"What happened? Why did he get the gun? Who is he looking for?"

"That's what I been trying to find out."

"Did you?"

"Him and Sonny Ray had some kind of fight over a basketball game this morning. Sonny Ray started getting after him bout who his father was. Andrew said he was going home to fetch the gun and coming back to kill them all."

"Where is he now?"

"Hiding somewhere. He gets crazy sometimes. Nobody wants to look too hard for him when he got a gun with him."

"Where are the others?"

"They home in their own houses. I been calling their parents."

"Have you or Esther called the sheriff?"

"Don't want to call the sheriff."

Of course not; he understood the danger of that. White lawmen wouldn't be careful how they disarmed a fifteen-year-old black boy. And Parker was on the point of asking, "What will Esther do?" when he realized that Esther would do nothing; Iva was going to do what had to be done. He realized also that she hadn't come to his room to relay to him the goings-on in the colored quarter on a Saturday afternoon, to instruct him with the example of avenging blood kin. She'd climbed those stairs to make demands, and she sat patiently on his bed, resting, gathering strength, thinking not of him but of Andrew hidden in some barn or thicket, awaiting Parker's comprehension so that they could depart.

Parker revised his question. "What are you going to do?"

"I need to find him before he hurt somebody. I need

somebody to take me hunting for him."

And Parker could only think what a target he'd make for his half-brother: white boy, issue of the same father, flesh-and-blood evidence of Andrew's stigma. If Andrew knew his father, he'd know his brother as well (and Parker knew Andrew, had identified him on the street, was sure that he would recognize him now)—the hated legitimate brother who had been spared. *Spared*—without forming the word in his mind, Parker had an instant's full consciousness of all its terrifying ironies. But he had no more than an instant, for he was aware of his own silence, of Iva's attentive wait for his reply, her patience in the nick of emergency. "I'll take you," he said. "Are you ready now?"

She was rising to her feet as soon as his lips opened, on her way, but at the door she gave final orders. "Better get some stout shoes and clothes on in case we got to chase him. I got a sandwich and some cookies wrapped for you to take with you. Soon's I make one more phone call, we can go."

By then she was in the hall, moving with all requisite speed; Parker heard the dial of the phone before he left his chair. He wasn't surprised that this errand fell to her; Iva was, he knew, the matriarch of her neighborhood, its venerable chief and grandmother. He'd gone once to pick her up and found her asleep on her bed, three small black children dozing against her bulk like puppies in the protection of their dam; he woke them and they scrambled over her, three diminutive mountaineers, and peered at him from the far side of the divide. He knew that Iva badgered his mother for extra money to buy toys and books for those children and others like them, and Andrew was a special case—having raised other Livingston children, she would inevitably have taken Andrew under her charge. She had told

Parker before that Andrew was a tormented boy, that Esther had practically entrusted his rearing to her. Some such knowledge of Iva came to Parker in a quick review as he pulled on walking shoes and a flannel shirt. He was buttoning the shirt as he passed through the door, and Iva called from the foot of the stairs, "I'm waiting on you."

Eleven

She led him out of the house into a vibrant and high-skied October afternoon. She had donned her coat and black field marshal's hat; the coat was a man's, and though its padded shoulders were unadorned, they projected with the assurance of epaulets. With her queue trailing from beneath the hat, her ample back bent but purposeful, she might have been the general of an expeditionary force—save for the empty shopping bag she carried, and her un-trousered, unbooted legs, her turned-over shoes. In any case, she marched to the garage with dispatch and waited for Parker to back the Volkswagen out; he leaned across the seat and opened the door for her; holding her hat to keep it from being knocked off, she committed herself to a heavy descent toward the seat, rotated her body successfully, landed on the vinyl cushion with a wallop that shocked the springs. "I just hope there ain't too much getting in and out of the car," she said.

"Where to first?" Parker asked when he got the Volks-wagen to the street.

"My house. I got half a mind Andrew might be prowling round there somewhere. I done called Mose to tell him to look out for Andrew, but he not going to do us any good. He so scared he couldn't hardly talk in the phone. I spect he got the place locked up tight."

Parker knew the way well enough and drove for a minute or two in silence. The car ran with the reliable and inimitable VW hum, the streets were familiar, but he had a vague and disturbing sense that something was amiss. As they entered niggertown (that was the only name he knew for it, and entering it was like the penetration of a frontier: the houses facing one street were occupied by white families, those facing the next were the dwellings of blacks; the alley which divided the backyards was a pitted and defoliated DMZ), he realized that it was Iva who was dislocated. For the first time in his life, she sat beside him in the front seat of an automobile. She'd invariably sat in the back when he'd driven her, and her presence now beside him—their shoulders almost touched, but she was intent, staring ahead through the windshield, deep tactician—in the tiny cab of the VW was enough of a lapse of tradition to be momentarily disorienting. Once he discovered that it was merely Iva's position which was unusual, his mounting fear was checked and he was grateful for her proximity. He was in foreign territory—hers—and though Iva couldn't possibly have inserted herself in the back of the car, still her front-seat passage appeared to make him a bidden visitor, an equal.

"How did Andrew get hold of a gun?" he asked.

"It's his. He saved up his money and bought it himself —the times I had with that child about putting that money to some good use. Twenty-some-odd dollars he saved up.

But he had to have the gun. He's mad to shoot at squirrels and rabbits."

"Were you able to reach all the parents of the other boys? Are all of them home now?"

"They sposed to be. But I ain't so worried about them. I know Andrew. I don't believe he gone to shoot anybody else—maybe Sonny Ray if he gets the chance, that's all. Andrew ain't no Jack Dillinger. What worries me is that he might shoot his own self. Off in the bushes somewhere, feeling low and miserable, got a gun in his hand—he liable to blow his own head off. That's what I been scared of since he got that gun."

That hadn't occurred to Parker, and when it did, his own fear seemed vain and base. Iva obviously did not consider herself in physical peril; her mission was to save. She did not allow herself to consider either the precedent of Philip Livingston: *blow his own head off*, she'd said, her voice as clear as the notes of a bugle. The dead were dead, the living might be kept in life, but Parker had felt a hot flush at the back of his neck—he'd thought at once of his father, could not share her certainties. "How are you going to find him?" he asked.

"Andrew just a mixed-up teen-age boy. He's not gone to run off to the swamp or catch the bus out of town. He gone to be somewhere he knows."

"Is Esther out looking for him?"

"She been out, but he ain't gone to come to her. He's running from her as much as he's running after Sonny Ray. I told her stay in the house and keep out of his sight. Let me find him."

"Is anybody else out?"

"I don't want nobody else out tromping around, scaring him worse than he already scared. He done talked himself into a place where he thinks he got to shoot somebody or something before he can come back. He ain't gone to shoot me."

They turned into Iva's street then, a sloping sandy lane off the main paved thoroughfare. Most of the meager houses were roofed and sided with paper, but they stood in neat bare lots, and the ingenious footbridges—all the decorative impulse of the residents had been spent on those bridges, and they were garnished with painted tires, flowers, metal animals, reflectors, and in one case a fading barber's pole—which spanned the running ditches on either side of the lane gave the place a cheerful, seaside look. "At least everybody staying indoors," Iva said, for the street was significantly empty, the life which normally would have spilled from the houses on so fine an autumn afternoon was contained within them. Even the basketball court—a small lot of packed dirt upon which the thump of a rubber ball was constant, the neighborhood's audible heartbeat—was deserted.

Iva's house, more plumb and substantial than the others, the only house with fresh paint and the only house under a shade tree, a brown and thinning pecan, was near the top of the lane. Her bridge was of stout planks, and the railings were mounted upon gigantic wrought balusters, huge and convoluted blocks of pine which had been turned on a lathe by Iva's husband, Mose. Parker drove the car across the fanciful bridge and stopped beneath the pecan tree.

"You stay here a minute. Lemme see what Mose been doing."

Iva pivoted and got her feet on the earth, gripped her hat and gathered herself. She left the car with a decisive heave forward, and with each step she took toward her porch the dry leaves snapped beneath her shoes. From the darkness under the porch two orange cats emerged to greet Iva. They stretched voluptuously in her path, expecting to be stroked, but she stepped around them. Other pairs of eyes glittered beneath the house; they seemed to be fixed upon Parker, like the unseen eyes at the windows of the closed and silent houses. Like Andrew's eyes—Parker believed that he could feel the boy's near presence in the pent street. Without Iva beside him, he felt exposed and he had to battle the fear which counseled him to sink down in the seat below the level of the windshield. His hands gripped the steering wheel and his arms were rigid, as if by muscular effort alone he could hold himself erect in the car.

"Mose! You in there. Open up this door." Iva hit the door with the flat of her hand and her voice sped clearly up and down the lane. For an instant her confidence seemed brazen, seemed to flow from an overbearing and insulting belief in her own immortality, and it angered Parker—why should he risk his neck for a deluded old woman and a wild half-black boy? But then he saw the curtain move in the front window, saw Mose peek out, rim of gray fur and eyes round as half dollars, looking at the large woman to whom he'd been married for forty years, asking, "Who there? Who that calling me?" A comic reflection of his own fear: *Ain't nobody in this chickenhouse but us chickens.* Parker was relieved, smiled, relaxed his grip—no use hiding from Iva or any other fate which could so easily find you out in your place of concealment.

For Iva had seen Mose too, and she moved to stand directly before the window. "Who I look like to you? The booger-man? Open up this door."

Mose's face disappeared. The lock rattled and the door opened for Iva, remained open as she entered the house. Parker could see her outline in the dim hall, wing of the lustrous hat and one military shoulder, but Mose was not visible, driven deeper into the house. It occurred to Parker that Iva had asked him to remain in the car to keep him from witnessing the worst of Mose's foolishness, a tender motive after all.

He could no longer hear her voice, but she reappeared at the door and waved for him to come. "You come on in and stay with Mose for a minute if you don't want to set in the car," she said. "I'm gone to walk out back and call Andrew."

She didn't wait for him. She came down from the porch and rounded the corner of the house, followed by the two loping cats, before he was out of the car. Mose closed the door of the house—no sense inviting trouble—but opened it promptly to admit Parker, bolted it behind him. "I'm scared of that boy," he said. "I ain't ashamed to admit it."

"I'm scared too," Parker said.

"Queen Iva say that boy don't mean to hurt nobody, but that gun he's toting don't know that, maybe Andrew don't even know it."

"You haven't seen him, have you?"

"Hatn't seen him and hatn't been looking, cause if I see him, he gone to see me too."

Then Mose took in Parker for the first time, and he grinned. "Ain't you growed yourself a headful of hair, though? I thought you been in the Army. They quit giving haircuts?"

"I've been out for a while now."

"Queen Iva told me you was home. How come you ain't been round to see me?"

Parker knew why, but he couldn't tell that grinning, grizzled old man. Mose stood before him in clean laundered khaki work clothes—Parker had never seen him in anything else—that were several sizes too big for him, as though they'd been bought for a growing child. The shirt was buttoned to the throat, the cuffs lapped over his shoes and touched the floor behind his heels. He inhabited the garments so tentatively that it was possible to imagine Iva dressing him each morning. Yet Parker knew that there was a wiry and able body muffled in those yards of khaki; Mose was a carpenter in the shop at the lumber mill, and had built with his own hands the house they stood in. And he knew that this man, who looked exactly as he had when Parker first saw him, as unchanged and solid as one of his own balusters, was entitled to an answer to that question; years have rights.

"Maybe you got yourself a girl," Mose said mischievously. "Queen Iva hatn't said so, but that wouldn't surprise me none, looking at you. Bet she can't keep her fingers outen that hair, like the song says."

Parker was grateful to be let off, but it hurt him to hear Mose dismiss his claim so lightly. Did he expect so little of Parker? Release him so casually? Parker only said, "I've been meaning to come, Mose. How've you been?"

"Bout the same, bout the same. Hatn't got smarter and I hatn't got richer, and I hatn't even learned to drive a car yet."

The old joke. Parker, at the age of thirteen, had been navigating the car in the driveway; Mose, who in those days did yard work on Saturdays, slid under the wheel to instruct him, had the car in a flowerbed three seconds later. Parker had forgotten, and the memory touched him. "You want me to teach you, Mose?"

"Too old now. Me and Queen Iva ain't studying no trips."

Mose's head bent forward and he listened intently. Iva

was calling behind the house, a high "Oooo-eeee, Andrew, oooo," a sharp and carrying note.

"She ain't gone to find him less he wants to be found," Mose said, "and he got no reason to want to be. Ain't no reward coming his way. He still ain't gone to have no daddy and he still gone to have to live with Esther. If I was him, I'd stay hid."

For the second time, Parker was jolted by the reference to his father, reference by omission. Mose was as bland as Iva had been; the father Andrew didn't have, the man who blew his brains out, was Parker's father too. For Mose, Philip Livingston was no more than the head of family who wasn't there when he was needed, and the loquacious black man continued: "Take somebody with a big stick to make me stay under the same roof with Esther if I was a boy like Andrew. That woman has got *hard.*"

"What's happened to Esther?" Parker asked. "I used to know her. She wasn't—" Wasn't what? He couldn't repeat Mose's *hard,* and he didn't know what other word would substitute.

"Take another somebody with another big stick to keep that woman straight, but it seem like each man she take up with is worser than the one before. How you like to be Andrew and see your mama living with a different man every month? How you like to have little bastard children to look after when your mama's out running around? How you like to have your mama's bad mouth on you all day long?"

Iva called again and interrupted Mose. She was still in the field of scrub cedar and honeysuckle immediately behind the house; those few acres ran on into the thick lumber-mill plantings of pine that stretched from there, the edge of Ewell, for miles.

"He could be back in them young pines," Mose said, "or he could be curled up under the honeysuckle close enough to hear me talking right now. Take a dog with a good nose to find him if he decides to keep quiet, which Queen Iva ain't being." Reminded of the danger, Mose had lowered his voice to a prudent whisper which became acerbic when he mentioned Iva's noisiness.

"Maybe he'll answer her," Parker said.

"He ain't coming in till he's shot something or till he's got cold and hungry. Too many people know he's out there for him to pop up out of the bushes the first time he hears Queen Iva calling."

Her cry was more distant when they heard it next. "She's headed for the pines," Mose said. "Chasing after that boy ain't gone to do her blood pressure no good neither. I told her before she can't look after every child that gets born, but she don't pay no mind."

Mose's whisper, however, was not grudging; Parker realized that it was simply the habitual admiring murmur of a well-married man. He thought: *This is Iva's husband talking to me.* Mose and Iva were husband and wife, had shared a bed, raised children of their own—simple facts, but they had the potency of revelation. Until that moment Parker had never imagined either of them in any web but that of the Livingston family. Yet the evidence—Mose's uxorious whisper, the photographs all about him in the respectable parlor—was plain as day, had always been if he'd had eyes to see it. Iva's two sons in gowns and mortarboards, Mose in a suit with a pinafored and pigtailed granddaughter on his lap—there was not one single photograph or keepsake of him, Parker, in that room. The only signs of Livingston influence were a refurbished table and chair, cast-off furniture which Mose had salvaged. Parker was in the resort of a different family, and he became aware that he and Mose had remained standing awkwardly, that Mose did not know how to entertain him there.

"You get in any of that fighting over in Vietnam?" Mose asked. He didn't even know where Parker had been for two years.

"No," Parker said. "They sent me to Germany."

"Germany? You lucky. Some of these boys around here been to Vietnam. Two of um been killed already."

"I don't know why they sent me to Germany," Parker said.

"Don't ask um. Who needs to know? Don't pay to investigate when you been lucky."

Mose squatted down and fiddled with a knob on the oil heater, but the gesture was a diversion. He couldn't ask Parker to sit down, was prevented by some sense of propriety. "How long do you think Iva will be gone?" Parker asked, and he almost hadn't been able to say *Iva*—in that house, addressing Mose, his unthinking use of her name seemed a presumption; he felt he should have said *Mrs. Freeman*.

"She didn't say," Mose answered, standing, and as if to rescue them both, Iva's voice sounded again near the house, a rising "oooo-eeee, oooo-eeee."

"She come back out of the pines, I believe," Mose said. "Maybe we can see her from the back."

So they went into the kitchen, and from the rear window they did see her, the top half of her body moving with surprising speed above the thick and weedy cover. Her feet must have been on a path, but Parker couldn't see it; from the window she appeared to be sailing on the waist-high brush.

"Don't get too close to the glass," Mose said, "just in

case Andrew happen to be out there."

But Parker was, for the moment anyway, no longer afraid of Andrew and he didn't believe that Mose was either. The old man's show of terror had been mostly for his wife's benefit, an installment of marital drama, household theatrics, the husband exacting his due notice and comfort, reminding his wife that he too needed her protection.

Iva was closer now, but Parker still couldn't see the path; the weeds parted before her like water cleaved by a ship's bow. She was making for the house, and when Mose opened the back door, exposing one weather eye, a tiger-striped cat streaked into the kitchen and Iva called, without breaking stride, "He ain't here. Let's go on to Esther's."

That order was for Parker, and Mose asked petulantly, "What you spect *me* to do? Wait round here by myself till he comes? And what am I sposed to do when he does show up?"

"Ask him to come in and set down and quit worrying everybody," Iva said. She had emerged from the weeds and stood full-length in the yard, hands shoved into her overcoat pockets. As soon as she stood still, the two orange cats which had trotted behind her began to luxuriate at her ankles.

"Call this one that got in the house," Mose said. "If I got to stay penned up in here, I don't need the company of no scraggly old cat."

Iva clucked, "Kit-kit-kitty," and the cat emerged from beneath the table and advanced willingly to the door. Parker followed it.

"Don't let her get you in a bad spot," Mose advised. "You don't want to mess with that Andrew or with Esther either one."

"I'll be careful."

"You too, Queen Iva," Mose said. "You look out, you hear? You too old for this running around."

"Let's us go," Iva said to Parker.

"Shoo, cat," Mose said when the tiger-striped cat realized the deception and bolted once more for the house. The door banged shut, and Iva led the way to the car.

Esther lived nearby, only a little way out the paved road, in what had once been a tenant farmer's house. The dwelling stood by itself under four big oaks, surrounded by the graying and rusted remains of fences and outbuildings. The disused pasture, now thick and thorny and inhabited by rabbits, was contained by the pines; the quickest way for Andrew to reach Iva's house or any other settlement would have been through the pines. Parker had thought that Iva's search was merely an intuitive stab—she expected Andrew to be where she looked—but he realized now that it was the logical quartering of the ground. At her own house she'd tried to catch Andrew at the end of his passage through the woods; from Esther's she'd attempt to overtake him.

Esther was waiting on her porch when they drove into the yard, and waiting behind her, dark curls at Esther's hip, black fingers hooked into her dress, was a child of three or four. The boy was barefooted and wore only a pair of soiled white cotton undershorts; he was shades darker than his mother, as smooth and glossy as though he'd been varnished. When Parker and Iva got out of the car, he shyly withdrew behind his mother and twisted her skirt, but Esther ignored him.

"Where've you been?" she asked Iva querulously. "I thought you'd be here an hour ago." She formed her words distinctly, but her voice was strangely flat and brittle, a reedy bray closer to Parker's speech than to Iva's.

"I been looking back of my house," Iva said. "That child" —and she meant the infant behind Esther—"ought to have more clothes on."

"You didn't find him? Has anyone seen him?"

"No."

"Are you going to call the sheriff?"

"We don't need no sheriff."

"Andrew is just going to kill somebody, that's all. He's already pointed that gun at me one time."

"I notice you still alive," Iva said.

"He would just as soon have killed me. He said, 'Get out of my way, Mama. I mean to shoot Sonny Ray and I'll shoot you too if I have to.' And he would have if I hadn't jumped."

"Better just go on back in the house."

"He's done everything else, but I never thought I'd see the day when he was ready to kill me," Esther said, and her voice was more tirade than lament. "It's no favor to me to keep the sheriff away from him."

"I didn't come to visit," Iva said. "I'm gone to look for him."

"And when you find him, you tell him he's not coming back here again till he's changed to where he's fit to live with."

Iva didn't answer. She set out for the pasture, and Parker took a hesitant step after her. "Should I wait here?"

"You better," Iva said. "If I don't find him quick, then you gone to have to help me hunt."

So Parker remained before the porch, and when he turned back to Esther her eyes were upon him for the first time. He couldn't tell if she recognized him, but her look was attentive and savage. Her head was drawn back and her nostrils flared with each breath, with each inhalation the cords stood out in her throat. Her dress—maroon, well cut from expensive fabric, surely a hand-me-down from an employer—was unbuttoned above the waist, held together only by her folded arms, but she made no effort to close it or to conceal the line of bare skin which showed. She wore no slip or bra beneath the dress. Tall, bony, light-colored, in high-heeled shoes and that bridge-club dress, standing three steps above Parker and staring down at him, she looked not just distraught but despoiled, and she would never have been mistaken for a harried housewife; she was a woman still capable of inflicting destruction.

"Who are you?"

"Parker Livingston."

Neither her face nor her body gave any indication of how she received that name, whether it came as a surprise or not. She merely twitched her hip once against the child's clinging hand, a movement as unthinking as the flex of a muscle to dislodge an insect, while she considered his identity and gazed at him. When she finally spoke, her harsh voice had the force of a blow.

"You got balls coming here."

Parker answered; he felt his lips move and heard his words, "Iva asked me to drive her."

"Just who do you think you are to show your face to me?"

Parker knew that he was in more real danger than he had been all afternoon. "I'm sorry," he mumbled. "I just wanted to help. I'll go wait for Iva in the car."

"Help? How are you going to help? You going to help like Philip did?" His father again, evoked for the third time that afternoon; at least Esther gave him his name, uttered it in a derisive burst that shocked Parker more than anything she could have said about him. He remained where he was, did not even turn in the direction of the car.

"You going to help Andrew? You going to let him be you? You want to change with him, try being Andrew for a while? Living here in this place? Or maybe you thinking of taking him back to your house, letting him live like a rich white boy. He'd appreciate that." Her lips drew back and without taking her eyes from him, Esther bent and swept up the child on her arm. The dress fell open and one breast was revealed. She saw Parker's glance upon it, but she did not try to cover it and a short, dry laugh escaped her. "That's right. You looking at a used-up nigger whore. First one you ever saw? Your daddy could have taught you things." She jogged the baby for Parker's attention. "And this is a nigger bastard, like Andrew is. The world's full of em."

And as she turned toward the door, she lifted the baby higher, a motion both contemptuous and triumphant. She entered the house and kicked the door closed. As it slammed, Iva's voice lifted for the first time, raised the cry that was to bring Andrew home, and Iva had only reached the tangled barn lot—it took Esther that little time to say her piece to Parker.

At first he couldn't move, as though the burden of her outburst pinned him to that spot before the slanting porch, as though the entire weight of the past descended upon him in her glare and language. He couldn't have said what emotions possessed him—pity, horror, grief, shame—but they seemed, all of them, to toil in the cavity of his body. He had to direct himself to turn, to move forward, and he walked very slowly and carefully to the car, concentrating on his balance, his arms held slightly out at his sides to keep him from falling, to catch him if he fell. And there, seated behind the steering wheel and leaning forward upon it, he was shaken turbulently. He didn't know how long it continued; he simply held on and tried to outlast it.

He didn't think at all, but he didn't have to think to know that his sight of Esther was the accusation and judgment he had sought since returning home. Not related to him by blood, kin only through the lost and maddened Andrew, Esther spoke for the wreckage of family, for love unhoused and forbidden to continue. It didn't matter how his father had found his way to Esther, what she had been then, what private or selfish needs corrupted the getting of a son; the act was its own promise. Father, husband, mother, wife— the primary names, oldest duties, surest sorrows, but grief met within the time-won bonds of family might be borne, grief outside them had no consolation and no end. In Esther, Parker had encountered that grief, seen the lineaments of the sorrows that lengthened into despair. *Look first to your family*—Iva's words, and lest he forget them, he heard her call.

Her voice had grown fainter, but it rose again in volume and clarity as she returned through the woods. She'd made one long cast at the edge of the pasture, and she seemed now to be enlarging the circle of her search. Andrew had yet to be found, but Parker believed that his own search had found its object in Esther. He discovered that, having faced Esther, he no longer had reason to fear Andrew. Blood brother to him, he felt that he understood Andrew's flight and his rage, and with that understanding came his first concern for Iva. Parker knew what terrible cruelties he himself had committed, the potential violence of shame, the sacrifices required by blood. He did not forget that Andrew carried a shotgun, and he opened the car door to hear Iva more clearly. When her voice faded, he was moving toward the spot in the pines where he had last heard it, and he was thinking of her, not of himself.

He was running before he heard the shot, past the barn and into the woods while the echo was sustained in the sharp air. He'd never been there before, but he ran immediately to the opening in the woods and sprinted deep into them on the path Andrew had worn. He did not notice the darkening as he entered the trees or the branches which lashed his face any more than he heard his feet on the pine needles; his ears were full of gunfire, the lasting shot, and his eyes strained forward for a figure in a coat and black hat. He did not think that he was running toward life or death but only toward the conclusion of that day.

The path led straight into the woods on flat ground and then turned to follow a wet draw to its source. The draw was full of briars and dense brush; the trees were thicker there, the light more obstructed, the path pressed more closely by the woods. Parker ran with one arm before his face, and it was still before him when he burst into the clearing at the spring.

He actually heard the water then and saw how the light became green as it fell through the trees, and he obeyed Iva before he saw her, smelled the gunpowder before he located the gun leaned against a stump. Iva's hand was lifted, turned to halt him; he was stopped. The earth there was a bowl, and in its hollow the essential water issued into a square wooden springbox before flowing in its mossed course. A stake was driven into the ground beside the spring; inverted upon it was a tin cup.

Iva sat upon the slope. Her legs were extended before her, her feet were at the spring's edge. One hand was lifted for Parker, the other held Andrew; those two simple human hands were enough to join and contain brothers. Even there in the trees, in the peaceful spring clearing which opened like the very eye of the woods, even dressed for shopping in her hat and coat, Iva was not outlandish but as serene as a tribal emblem planted in that fertile spot. Andrew was curled against her, head and shoulders buried in Iva—the position of an infant, but he seemed to rest there easily. His back rose with each calm breath; comfort had been that quick. Parker did not have to be told what had happened. He knew as certainly as if he'd been Andrew. When he had heard Iva's piercing call, he had discharged the gun at the general sky, defiant capitulation, and accepted Iva's arms.

Parker waited where he stood until Andrew lifted his head and saw him. "It's all right," the boy said to Iva, and Parker knew that was his permission to approach. He squatted beside the spring and lifted the cup from the stake and drank.

"You act like you thirsty," Iva said.

"I am."

"You better rinse your face too. You look like the cats been after you."

Parker touched his cheek and his fingers came away bloody—the sharp branches. He knelt beside the spring and splashed his face with cold water. As it settled, the water was so lucid that the black hat and watchful brother's face reflected upon it seemed to rise toward him from the bottom of the source, transmissions from the earth itself.

3

Twelve

The next morning, Sunday, a hard rain was blowing against Parker's window, but the telephone, and not the rain, awakened him. He roused himself at once to answer it, for he thought that he was alone in the house; his mother hadn't returned when he went to bed. He reached his door and opened it before he heard her downstairs in the kitchen, heels on the tile floor, the phone lifted from its cradle, her voice. She was home safe, thank God; his relief amounted to a grateful prayer. He'd had time—seven groggy steps from his bed to the door—to dread the phone call, to remember that last night he'd been on the brink of calling the highway patrol and the hospitals to try to locate her. He listened for a moment to make sure that he really had heard her, for his mind didn't entirely trust the report of his senses; consciousness had resumed while the body still struggled toward wakefulness; his throat was clogged, mouth scaly, his penis erect, and his bladder imperative. In that state he listened and willed his ears to clear; his mother's voice was indistinct, but it was still her voice, and

Parker hurried to wash and dress himself.

He'd come home yesterday to await his mother, anxious to see her, armed with apologies. He'd begun to think of her even before they left the spring, when he saw Andrew in Iva's arms—under the needled and prismatic light, with that vision before him, he knew that contrition was a filial duty and he saw its reward. And when they'd walked out of the woods (Iva first, carrying the gun, beating back the branches with it) and Esther came to her door, he had to bite his tongue to remain silent. *Forgive him,* he wanted to cry, and to Andrew, *Forgive her.* Iva stood between them as a kind of arbiter, to keep harm at a minimum, and at last suggested that Andrew might go home with her for the night: "Y'all both have time to think about it till tomorrow." Esther's anger then turned upon Iva, and Iva bore it patiently: "You know what you saying ain't true, Esther. I hatn't tried to come between a mother and her son." Parker had to stand by as an observer, but each second of his helplessness sharpened his longing to reach home and his own mother. He drove Iva and Andrew back to the house Mose was guarding, but he did not get out of the car; he continued straight to his own house.

She wasn't there. He made himself coffee and watched the last of the afternoon's sporting events on the television. During the news he fixed himself dinner—canned stew and a salad—because he didn't want to go out and risk missing her when she came in, and he'd already begun to fear a phone call. His fears annoyed him: why, on this day, should she meet with accident? He thought of McKemeny, but he simply couldn't believe that his mother had fled to him— who would take misery to that lout? There had to be an explanation for the length of her absence, but nothing seemed simpler to him than catastrophe. As he watched his way through the schedule of evening programs (family comedies, and they all included a wretchedly fraudulent tear-jerking moment, but Parker was moved nevertheless; he was moved also by the intrusion of the candid ads, where embarrassed men and women testified to the efficacy of sinus decongestants and headache remedies; they were so bewildered and proud to find themselves before the camera, their lives seemed so precarious, one more question and they'd break down entirely, choke on sobs as they announced, *Yes, it certainly worked for me*), hour after hour of it, his nagging fears grew to alarm. At eleven o'clock, the late news, he was ready to telephone the hospital; the phone was in his hands, his finger on the dial, but the questions he foresaw prevented him. *What time did she say she'd be back? Where did she say she was going? Have you tried to reach the friends she might have visited today?* He couldn't answer any of them.

He went to bed, and though he didn't expect to sleep, he discovered that his body at least was very tired. Left to itself, his head, that part of him severed by the top border of the sheet, might have roared on through the night. But body prevailed, for he did sleep and he was not interrupted by the customary dead-of-night insomnia. He slept, and now, when he finished brushing his teeth, his clock read ten past nine; he'd thought it was much earlier, but the sun's height couldn't be established through the gray and rainy air. He pulled on his clothes quickly, the usual jeans and the flannel shirt he'd worn yesterday, and he went downstairs.

His mother was dressed for church. She sat at the breakfast table, her spine not just straight but tense, her eyes upon the window, where the rain streaked across the glass. Her breakfast was spread neatly before her, excavated grapefruit and wheat-germ toast with precise bite marks that might have been stamped out with a cookie cutter. Her fingers tightly encircled the throat of her coffee cup; the base of the cup rattled in the saucer, and the surface of the coffee rolled in tiny undulations against the white china rim.

"Mama!" The word escaped him as a cry, his relief turning to dread, his intimations of disaster all revived. It was not his approach which had imparted a tremor to her hands; he realized that at once, and he asked urgently, his voice already inflected for sorrow, "What is it? What's happened?"

"That was Dr. Price that called," she said, rotating her head toward him. The movement required enormous deliberation; her shoulders did not shift a jot. "Queen Iva had a stroke. She was taken to the hospital early this morning. She's in a coma."

"But she's alive? She's all right?"

"The stroke is a serious one, but there's no sign of heart failure." The words were uttered in a voice from which emotion was carefully eliminated, as though her entire concentration was required to repeat faithfully the doctor's bulletin. The message was bare and unrelieved, and there was no flutter at all of the irrepressible delight which those who relay information of mortality nearly always experience: for an instant the power of death seems theirs, and they cannot help but glory in it.

"When did it happen? When did she go to the hospital?"

Futile questions, and Parker knew it; the available details, schedules, itineraries, diagnoses would explain nothing. Still, his mother replied in her eerie voice, "Mose found her unconscious beside him in the middle of the night. Her breathing woke him up. She was gasping. He didn't know how long she'd been that way. He called the ambulance right away."

Stroke. The word itself was so unmedical, so ordinary, had been used so familiarly by Iva as threat and prophecy, that for Parker it evoked only the image of brightly dressed women under flowered parasols in a tropical climate, palm trees and a yellow sun; a decorous fainting, warm prostration, occasion for rapid fanning and smelling salts. He knew well enough that a stroke was a cerebral hemorrhage, but its actuality—this rainy morning, his mother's coffee, the ring of the phone, and beyond the mundane data the possibility of life ending, principle leaving the phenomenal world—would not yield to any idea he could form. He asked about what he could grasp.

"What are they doing for her? Is there any way they can treat her? Will she be paralyzed?"

"Her left side is paralyzed now. Dr. Price says that's usual, but it probably won't last. He said they tried to bring her blood pressure down."

"How long will she be unconscious?"

"They can't tell."

"How dangerous is a stroke like this? Did he say?"

"No. Patients with high blood pressure have strokes," she said, as though axiom sufficed. But then she released her coffee cup and pushed herself back against the chair. She gripped her hands in her lap and turned her face back to the window. The rain beat down, and upon the straight wooden chair she appeared braced and solitary in an immensity of disorder. Her neck was rigid, and her voice was factual and determined: "I don't think I can stand it if anything happens to Iva."

"Mama." Again the cry, her name; he touched her shoulder and her arms reeled him in, surrounded his waist, ferociously drew him near. Her complete force was exerted in that embrace, her chin was above his belt buckle, her face ground against his shirt as if she meant to leave an impression of it in the flannel. He looked down upon her head, the sheaf of combed hair which loosened before his eyes, and he could only think that absolution came without his asking. And despite his joy, her reach was so humbling that he was embarrassed for her; he wished that she had let him kneel, that she had not stranded him in air above her, that he could do more than calm her shoulders with his hands.

When she withdrew her face, she wiped her cheeks with her napkin. "I'm sorry," she said. "There's no reason for me to be so upset now. Dr. Price can't tell yet exactly how serious the stroke is. But all this last week it seemed that something terrible was going to happen to one of us. I don't know why."

"It's all right, Mama," he said, and he did kneel beside her then. Her back slumped, and she leaned forward over the table, face in her hands, each breath an attempt to clear her emotion.

"I knew when the phone rang that it would be—something, I wasn't sure what. That probably sounds very foolish and superstitious. But, Parker, I was terrified yesterday in Montgomery. I was afraid to come home. I was afraid even to call." She tried to laugh at herself, and her shoulders heaved under his arm.

"What did happen?" she asked. "Mose is at the hospital. He told Dr. Price some story about you and Iva looking for somebody. What was it?" She lifted her face toward him, imploring, expectant—he might tell her what she needed to know.

"Andrew ran away from Esther," he said. "There had

been a quarrel with some other boys and he went home and got a gun. Esther called Iva for help."

"Did she find him?"

He told her how Iva had looked for Andrew and how she had found him, but he did not describe his own meeting with Esther.

His mother nodded when he finished. "He said the stroke might have been brought on by something like that, that kind of excitement and activity." And after a pause she added, "That poor Andrew. He'll blame himself for it."

"No," Parker protested. "Iva won't let him." But how could she persuade Andrew otherwise? Hadn't he set out to inflict suffering? Parker and his mother were both silent.

"I was on my way to church," his mother said finally. "I suppose I might as well go."

"Are you going to the hospital?"

"I'll stop on my way back. I'll see if I can catch Dr. Price and find out anything more. I want to see Mose too."

She stood up and placed her head against Parker's cheek. The movement was awkward and she pitched forward; it was the first time that Parker had ever been conscious of embracing her full weight.

After she'd left—raincoat, umbrella, her car a looming specter in the rain—Parker prepared himself a spartan breakfast. He ate, and he faced another morning in an empty house, but he did not feel alone. The house seemed to be entrusted to him by his mother and Iva, and he cleaned up the breakfast room and the kitchen—a small enough gesture, but still it was conceived as an act of stewardship, and it was undertaken to ready the house against their return. He'd have been grateful for other chores, for any activity that suspended thinking (not thinking, really;

211

guessing and *fearing*), but the rain kept him from any out-door task and no further housekeeping was needed. The dishwasher chugged away and Parker retrieved the damp newspaper—it was delivered in a plastic bag and wasn't a total loss—before he thought of his deposition. Only the strangeness of finding himself seated in the library in the morning reminded him of it; he knew that he'd strayed from his routine. He did not want to continue the deposition on that of all mornings, but he failed to convince himself that he was interested in the news. He'd heard it all twice on the television the night before. So he gave in reluctantly; at least it would keep him occupied until his mother returned, and he would be that much nearer the end of it.

To his own surprise, he wrote with fluency. He did not pause for coffee or cigarettes, did not fiddle with the desk lamp or get distracted by presences in his room, did not labor to achieve neatness. He merely attempted to fulfill the letter of Booth's instructions, and the deposition slewed onto the page like the rain on the window. The meeting in Amsterdam, the stop at Rhein Main, Newark, Everly—he covered thousands of miles in twelve pages (but his handwriting grew larger and more open, began to slant forward precipitously because of the pace) and accomplished several weeks in two hours. He got himself and Arthur almost to Ewell in that one session, a fact which provoked self-deprecation: he'd have finished long before, he thought, if he hadn't been filibustering.

And he'd actually been able to compose with a divided mind, for during the last hour he'd been more alert for sounds of his mother's arrival than he was to the activity of his pen. She should have been home by then; delay boded poorly. He feared for Iva, with the usual inability of the healthy to conceive of bodily failures. His own corporeality was effortless as air and seemed as little vulnerable to cessation; his consciousness and emotions swam in a medium which had nothing to do with bodiness. So fear was really the only way he could accommodate Iva's stroke, a vague fear which, like his vigils of the previous day and night, should have brought home to him the limits of what love can save.

He put the deposition away before his mother returned, driven downstairs not only by his impatience to see her but also by an unprecedented urge to cook for her. Sunday was the day of ample breakfasts, or had been while his father was still alive, the one meal of the week when the family was certain to sit down together at an abundant table at a fixed time. He couldn't bake biscuits, but he could scramble eggs and fry sausages and boil grits, and the pots and pans were working on the stove when he heard his mother arrive.

She saw him at the kitchen window as she crossed from the garage to the house. The rain had settled to a steady gray drizzle, and her black umbrella was raised against it, but her smile pierced the weather; Parker knew that she carried happy news. She shed her coat and rubber boots in the back hall, shook her hair exuberantly after she unknotted her scarf, and told her son, "They let me see her. That's where I've been so long—not in her room the whole time, I only went in for a minute—but at the hospital talking to Mose and Dr. Price."

"She's all right, then? She's not in any danger?"

"She came out of the coma right after Dr. Price called here. It seems as though she just woke up—I didn't really understand. Anyway, she's alert and she knew who I was. She couldn't talk—Dr. Price went into the room with me and told her not to try—but he wanted me to visit her anyway. He says patients are very frightened after something like that. They don't quite know what's happened, and it reassures them to have visitors and see familiar faces. Mose went in to see her too."

"Could she move at all?"

"It's only her left side that's affected, and really I wouldn't have been able to tell if I hadn't known. Her left eye is sort of droopy, and her mouth is funny—you know how you look after the dentist gives you a shot of novocaine. But I thought she looked fine, and Dr. Price said the stroke may not be as serious as it seemed at first."

His mother had fully emerged from her rain gear by then, and she'd kicked off her damp shoes as well. She hugged Parker cheerfully, and the instant during which he felt deceived, cheated for having prepared for the worst, passed so quickly that he scarcely noticed it. His mother sniffed and advanced into the kitchen on her stocking feet.

"You're fixing a Sunday brunch—that's perfect. It's just what I wanted. I didn't know you could cook. I love the smell of that sausage." She commenced a hopping, playful dance. "Oooo, this floor is cold on my bare feet. Let me run up and get some slippers on."

She returned at once, her feet furred to the ankles. "Can I help you do anything, Parker? This is so lovely, to have a big hot breakfast on a rainy Sunday. And I'm so relieved to have seen Iva."

"Did Dr. Price say when she'd be able to have other visitors? I'd like to go see her."

"I'm sure it will be all right to go tomorrow, but you'll probably be allowed in for just a minute."

"How long will she be in the hospital?"

"He wants to move her as soon as he can. He was funny —you know how he mutters. He said the hospital was the worst possible place to recover. He wants her to go home, but she'll need to be looked after there. Poor old Mose will have to have help."

"How is he doing?"

"He was grand. He was really very calm. He seemed to understand everything Dr. Price said. He was much steadier than I was."

"How long does Dr. Price think the paralysis will last?"

"He says it usually doesn't last very long. She'll have to go at things slowly because of her age, but he thinks the best thing for her is to be as active as she can be without wearing herself out. But all that's a ways off—she won't be able to do anything for a while."

"This stroke won't affect her mind, will it? She won't lose her memory or anything like that?"

"He said there's a chance of that. People who have strokes sometimes get very fussy and crotchety, but that usually goes away with the other effects. By the way," she added, "Dr. Price said he ran into you at the football game the other night, and he and Mose both made cracks about your hair."

"Maybe I should wear a net while I cook?"

She laughed. "I think I like it now that I'm used to it, but when you first came home, you did look awfully strange to me. And you had Arthur with you—I didn't mind that, really I didn't, even though I'm sure you thought so. I was just surprised. Somehow I expected that you weren't going to be different at all after two years away."

A month-long silence was broken; she spoke Arthur's name without hesitancy. She was seated in Iva's chair to be near him as he stirred the eggs, so relaxed that she seemed lost in dreams. "And then there was all that trouble. I know it wasn't your fault, but you'd just got back and I didn't know what to think. Amsy told me what happened out there at the lake, and everything was so confused for a few days —oh, Parker, I'm sorry I let things get off to such a bad start. I know that it's been terribly hard for you since you've been home, especially being here all alone. I haven't been much help. I wish that Amsy hadn't gone off to school right away."

"I wish so too," Parker said, but despite his mother's complete and gentle apology, he didn't know how to begin his own. Her warmth was more intimidating than severity would have been. In her present mood, indulgence was plenary, and he'd expected, even rather desired, the chastising rigors of an opposed, full-dress contrition.

"It was very silly of me to be so touchy about your father's room, too, but I didn't know what to say to you about it. There was no reason why you shouldn't have worked up there if you wanted to."

She stopped abruptly and sat forward in the chair, her face molded by concern. "Did you move the pistol, Parker? I found it in the bureau yesterday morning."

He'd forgotten the pistol, the test he'd arranged for her, and in his chagrin at being caught out in such a juvenile prank, he was scarcely able to answer, "Yes, I did."

"I looked for it when I cleaned up after Frank left, and when it wasn't in the drawer I was petrified—I thought he'd taken it. . . . But why did you move it?"

"To see if you'd find it," he said. "The eggs are ready. Go sit down at the table and I'll bring you your plate."

She obeyed him and went to the table, but her expression was puzzled. He had more to account for than he'd thought, but he attempted an explanation when he placed food before her.

"I had the feeling, not exactly that you were spying on

me, I knew you wouldn't do that, but that you were watching Daddy's room. Why do you keep it so sanitary and antiseptic? Why don't you just close the door on it and forget about it?"

"I don't go to any special trouble," she said in an offended tone. "I like to keep the house livable. I've always cleaned that room."

"I don't mean that you ought to neglect it. It just bothered me that everything of Daddy's is still there, all his clothes and even his pistol. Why did you keep it?"

"It's not something you just throw out," she said. She hadn't touched her food, and she seemed baffled and hurt by Parker's questions. He knew that they were reproachful, though he did not mean them to be.

"Please, Mama, eat while it's hot. It doesn't matter why you kept the pistol up there—it was stupid of me to move it. But everything was so neat and orderly, as though nothing had ever happened, and that was the way you treated me, too. So I thought if I moved the pistol, you'd have to say something."

"Was I so awful, Parker, that you couldn't tell me any of this before?"

"I wanted to, but even that day when we talked on the lawn—I don't know what was wrong with me. I think I wanted to blame you and Daddy for everything that had happened to me. Everything I'd done," he corrected himself.

His mother lowered her head and spoke softly: "We . . ." but she didn't finish her thought.

"Eat, Mama, it's getting cold," he said.

She obeyed again. Even without biscuits, it was robust and belly-filling fare, and after they'd once begun, they both ate with gusto. His mother praised him; she said she hadn't eaten a solid meal for days.

"What about that steak and soufflé?"

"You know, I really think he overestimated his skill."

"I'm sorry for everything I said that night."

"I ought to thank you. It taught me something, the way he baited you. We had an ugly battle right after you left."

"That only makes it worse that I said what I did later on."

"Let's not talk about it," she said.

But he couldn't repress one final question: "You didn't see him yesterday in Montgomery?"

She laughed. "Do you really want to know what I did? I went shopping in the morning, then got into a ladies' gin-rummy game at the Country Club in the afternoon and lost seventeen dollars, and then I went by myself to a double feature at the drive-in."

"I hope they were good movies."

"They were both Beatles movies, and I went because they made me think of you. Maybe it's the hair, after all. I didn't suffer as much as I thought I would."

Parker did see Iva the next afternoon. He had agreed with his mother that they should visit separately, in order to provide company at two different times. Mrs. Livingston returned from her visit with a cheerful report of Iva's condition, and Parker later went to the hospital alone. When he asked for Iva's room at the desk, the receptionist gave him a visitor's card and told him someone else was already with her.

Parker went to the room anyway, expecting to find Mose with his wife. He tapped on the door, which was already ajar, and opened it without waiting for a summons. He entered, and Iva filled his appalled sight. She was prodigious. Upon a mattress as high as his waist, covered by a sheet and hospital gown, she looked like a huge polar beast, and the standard hospital furniture appeared to have been designed for a different, smaller race. Her skin was oily and shone as though freshly anointed. The only sign of her recognition was the movement of her right eye and a slight lifting of her right hand. Acknowledgment, but no greeting. Prostrate, motionless, she was not acquiescent, and the labor of her huge body seemed to be wrath. Her right cheek puffed with each stertorous breath, that discharge the single but unremitting index of leashed force.

The other visitor was Andrew, and he was standing on the far side of the bed, in front of the flowers banked on the window sill, his face wary, alert, distrustful. One of his hands stroked Iva's left arm, and his posture was so protective that Parker felt he had blundered upon an intimate scene.

"How are you?" Parker asked. "Are they taking good care of you in here?"

"She not sposed to talk," Andrew answered for her. "She can't talk too good yet."

Parker nodded, but he wondered how Andrew had become the custodian of medical information. Dr. Price? More likely that Mose had told him. "I hope you're comfortable," he said to Iva. "Mama told me that Dr. Price was real pleased by how well you were doing. He said you'd be home in a few days."

The most trivial kind of encouragement, and it had no visible effect upon Iva. Parker noticed now the clamped squint of her left eye, numb wrinkle at the left corner of her mouth. *Permanent damage of brain substance:* that was what Dr. Price had actually told his mother.

"Did Mama tell you where she was all day Saturday, when we thought she'd gone to Montgomery? Well, she was in

Montgomery, but guess what she was doing—she went to the movies there, to two Beatles movies."

He wanted Iva to know of the reconciliation which had taken place, but he couldn't tell what she gathered from his speech, or even if she understood the words of it. Andrew's presence made him self-conscious, and his efforts at cheerfulness resulted in this bogging chatter. Why had his mother been so buoyed by her visit? Iva was incapacitated, and there at her bedside her suffering became material to him for the first time; he felt acutely how the resources of that body struggled to harness themselves to cure. *Brain damage:* tissue scorched by blood, the life-sustaining functions continuing without government. That was the origin of Iva's wrath. Her stroke contained no mystery, but delivered her to fierce incomprehension; she lived still, experienced the sensations of life in the body, but she was not restored; intelligence knew only deprivation.

"You'll have a good rest here," Parker said helplessly. "You'll be on your feet in no time."

"She doing the best she can," Andrew said in a tone of reproach. His voice announced plainly, *Don't aggravate her with foolish hopes.*

"Has Dr. Price been in?" Parker asked.

"He was here when I got here," Andrew said. "I come here straight from school."

"Is everything all right now?" Parker meant to ask if he'd gone back to Esther, but stopped, thinking he shouldn't mention that in Iva's hearing, shouldn't pry in case Andrew had not yet returned home.

But Andrew answered calmly and with some pride. "I'm staying with Mose now. I'm gone to stay there for a while and help him look after Queen Iva when she gets back home. Dr. Price says I can be a help to her."

220

So that had been arranged. Parker was mindful of his selfishness—he hadn't thought of what real service he himself might render Iva, hadn't even brought flowers, simply bestowed his presence—and he was jealous that Andrew should enter Iva's need so much more naturally than he did. His half-brother's sympathy was more substantial and generous than his, and Andrew seemed to realize that as well as Parker did. Parker asked Andrew about his schoolwork, and they chatted over Iva for a few more minutes. At one point Parker was on the verge of announcing a vague philanthropic intention; in the last two days he'd idly considered that he had an economic responsibility to Andrew, a familial duty to keep clothes on his back and money in his pocket, to see him through school, to foot the bills or get his mother to foot them, and these speculations now assembled in a wish to make their relation clear. He imagined that Iva would be pleased, but he wasn't able to make the offer, not there in that hospital room. He looked at Iva and he fathomed his own motive, and he took his leave very soon after.

He returned to the hospital the next day and found Iva alone, but he felt no more comfortable than he had in Andrew's presence. He tried again to describe his new and affectionate harmony with his mother, and he joked about their clumsy efforts to run the house without Iva's assistance, but his sympathies emerged in what sounded like bland pleasantries, languid banter. On the third visit—again he went as soon as visiting hours began at two o'clock, before Andrew was out of school—he told Iva that he had at last finished the deposition. He was anxious to tell her; he didn't quite know why. She responded to his news, lifted her good hand and strove to speak. The right half of her mouth moved and she produced a gnawing rasp. The machinery of speech seized and ground upon itself to achieve that utterance, and her face was pinched more tightly into its agonized twitch. Parker distinguished the words "you" and "done," but he immediately tried to quiet her. "I take it to Booth this afternoon," he said, "and that's the end of it." His assurance had the fervor of a promise.

He had finished the deposition with all the aplomb and velocity he'd expected. His memory had served him faithfully and provided the data Booth had requested: the number of shots, their timing, even the accompanying remarks. Parker would have sworn to the verbatim accuracy of the deposition. He did not dwell on his contribution to the discovery of Kin, nor did he gloss over it. That was the only piece of the deposition that surprised him; he'd dreaded that final confession, but it unspooled itself in ready language. Words, words, words—he knew they mattered, believed that the past resided in them, and acknowledged their power, but it was no longer an intimidating power. He did not feel that he had to seal off the past; he felt sure enough to let it flow into the present. When he reached the end of the deposition, after all the facts had been recorded, he was able to write a conclusion.

You'll recognize an inconsistency in this document. The first part of it won't be much use to you as evidence, and I suppose I could keep it and give you only the second part, the part you asked for, but I'm going to pass the whole thing on to you. I hope you won't be offended by the tone of the first part and that you'll read long enough to get to this apology. I'm sorry for all the insults. If I had the deposition to begin over again, it would be less cockeyed. The reason that I'm giving it all to you is that the first part clears me, I think, of something I'm sure you've suspected: that I've been pressing for prosecution in order to get myself exonerated. I hope that the deposition will prove to you that I know I can't be acquitted, freed, or even pleased by anyone else's guilt. There's no satisfaction in knowing that others are capable of the same crimes that I am. I honestly don't know any longer if I want the case to come to trial. It *should*—that's the last time I'll tell you your job and the last time I'll apologize. I just don't know if I want it to because I don't know what good could come from it. Maybe a verdict would deter some white man at some future time from taking up his gun—that's something. But shouldn't that man be more than deterred? Shouldn't his very desire be extinguished?

Here we are again, the difference between justice and law. And all we need to do to accomplish justice, to extinguish that desire, is change history. Well, I don't believe that any longer; I think it's a question of how we inhabit our history. If we can't overcome it, we can at least gain possession of our lives within it. And we *have* to do that; otherwise we are subject not just to those murderous desires but to the griefs they engender, to sorrows that increase, to despair. Who can bear them? Who can bear them if they are not his own, if he has not made them his own, if they are the merely inevitable, the merely fatal burdens that history has thrust upon us all? We have to occupy our history as we occupy our homes, as the place from which we see most clearly, not as the place which robs our vision of dimension.

But that's enough. It certainly sounds like enough. Sorry —I do keep on apologizing. But this is what it's come to, a heap of Blue Horse paper, a couple miles, I bet, if you stretched it all out in one straight line, of penmanship. Maybe you will be a better reader than I was a writer and therefore, as the Good Book says, into your hands I commend it.

Thirteen

The dogs were far out ahead of them, the bells on their collars tinkling as they searched the field. The big-boned, barrel-chested male pointer loped with his muzzle held high, sorting the slight breeze for the scent of quail. The smaller female worked the brushy edge of the field in cover dense enough to hamper her, advancing in nimble hops, every few minutes standing upright on her hind legs to look back for Booth. Even reared back like that, the weeds were high as her collar, and the men had only occasional glimpses of her trim white body sprinkled with liver-colored markings as she forced her way through honeysuckle turned copper and the pink and crimson shoots of brambles. Intent, deliberate, avid, the small bitch exhausted that terrain with a ferocity which made the dog's handsome stride seem vain and dopey.

"When that bell stops, she's got em," Booth said. "There may be classier dogs than Ticky, but there aren't very many that find more birds than she does. Look at that tail going now. She's got some scent."

He began to walk toward her, excited, almost trotting, and Parker had to press to keep up with him. Booth was talking to the dog, encouraging her—"Whoa now, Tick, easy girl, whoa now, pin em down, careful now"—but the words were not commands. His voice was a primitive croon, huntsman's immemorial wail, of which he was probably no more conscious than he was of Parker stumbling along behind him. His cries were open-throated and, to Parker, as incongruous as a yodel, for even in his bird-shooting costume—leather-faced trousers, drab shooting jacket, Gokey boots—Booth managed to look professional and desk-bound. He wore his black-rimmed glasses, his hair was stiffly combed, and his cheeks were as clean-shaven, smooth, and hairless as wieners.

"There. She's got em. Dear God, look how staunch. There, Ticky, hold em now. Good girl, Tick. Do you see that?"

And without taking his eyes from her, without slowing down, he called the male to come and back her point. He'd already raised his arms and held his automatic shotgun ready before him, not at his shoulder but his finger was on the safety. Parker was still behind him and he hadn't seen the point yet, and he was as curious and perplexed as the male dog which ambled in the direction of the shouting. Parker carried a loaded double-barreled shotgun and he concentrated on keeping it pointed at the sky. The gun was Booth's, as were the dogs and the idea for the hunt and even the jacket Parker wore. Booth had outfitted Parker and given him a two-minute lesson in gun handling before they cast the dogs. Parker's hands were sweating, and he held the gun as though it were atomic. He didn't know what to expect from it or the dogs or the quail; his errand in that November field, chasing after a monomaniacal pointer bitch and a similar lawyer, carrying a weapon that had been forced upon him, was not at all clear to him.

He was annoyed by Booth's obliviousness. The invitation to hunt, he knew, was Booth's response to his deposition; it had seemed peculiar enough—why did Booth think that he'd want to discuss it with a shotgun in his hands?—but he'd thought the invitation was kindly meant and he'd accepted it. Now, fifteen minutes after they'd left the car, it seemed as though Booth had forgotten him in the passion of blood sport; he and the pointer were honed to kill the small birds crouched somewhere ahead of them. But, ignorant as he was, Parker felt the pitch of emotion as they converged upon the quail—the jangling bell of the male dog, the dry weeds snapping underfoot, Booth's instinctive cries—which declared that edge of the field and woods the arena of violence.

The male dog saw Ticky at the same time Parker did. His head lowered, his neck stretched forward, he seemed to glide through the weeds and then clenched into a point that reproduced the bitch's. Motionless, taut, their shoulders and spines raised under their skin, their tails curved and rigid as scimitars, the dogs had narrowed it to these few yards of weeds. The bitch's left forepaw was slightly cocked in an imperious economy; the dog's snout twitched as the quail's fatal musk touched it. Bred to this moment, shaped and formed for it, straining in every cord and bristle, both animals scanned the earth and air before them with exulting senses. In their wild and savage paralysis, Parker hardly recognized dogs at all; these creatures were animated by predatory essence.

"Good Gravy, good Tick. Steady now. All right, they've got em nailed down. They'll probably flush toward the woods. You go in on the other side of Ticky."

227

They closed. They passed the male and it stepped forward, the bell clanged, Booth issued a sharp command. They drew even with the bitch, and Parker's gun came up as Booth's had, chest high, one finger on the front trigger and his thumb on the safety. He looked at Booth, but Booth was gazing at the air in front of him, and he looked down into the tasseled weeds as though he might see the birds there.

He didn't, even though they rose exactly where he looked. He heard them before he saw them, a squeal of wings and humming air, then gray and brown blurs, generative ideas of earth until they were head high and fifteen yards out; there they seemed to pause or hover, in stasis between rising and level flight, and there the great rush became clarity and the birds suddenly appeared, materialized in all their gorgeous detail; the covey of twenty was aloft, not as if they'd risen from the earth but like a distillation of the air.

He was able to focus on them just as Booth's gun went off. He saw the blue puff of feathers, the bird which fell not as if had been overtaken but had met the shot coming toward it. A second and third quail fell, folded, and dropped, and Parker knew that he too had shot, although he was not aiming the gun and had not swung on any target. Then the air was empty again, not just empty but deserted, and the sound of the guns dissipated, and he heard the bitch snorting and the convulsive flapping of a downed bird.

"I tripled! What a covey! I hit three goddam birds, just one-two-three, left to right—that was a textbook rise. Did you hit any?"

"I don't think so," Parker said. "I really wasn't ready for them."

But Booth wasn't listening. He called Ticky to him and led her out to retrieve the birds. "Dead, dead, dead," he repeated, "hunt dead, Ticky, dead, dead, dead." The little bitch rooted with her nose to the ground and found the shuddering bird first. It was still alive when she delivered it to Booth. He held it by the neck and twirled it a few times, grinned, and tossed its head into the weeds. Its neck was a bloody excrescence. "Too much torque," Booth said, and the headless bird expired in one last unbelievably rapid spasm of its wings. Booth shoved it into his jacket pocket. "Dead, dead, Ticky, hunt dead, dead, dead."

When the bitch had retrieved the other two birds, Booth asked him again if he'd hit any. "Too bad," he sympathized. "That was a classic rise. But we'll get up a couple more coveys and we ought to get some singles shooting. First time you ever shot at a quail?"

"Yes. I've shot dove before, but never quail."

"What you been doing till now?" Booth smiled, but he was serious when he said, "I must have seen Ticky point a thousand times, but every time is like the first time. My heart just pounds when I go in behind her, I mean it pounds like a hammer. Quail in front of your bird dog must be the purest excitement in the world. There's nothing like it for me."

Parker shrugged. He knew approximately what Booth was trying to convey—why else had his gun risen and fired? He hadn't willed it, hadn't even thought of shooting, but the stock had met his shoulder and his finger had pulled the front trigger. He wasn't conscious that he'd shot until he found himself still pulling the front trigger, trying to fire the second barrel, and by then he'd seen the birds fall and he was dismayed.

"What do you think? You want to try to scare up another

covey now? We ought to give these birds some time to settle and put down scent before we hunt for them. Looks like we might be into some birds today if Tick finds em all as easy as she found those."

"Whatever you say."

"Skedaddle, Tick, hunt em. Off you go. You too, Gravy, you good-looker. Hunt em now."

The male had to be chased from the heavy scent, and then the dogs were in front again, the bells going, the scene in that Alabama field as idyllic and crisp and melodious as a Swiss postcard. Ahead of them were the free-running dogs, expanse of muted and burnished autumn colors, ocher and copper and ivory, impinging evergreens; above them was a sky which maintained its blue to all horizons, a composition of air, so that the unfelt work of lungs procured the very taste of it and breathing was like seeing. But as he walked forward, Parker had to squint because of the sun streaking the barrel of Booth's gun and he was as pained as if he carried them himself by the bloody weight of those three feathered carcasses in the pocket of Booth's jacket.

"The mistake most people make," Booth said helpfully, "is they're looking at the bushes or the dog when they walk in on a covey. You ought to be looking out in front of you where you expect the covey to get up, and that way they fly right into your focus. You're waiting for them, and you can get a real hold on them. You can get em to sit right on the end of your gun."

Parker didn't answer, but Booth did not need any prodding to expatiate. "The old-timers say you ought to wait till they reach the top of the lift and you can tell the cock bird from the hen. The cock has a white stripe across the eye like a mask, and the hen has a buffy-colored stripe. When you can see that, when they hang up in the air before they turn, that's when to crack them."

"How many hens would there be in a covey like that one?"

"Three or four to every cock. That's a good big covey. It hasn't been shot into much. But when a covey gets thinned down to eight or ten birds, it's criminal, just criminal, to harvest any more birds from it. You're liable to leave it without a cock, and even if you don't, the varmints might get into the birds. The foxes and snakes will be after them, and the coons and skunks are always nosing after the eggs. Quail have good big broods, but they need them to survive."

Without warning Booth accelerated his pace. "Look at Ticky," he called back to Parker. "She's making game again already."

They hurried toward the bitch, but she couldn't pin the birds down. She canvassed a small area where spiky stumps and rotting treetops were hidden in the brush and the berried prongs of sumac clustered like antlers. Her tail beat upon the rattling weeds, and she gulped noisily as if drowning in the scent of quail. Parker found himself hoping that the birds were gone, transfixed as he watched her by a fear that she would coil and lock into another point. Booth separated the weeds in front of him with one boot.

"You ever seen a roost?" he asked. "That's what she's on to. It's good hot scent, but the birds probably got off the roost and moved out into the field somewhere to feed."

"What's a roost?"

"Look here."

At Booth's toe was a neat circle of white droppings, and the grass about it was lightly beaten down and blackened. "They get in a circle with their tails together, looking out in all directions, like a wagon train circled up to keep off the Indians. Other animals make rings like that too, animals that stay in herds, and they put the young ones and weak ones inside to protect them from danger. It's an amazing thing, isn't it, the way they know how to look after their own?"

They found several other roosts within a few steps of the first one, the domestic encampments of quail. The ground thereabouts was dotted with mounds of guano; the gregarious birds seemed to have moved to fresh sites as housekeeping dictated. The discovery of the roosts was enough like the invasion and ransacking of family privacy to silence even Booth. The bitch lost interest in the place and began to hunt about its edges, seeking newer trace of the covey. The carefree male dog made a pass near them and kept on motoring, but it was he who found the covey, who spun in mid-stride and alighted in a galvanized point, all motion truncated. Parker had been watching him, but Booth didn't see him until he noticed the cessation of the bell.

They closed again, and as they did, Parker wavered. He didn't want to shoot this time, but he didn't know how he would explain his refusal to Booth, and when the covey rose, he deliberately fitted the gun to his shoulder and lowered his cheek to the comb of the stock. He selected a bird at the edge of the covey, fired once and missed it, heard Booth firing but kept his eye steady on the bird as it circled, moved his finger to the rear trigger and waited until he saw the gun's bead in front of the bird. Minutes seemed to have passed, but the quail's rounding flight had kept it within range as he trailed it, and he knew before he fired that the bird was going to fall. He pulled. The bird's wings dipped and its head fell forward like a weight and dragged the body after it.

"Good shot," Booth exclaimed. "You stayed on that one long enough. I had time to reload while you were swinging on it. I knocked down two," he said. "It looks as if this is going to be a banner hunt if Gravy finds birds by himself and you hit the second bird you've ever shot at."

The bitch had gone forward to fetch Booth's two birds, but Parker did not yet move to retrieve his own. He could see it from where he stood, for it had fallen in a patch where the weeds were flattened down. The quail was a cock—Parker saw the white stripe, the white at the throat—and it was not dead, was not crouched, and though it must have known that its camouflage did not avail it on the smooth bed of yellow weeds, it made no effort to conceal itself. The head was raised and turned toward Parker.

"Hunt dead, dead, dead."

Booth was leading Ticky toward the bird, but before they reached it, the excited male dog romped by. Instead of fetching, the dog pointed again, its snout not three feet from the bird.

"Would you look at that? That damn bird is staring Gravy right in the eye. Good boy, Grave, good boy, you hold now. Don't you bolt on that bird. Are you reloaded, Parker? This bird looks like it might jump up again."

Parker approached. He could see that the bird's exquisitely plumed back rose and fell with breathing, that its eyes surveyed dogs and men without flinching. Some unthinkable pain had converted its fear to wrath, the instinct for flight to a readiness to confront the four huge creatures which advanced upon it.

"You be ready to shoot," Booth said. "I'm going to reach down there for it."

He squatted slowly and extended his hand, and when it neared the quail, the small head snapped back and the tiny beak opened in threat. Booth's hand jerked away from the bird, and he laughed at himself as he reached forward again and seized it by the throat. He spun it to wring its neck, but there was no beating of wings or closing of claws. This bird simply died.

"That beats anything I've ever seen," Booth said as he examined the bird. "This fierce little cock was ready to attack me. I wonder where you hit it to make it behave like that?" He parted the feathers to look for injury, but he found none. "Looks to me as though this bird died of anger," he said, "but it sure came down hard when you shot."

Booth tossed the dead bird toward Parker, but he stepped out of the way and let it fall to the ground. Booth laughed again. "I don't blame you for being scared of that one. That's the meanest little quail I've ever done business with."

Parker lifted the quail with his fingertips, but he didn't study it as Booth had. He tucked it into the pouch on the left side of the jacket to remove it from sight. He felt its weight against the top of his hip, and he discovered that he had blood on his hand, not a smear but a quaking and brilliant puddle balanced on the web between his thumb and forefinger.

"Let's go on up to this point of woods," Booth said. "There's a big cornfield off to the right, and we can sit down for a while and let the dogs work through there."

The corn had been harvested, and from the high end of the field they could see the dogs roaming swiftly above the

234

stubble. They coursed down the half-mile rows, more like sight- than scent-hunters, and waves of doves swelled up in front of them. The male ran up two crows which took wing with bitter squawks. As the black birds rose, the dog in pursuit of them, the sun transformed their backs into decks of silver, twin planes of dazzling radiance, and they escaped as if by metamorphosis.

"The dogs would need a powerful stroke of luck to find quail in thirty open acres," Booth said. "We can keep an eye on them from here. We'll let them work the field by themselves for a few minutes. We couldn't keep up with them out there anyway."

Booth ejected the shells from his gun and sat down beside Parker on the edge of an elevated farm road. "You know that I didn't ask you to come out here to hunt. The birds are a bonus. I want to talk to you about the deposition."

"You've read it, then." And though he enunciated that fact carefully, Parker couldn't help thinking that Booth had kept the deposition for longer than three weeks—slow reader.

"Every word," Booth said. "I admire you for taking the time to write it. I think I realize what this case means to you, and that's why I didn't ask you to come by the office again. The case means a lot to me too, and I want you to know that."

"I'm sorry, Booth, for some of the things I wrote, especially at the beginning. I felt as though I ought to go back and start the whole thing over."

"Most of what you said was quite valid. I had it coming. I thought the deposition was very honest and very forthright and it made me examine my own motives."

"I know it was four times as long as it needed to be. I

didn't feel right about shoving the whole mess into your hands."

"It made a strong impression on me, and, as I said, I don't want you to think that a case like this or a deposition like yours is all in a day's work for me. You deserve the best explanation I can give you, and since we haven't communicated very well in my office, I thought we might try an out-of-doors conference."

Booth removed his glasses, blew on the lenses, wiped them with a handkerchief. He actually seemed nervous, and he had struggled to sound humble. But *explanation*—the only thing which could need explaining was a disinclination to prosecute. Exactly what Parker had always expected, but now that Booth's refusal was imminent, he felt the extent of his disappointment.

"I hope you'll understand my position, Parker. I'd hate for you to believe that I was just washing my hands of the case. In your deposition you have some shrewd insights into my predicament—"

"You're not going to prosecute," Parker said.

"I don't see how it can be done," Booth answered quickly, replacing his glasses and turning to face Parker. The sun made bright, blind discs of the lenses. "It hasn't been easy to arrive at this decision, and I assure you that I haven't reached it without long and careful consideration. I read your deposition very particularly, and the reason it's taken so long to get back to you is that I've had several meetings with Sheriff Flood and I've also questioned Sessions and Bates. After reviewing the evidence available at this time, I see no way that the state can bring charges of attempted murder."

He'd recovered his idiom, the bland and formal language

of authority, but the words seemed as evasive as the glare on his spectacles.

"They threatened Arthur out there at the lake. They weren't interested in the rest of us. They had loaded guns and they shot them. What else do they have to do?"

"The only feasible charge is aggravated assault, but I doubt even that would stand. According to your deposition, they never actually threatened Arthur's life. They asked him to come out of the house, and, given the circumstances, I think a jury would require more."

"What are the circumstances? That Arthur is black? They did threaten to kill him. That's what all of us understood. Why do you think Arthur left the house? And then they fired at him—why isn't that attempted murder?"

"There's no proof that they shot to kill. When I talked to Arthur the day after the incident, I asked him if he had heard any shots hitting near him on the ground or in the water."

"How could he have noticed that? He was running for his life."

"He might have noticed. A bullet from a high-powered rifle has quite an impact. But he didn't remember seeing where any of the shots hit."

"What does that mean? You think they weren't shooting at him?"

"It means he can't testify that the bullets landed near him, and, as a matter of fact, I don't think they were shooting at him."

"Because Arthur didn't hear the bullets hit? Why did he act dead, then?"

"Deputies were out at the lake with metal detectors for three solid days. They didn't find a single spent bullet anywhere near where Arthur fell."

"Most of them could have gone into the water."

"That's possible, but you'd think they'd find something in three days—if there was anything to be found."

"Is that evidence?"

Parker's tone was bitter. Booth's condescending explanations galled him, indoors or out. He watched the dogs, two barely visible specks at the distant end of the field, hunting more slowly now, tired by their initial burst. This whole day, weather and dogs and birds, seemed calculated to purchase his acquiescence, an ambitiously orchestrated bribe, and he resented it more than he would a curt dismissal in Booth's office. Booth paused, and when he spoke again, Parker could hear that he'd attempted to make his voice more vernacular—just two Alabama boys chewing the fat during the hunt.

"I had a kind of peculiar interview with Sessions. Do you know him? You said you recognized him in the car, and you couldn't have seen him for two years."

"I remember him from school, that's all. He must be seven or eight years older than I am, but I knew who he was."

"Still, to recognize him after such a long time."

"Ewell's not such a big place. He's been around. I kept seeing him. Why should I have forgot him?"

"Claude Sessions is not a dummy. He wasn't reluctant to tell me what had gone on out there at the Hirts'."

"You believed his version?"

"Let me tell you what he told me. He said they'd seen you on the road—he doesn't deny that at all—and they followed you as far as Kingberry. They recognized Dotty Hirt and they knew about the lake, knew where it was, so they were sure you'd gone up there and they came on back to town."

"Does he deny that they were out there later?"

"No. He came back to town and let the others off—they all live right near one another—and he went home to eat. He had a fight with his wife over something, and he says she broke a pitcher over his head and he left the house. He went back to Bates' place and they spent the afternoon tinkering with Bates' car and drinking beer. Fuqua came by, and somehow the subject of Arthur Kin came up, Sessions doesn't remember how."

"One of them just accidentally mentioned it—how odd. What's the point of this, Booth? Am I supposed to feel sorry for Sessions?"

"The point is that they decided among themselves before they left that nobody was going to be hurt. Sessions said he made the others agree to that."

"So they shot out the windows and the lights so that they couldn't see what they were doing. That's playing it safe."

"They could see you clearly. They knew they were shooting fifteen feet over your heads and they weren't much more than fifty yards away. They were confident they had plenty of margin. I know for a fact that Sessions and Bates are crack shots, and they were the two shooting. Manley Fuqua was holding the light. He didn't even have a gun."

"They didn't turn the light on until after Arthur had left the house."

"But they never shot blindly. They shot out the lights first and they didn't shoot again until just before Fuqua turned on his light, but those shots were fired wide of the house. That corresponds with what you say in the deposition."

"And Sessions told you they didn't shoot at Arthur."

"He was ready to swear that they didn't. They left as soon as they saw him go down. Sessions was sure that Bates had shot him, because he knew that he himself had been firing into the air. But when he accused Bates, Bates claimed that he'd been shooting over Arthur's head too. And then Bates accused Sessions of killing him, and they accused each other of lying. It occurred to Sessions that Arthur might have done exactly what he did, pretended to be shot. The only other possibility was that he'd fallen down, but he didn't get up and run again, or that he'd had a heart attack. So Sessions thought that he must have been playing possum, but they didn't hang around to see. Whatever had happened, it wasn't what they intended. They came back to town right away, and they parked across from the courthouse to see if anything was reported. Fuqua actually went over there while the deputies were assembling and asked one of them that he knew what was going on. The deputy wasn't sure. Sessions didn't find out till later what had happened. Two of the deputies went to the bus station for coffee when they got back to town, and he was there waiting for them. They told him that nobody had been hurt."

There at the edge of the immense cornfield the story sounded possible, even persuasive. As he listened, Parker found it difficult to doubt that he was hearing truth. He had never really believed that Sessions and Bates and Fuqua were cold-blooded assassins. A family misunderstanding, a broken pitcher, the muddled and beery stretch of a Saturday afternoon, habitual contempt, available weapons, the fulfillment of boasts and fears, the horrified realization that their mission was fatal, that idle imaginings created a death —it was too near Parker's own experience for him to doubt its likelihood.

"They might not have intended to harm anyone when they went out there," he said, "but what makes you think they didn't change their minds when they saw Arthur? They had guns, Arthur was running—why not shoot at him just to see if they could hit a moving target?"

"It might have been tempting. You can't tell what anyone will do with a loaded gun in his hands. But I believed Sessions, and Bates corroborated his story."

"What about all the gossip in town, then? Am I just wrong about that? Haven't Sessions and Bates let everyone believe that they went out there to kill?"

"I asked them about that. You're right—the public story is that they went out there to kill Arthur and just plain missed him. Sessions knows there's no glory in that reputation. I think he's ashamed of it, and that's really what convinced me that he was telling the truth."

"Ashamed of what? Of missing?"

"No. Ashamed to be thought of as a killer, ashamed that he hasn't had the guts to set the story right."

"But that's exactly what people would have thought— that he was a killer, but he missed his shot—if everything had gone the way he planned and Arthur had never faked it. They weren't going to keep it a secret that they went out to the lake."

"They wouldn't have claimed they wanted to kill him, I don't think. That all got started by the deputies. None of this matters, though. The point is that Sessions lived through a long couple of hours thinking that he'd somehow killed Arthur, and it make him sick, and he knows that the people who have spread the story, most of them anyway, don't have any respect for what he did. There are a few punks who might think that Sessions is a big man, but he knows that most people around here think he's lower than dirt. Parker, I got the impression that Sessions would actually welcome the opportunity to swear before a judge and jury that he never intended murder."

"So you think he's being punished enough by getting a reputation around town as a nigger-knocker."

"That's not called for."

Booth was very calm, and Parker regretted his outburst. He knew that Booth was trying to do him a favor by explaining all this, but all the lawyer's thoughtful and decent forgiveness began to sound like a complacent retreat. Booth wanted understanding to equal condoning, the reckoning of Sessions' confusions to constitute acquittal—*error*. There was the origin of continued self-deception, the principle which maintained the illusions of civility, courtesy, and hospitality. *Ain't it terrible what Claude Sessions and those others did? Down here in Ewell we ought to know how to treat our black folks better than that.* But Sessions' confusions were their own, as they were Parker's, and until understanding contained that acknowledgment, justice could not begin.

"Shouldn't there be a trial anyway?" Parker asked. "Suppose it had been a white man they shot at. Would you try the case?"

"That's a different case."

"But suppose the circumstances were identical."

"I've already told you, Parker, that it's my own personal conviction, based on your deposition and on the other evidence, that Sessions and Bates did not try to murder Arthur Kin. My opinion wouldn't be any different if he had been a white man."

"And you're not going to press charges for assault either."

"Here we've just got to be realistic. The case would come before Judge Waggy, and there would be tremendous wrangling about what exactly was said, and the most we could expect would be a suspended sentence. Does that seem worth it?"

"It does to me. Otherwise these rumors persist, and everyone believes that Sessions shot at a black man and got away with it. He just had to pay for a few broken windows."

"But if I get an indictment and prosecute the case and nothing comes of it, isn't that even worse? It's on the record then. That makes it official that they got away with it. We've got to decide on the lesser of evils."

"I don't agree."

"I know you don't," Booth said with asperity. "You want a symbolic gesture. You want me to enter a moral plea, not a legal one. Let's try to remember the facts: Arthur Kin is still very much alive, and we all of us—me and you and Sessions and Bates and all the people of Ewell as well as Arthur—are damned lucky that nothing worse happened. I'm not defending Sessions and I'm not trying to spare myself, whatever you may believe. You have a load on your conscience, but that's a private matter, Buster, not a public one, and don't make the mistake of thinking that it is."

Booth stood up and dusted the seat of his trousers with his hands. Parker was stunned by the abrupt and venomous conclusion of the interview; he hadn't been aware that Booth was toiling under such restraints. Booth blew a sharp blast on his whistle to summon the dogs back to him, shoved three shells into the chamber of his gun, and grinned at Parker as if nothing at all had been said between them. "You ready to get after em again?"

As he rose to join him, Parker's left arm fell at his side upon the dead bird in his jacket, a lump like a tumor.

Fourteen

In the crowded Montgomery airport, waiting for Amsy on the Tuesday before Thanksgiving, Parker wished that the terminal was more auspicious, but it seemed better designed for partings than for greetings. A hundred spotty windows looked over a barren field containing an enormous asphalt cross; five hundred people stood or sat in ranged orange chairs and stared out those windows. What were they watching for? For daughters, sons, sisters, brothers. And what did they listen for? For news of them, relayed by the crackling public-address that made itself heard above a substratum of noise, a shuffle and din in which footsteps could not be distinguished from engines and voices were mingled with the heating system. But the kids were coming home for the holidays, they were out there beyond those windows five miles high over South Carolina or Georgia, and their parents, Parker supposed, were prepared to receive filial embraces. He had already watched two deplanings and seen enough of disappointment. This is my daughter? This my son? My father? This is what I came home to? This is what I waited for? They didn't embrace, they just bumped into each other; they shrugged, they shifted from one foot to the other; they looked vacantly at the life-insurance machines and the enormous clocks as they drifted toward the baggage claim, but nothing provided much information about where they were and they didn't seem to mind.

He minded. He left the building and stationed himself on a bench near Gate 4, where the plane bearing his sister was scheduled to arrive. His sister, his sister—he realized with alarm that he didn't even know what she looked like. He tried to remember; he gazed across the level field which seemed to meet the wall of the sky at a right angle. The field was like a floor, the sky rose in subtle combinations of blue, the violets and azures contained—nothing, or at least not Amsy. The sky was not, in any of its hues, the color of her eyes. He described her to himself, but the description—medium height, longish blond hair, rather lean—was so vague that it frightened him. If he didn't recognize her, would she recognize him? Could he watch the passengers file out until a girl answering his very approximate idea of her smiled at him? He couldn't, because she might not smile. Parker shivered. The sky did contain wind; it rattled the flashing on the roof of the terminal and it rattled his jaw.

He was chagrined by his lapse and both annoyed and bewildered by his agitation. Amsy was coming home for Thanksgiving—that was simple enough. He was meeting her at the airport. She was, presumably, aboard Delta Flight 212, due to arrive Montgomery at 4:15. Those were the facts; he made a litany of them. Surely her presence, no matter how strenuous, would be preferable to her absence. But what had she done all fall? Why hadn't she written?

What judgment had she passed? For a panicky instant he feared that she would refuse to speak to him, but the instant was only an instant. Her fall, he guessed, had been as excruciating as his own, and if her high-flown idea of him hadn't survived the fall, if he was no longer an important figure in her life, there was no real damage done. He didn't want to be an important figure in her life; he wanted only to be her brother.

The plane was late, delayed in Atlanta. Parker, on his bench, attempted without success to locate the origin of the voice which made the announcement. He did, however, identify the plane in the sky while it was just a tiny flake of silver, long before the voice told him to look for it. A tiny flake of silver, and at that distance completely silent, but the sky did after all contain his sister and was about to deliver her to him. It had engendered a Boeing which grew larger by the second and very noisy as it descended above the row of pylons. Parker got to his feet and stamped them, closed his coat at the neck, puffed rapidly to send warm air to his lungs. The wind increased materially as the jet lumbered to its dock, or perhaps it was only the whine of the engines which sounded like wind. The ground crew wheeled a staircase out to the plane and blocked it; the port opened in the fuselage; the passengers tottered out as though they were just learning to walk. It wasn't easy in that wind. They had to hold skirts down, hats on, coats shut while they scanned the faces gathered at the fence to meet them.

Presently the Boeing engendered Amsy—her name came readily to Parker when she appeared, full-grown, in the port. Wearing a subdued green outfit, holding a white and sizable cowboy hat in her hand, she ignored the wind. Parker shouldn't have recognized her, for she had lopped off most of her hair—and she looked more like her mother than like herself. She spotted him and she did smile; she defiantly jammed the hat over her short hair and skipped down the steps. There was no doubt that she was Amsy. She was lithe, nimble, and so familiar that Parker thought that his anxieties, some of them anyway, were at an end. She had no trouble running to him, and she positively leaped into his arms, bending the brim of her creamy hat against his forehead. "Oops," she said and removed the hat. "Hug me, Parker, we're supposed to be engaged." Her voice in his ear was breathy, confidential, dippy. "Of course our children would be hemophiliacs or whatever, and we're both much too good-looking ever to be happy together."

He craned his neck to get the distance he needed to look at her.

"Hush. Don't say anything." She pressed her mouth against his to keep him silent. "I'll explain later," she whispered, "as soon as a certain party is out of earshot." She made her eyes travel dizzily in their sockets, indicating with them a stocky and spiffy collegian who had followed her off the plane.

But as soon as the undergraduate had passed them, she released Parker and her head drooped. She shrugged, she shifted, she punched at her hat. "I don't know why I ever bought this thing. Every time I wear it I feel like a splashy idiot."

"It's gorgeous."

"Do you think so? I don't know who I think I am when I put it on. I just wanted it to cover up the mess I made of my hair."

"Why did you cut it?"

"I don't know," she said, and gave him a short, imploring look. "I was just tired of it. I was tired of everything. I even tried to get people to call me by my real name.

Amanada. It sounds like an appliance."

"I like your hair that way."

"Aren't you sweet?" She spoke with a gooey drawl and she immediately apologized. "It's strange standing here with you," she said. "I think we came down too fast. I feel like I'm still talking to that wonk on the airplane."

"Do you want to tell me about him? And why we're engaged?"

She did tell him, but she did not want to fetch her luggage until the wonk had vacated the area, and her voice was as flat and muffled as all the other voices in the terminal. Walking beside Parker, not touching but moving forward beside him as though yoked, she droned through a yarn that, Parker thought, would ordinarily have inspirited her. It was a boy-meets-girl story, but she didn't have much heart for it; she'd told her flight companion that she was engaged, that her intended was awaiting her at the airport, in order to discourage his advances.

"Let's stop here, OK? They haven't unloaded the plane yet."

They were in front of a souvenir counter and Amsy began to finger the artifacts, the mugs, ashtrays, paperweights embellished with confederate flags, the plates and bowls with representations of the statehouse baked onto them, the cardboard rebel hats. She picked up a T-shirt and held it up to her shoulders as though trying it on: SOCKET TO ME, the shirt invited, and a cheerful, glowing light bulb was depicted beneath the writing.

"I want it, Parker, I want it."

"It's two ninety-eight," said the woman behind the counter.

"Only kidding."

She refolded the shirt carefully and replaced it, smiling

at the attendant. When she turned away, the woman pointed out that she'd forgotten her hat. "Thanks a million," Amsy said as she retrieved it. "Happy Turkey Day." She tugged at Parker's arm and held on to it as she propelled him away from there.

"I didn't come home to act like this," she said. "This is ridiculous. I practiced what I was going to say to you. I had speeches all worked up."

"Am I going to hear them?"

"Not now. Not here. I'm not ready to deliver them. I have to calm down first. Why did you meet me here? I didn't expect you. I thought Mama would come for me."

"She's at home making your dinner. She has someone for the cleaning, but she's done all the cooking herself since Iva had the stroke."

"How is Iva? Is she doing any better?"

"She's home now, but she's still in the wheelchair."

"Mama said that she was talking again."

"A little. She's still a long way from being well."

"Poor Iva," Amsy said, and her grip tightened on Parker's arm. "I picked a bad time to leave, didn't I? I feel about as faithful as a cat."

"There's nothing you could have done for Iva."

"But maybe I could have done something for somebody else. Maybe I could have done something for me—instead of cutting off my hair."

Parker returned the pressure on his arm. "This is the first time I've ever gone for a stroll in an airport," he said.

"How do you like it?"

"In this company I like it more than I can say."

"I like the company but not the place. I want to get out of here. Let's go see if Tubby has got his bag and left."

The baggage rack was empty except for Amsy's one

enormous suitcase. Parker remarked that it seemed heavy for a five-day trip; she answered that she had been carried away once she started packing. As he lugged the bag to the car, she told him how she'd stripped her room completely and stuffed everything into boxes and suitcases.

"Are you thinking of not going back?" he asked.

"I just couldn't imagine my future."

And during the short walk to the car, keeping her hand on his sleeve, she supplied him with some of the details of her fall semester. She hadn't been able to study, didn't seem to get on with her friends, hadn't even been able to sleep unless she got one leg hooked over the edge of the bed, "sort of an anchor," she explained. She went to every movie in Roanoke and sat all the way down front, where actors' eyes were big enough to fall into. Parker listened, but he didn't know how it all added up; she didn't slow down until the suitcase was in the back of the VW and Parker was fiddling with his seat belt. "You all strapped in?" he asked.

"For what? Is this drive to Ewell so death-defying?"

"You don't know what you'll meet on the local roads."

"What does that mean? Is all that a joke now?"

Her voice sounded genuinely angry, and though Parker regretted what he'd said, he was relieved that it had interrupted her giddiness. "No, it's not a joke."

"What did *you* do all fall?" she inquired, and he could hear that she tried to keep her voice equable. "Mama told me that you were writing something for Booth, some sort of testimony."

"A deposition."

"What is it? Am I going to read it?"

"I want you to."

After dinner he put the deposition into her hands. She opened the binder and glanced into the thing. "Uh-oh," she said, "it's pretty long. I hope it's not tedious. My concentration isn't very good these days." When he promised her that she could finish it in an hour, she carried it off to her own room and he went to his to wait for her. He tried to read—he was halfway through *Sanctuary*—but he was the one who couldn't concentrate. On the other side of his bedroom wall his sister was turning the pages of his deposition, and he couldn't even guess what effect it would have on her. When his mother read the deposition—she had asked to see it—she had only thanked him when she returned it. "And I want to apologize for something I said, Parker," she told him, "that thing about your father." Parker didn't know what she meant until she added, "That night when Frank McKemeny was here. I said you would never know what Philip was like. I'm ashamed to remember it," she said, and so was Parker. They couldn't say more than that; it wasn't easy for them to acquire the habit of talking to each other. Well, Amsy would talk; he just wished that he could predict what she might say. He waited, read, turned a page or two and realized that he hadn't absorbed a word, put on a record, smoked a cigarette, drank a cup of Sanka. He was ready to go fetch her when her door finally opened and she banged into his room.

"The scribe," she said. "You must have a fantastic case of writer's cramp."

"The critic," he said, turning in his chair.

"I'm not a critic, I'm a character. I'm in this book." She hefted the deposition and stretched herself voluptuously. She realized what she was doing, but didn't know why she was so uncontrollably brassy. She charged it to the music, a funky album by a group called the Doors, stoned-looking artists who had posed for the record jacket in a weedy field with a knee-high sunset behind them.

"Mercy, Parker, you're not turning into a freak, are you?"

But she didn't mean to mess about. It occurred to her that Parker had been waiting for her to finish the deposition with an expectancy that deserved a better response than dormitory brashness. He didn't answer her question but looked down at his book. She thought she had best say what she had come to say. "Well, I read the deposition, the whole thing."

"And?"

"I'm glad you let me see it, I'm glad you wrote it—and, Parker, I'm sorry. It was low of me to run out on you in September."

"I don't blame you for that."

"Come on. Let me apologize, will you please?"

"You don't owe me any apology."

"I feel as though I do," she insisted calmly.

"I don't know why."

"Because I see now that it wasn't over when I left, not even the worst of it was over. I knew that anyway, for myself —it was worse at school than it was those few days here, and it was worse for you too. I can't even claim that I learned anything in class. You know the only thing I remember? This Shakespeare professor with a head like a turnip saying, 'Melodrama is for those who haven't the resources for tragedy.' I wanted to fly out of my seat and put a few lines in his face, a few melodramatic lines."

"Why didn't you?"

"Scared to," she said. "Oh, Parker, you blame yourself for too much. That passage where you say your hand is a gun—you don't ever come out and actually say it, but you imply it, and it's loony. Your hand is just a hand. You got

252

scared and you ran out of the house. I could just as easily have run out of there as you."

"You didn't, though. I did."

"What does it matter? They'd have found Arthur sooner or later with that light."

"I don't think so. They didn't even know he'd left the house. He'd have been in the woods by the time they started looking for him."

"Why are you arguing with me? You ran out of the house and Arthur happened to be where you pointed." But he had reason to argue, and she knew it. She'd been a little disingenuous; she began again. "I just don't think one lapse cancels out everything. You're judging yourself a lot harder than anyone else does."

"I don't think so."

"I do. I *know* what you did—but, Parker, that's not what you wanted to do."

"I don't see what wanting has to do with it."

"It has everything to do with it. With Arthur you had to be thinking all the time, thinking what was right, before you could make a move. But that's what you *wanted* to do. It was when you stopped thinking that you ran out of the house."

"That's one way to put it," Parker said dryly. "I regressed."

"Don't be that way with me," Amsy said. "You know what I mean. You brought Arthur here, you were trying to help him, you were self-conscious the whole time, you were *thinking*. You just couldn't forget what he was."

"Could you?"

"No, I couldn't." She hesitated; she had the impression that this subject was as important as any they knew of and she wanted to be certain that she was scrupulous and exact. She had been conscious of the color of Arthur's skin, and reading the deposition had opened corridors in her own past. It had made her feel rather delinquent for having considered so little her relation to the black people who'd always surrounded her. But though she had been exposed to the same lore Parker had, she could not define or articulate any particular attitude toward those people. She wasn't able to think of them as belonging to a race—it was that simple and it had seemed, while she read the deposition, that deficient. Had she, after noting the color of his skin, treated Arthur any differently than she might have treated another man? She considered. Arthur was affable, amusing, even attractive to her, but she had never for a moment viewed him as a candidate for romance. She hadn't forbidden herself to view him so, or at least she was not aware that she had. As for sex, she had noticed the volume of groin in that little yellow bathing suit of his, but she was certain that her curiosity about it was academic. No, he'd been an outsider in an unpleasant situation; to make him feel more welcome, after the incident on the highway and the unfortunate treatment he'd received from her brother and her friends, had presented itself as a civic duty. Was she deceiving herself? She looked carefully at Parker as though she might find the answer in his face, and she was confident enough to say, "I couldn't, but I didn't have to think about it the way you did. And he wasn't so important to me—he was just someone you brought here for a day."

When Parker didn't reply at once, she said urgently, "Parker, don't you see? What you did was just backsliding. You gave Arthur a ride, you brought him home with you, here to this house—you did all you could for him. You didn't bring him here to get shot at; you brought him here to help him out. I'm sorry to keep telling you what you did, but you think worse of yourself than I do or than Arthur does."

"When did you talk to Arthur about it?"

"While he was still here, before I left."

"He never said anything to me."

"How could he? You didn't make it very easy for him—or for me either. You were sort of unapproachable."

"What did Arthur think?"

"He thought it was pretty frightening, but he knows who did the shooting. He knows it wasn't you."

Parker didn't entirely trust Amsy; he thought her manner was a little too therapeutic. Although he wanted her forgiveness, he wanted it measured to his failure. "Why was Arthur so set against the trial?" he asked.

"He just wanted to get out of Ewell as fast as he could —can you blame him? And he didn't think a trial would amount to anything. He said it would just stir up more trouble, and he didn't want us to get dragged into it. He said we were the ones who'd have to live with it."

"That sounds like an excuse."

"It's not an excuse," she said indignantly. "That's what he believed."

"Didn't you too?"

"Didn't I what?"

"Believe that there shouldn't be a trial."

She colored. She had believed that, but her opinion had never amounted to much more than getting back at Parker. In her eyes her brother had fallen from grace—not just for what he'd done at the pond, but for the guilty righteousness which had followed—and she hadn't been able to bear what she saw. And so she had sided with Arthur and she'd fled to college, where she kept track of herself by repeating,

255

I am not the one involved. There wasn't much consolation in
that slogan; it didn't help her define her own situation, nor
did it do much justice to the more immediate plights of
others, from whom she was separated. She was not the one
involved, she told herself, but when she looked about her,
the world seemed to be composed of awful strangers. She
had begun to long for Parker, and now, seated near him—
she had improved her posture on the bed—she was cross
with herself for blushing, and angered by the need to blush.

"All right, I did believe that. I think I was wrong. They
broke a law, they ought to be tried. That's really what I
thought all along, but I was too mad at you to say so. You
were acting so holy. If you remember, I wanted to call the
sheriff after they bumped us on the highway."

"Are you still mad?"

"Yes—at you, at myself, at all of us. We were all pretty
dumb. And Sessions and those people ought to be put
away. Are they going to be?"

"No."

"What do you mean, no?"

"Booth isn't going to prosecute."

"Why not? What's the point of this deposition, then?
How do you know he's not going to?"

Parker smiled at her broadcast. He described the hunt
with Booth and repeated what the lawyer had told him
about the testimony of Sessions and Bates. Amsy listened
soberly and sat up very straight, as if the arrangement of
her vertebrae had something to do with hearing. She asked
Parker to please turn off the record player, and he did. He
tried not to bias his account of the legal situation; he explained as well as he could Booth's predicament and he
admitted that Sessions' version of what had happened
sounded plausible to him. The chore of explicating so

much would have oppressed him if he'd had any audience but his sister, whose emotions as she listened were so material to him that he felt he could have plucked them from her cheeks and forehead. He couldn't help smiling at the changes in her face, and he continued until he had summed up as much as he could of the case.

"Booth Lovelace is unregenerate," she said.

"He's probably doing what he thinks is right."

"How can you say that?"

"I don't think he's an evil man. He's ambitious and shrewd and practical, but he's not evil."

"What about Sessions and that crowd? Poor babies, I suppose they're just misunderstood."

"No, I think they should have been tried—maybe not for attempted murder."

"I don't get it. You think the absolute worst of yourself, but everyone else is the victim of circumstance. You're just looking for somebody to nail you to a cross."

Her vehemence was so surprising that he laughed. She was sitting cross-legged on his bed, his sister with her hacked-off hair, the image of his mother. In her anger she spoke to him with what sounded like perfect sincerity, with emotion as pure and substantial as an unthumbed fruit.

"Don't laugh at me. I'm not kidding. It just doesn't make any sense. Do you think those crackers should be on the loose? Do you think Booth ought to be able to hush up the case? I bet the sheriff told him to leave it alone, and probably Mr. Hirt did too."

"Of course I'm disappointed."

"Of course," she snorted, mocking him. "I'll tell you what *I* am—enraged."

"There's nothing we can do about it."

"Couldn't we get some other lawyer?"

257

"Booth is the State Attorney. He's the only one who can bring charges."

"Booth Lovelace is . . . is . . . and you . . ."

He laughed again, and this time he knew the laugh was an acclamation. He took his sister's anger, the flush of her throat and forehead, as proofs of a bracing intimacy that could withstand the clearest insights and most unflinching judgments. His laughter continued, releasing, elating, and it lasted long enough to begin to alarm her, long enough for her to answer it with a perplexed smile, but she was not prepared to be routed from her indignation.

"Would you mind telling me what's so funny?"

"You are. Seeing you again is." She didn't appear satisfied with that answer, but he didn't know what more to say.

"How much is there I still don't know?" she asked, asperity in her voice. "I've read the deposition, I've seen Arthur, I'm looking at you right now, and I still don't have an idea why you brought him here."

"I thought we talked about that the first night I was home."

"You told me what happened in Amsterdam, but you never finished. Isn't there more? Didn't you ever like him at all? Was he just some poor strange black guy who walked into this mess? Were you always as rotten toward him as you were when he was here?"

"You're not making your questions very easy."

"Why should I?"

"To be kind to me."

"Were you ever kind to him? Kind without having to think of it, without congratulating yourself for it? Tell me what happened after Amsterdam."

"I bought him a train ticket to Frankfurt."

"After you'd lied to him about the amount of money you had?"

"I still bought the ticket."

"What about his girl?" Amsy asked. "Did you ever see her again? Or is this another story with all men in it?"

"She came to the train station with him."

They had arrived at the last minute. Arthur was wearing a beret and dark glasses, carrying his duffel bag and escorting Katrin. Parker had a better look at her as they came through the mobbed concourse than he had had in the café; she was solid and stocky, thick-limbed and plain-featured, yet she might have been comely with a glow of color in her cheek and energy in her step. She was not just pale but drained and ashen, and she submitted entirely to Arthur's guidance to pass through the pedestrian traffic toward the gate. Despite his impatience, and despite all his doubts about the motives for their liaison, he was rather moved; he thought that he was watching the last minutes these two would ever spend together. There wouldn't be, for them, any consoling possibilities—no promises to return, no illusions of a palmy future. Their time in Amsterdam, Parker thought, was all of love they were to know; that's what they must have seen when they looked at him and the hissing train beyond the gate, the station clock and the conductor flourishing his ticket-puncher. No wonder that Katrin used the weight of her body to oppose the time, no wonder that Arthur wore a stoic expression.

"We here," Arthur said. "How much time we got?"

"Just a minute or two. The train's already been announced."

"You got the tickets?"

"Yes. Look, why don't I go ahead and get on the train? You wait here with Katrin until they get ready to close the gate. I'll give you your ticket."

"She can't go down on the platform?"

Katrin asked the conductor a question in Dutch; he shook his head no. She then looked at Parker as if it were in his power to help her, and while there was no accusation in the cast of her face, Parker scuffled busily and lifted his own two suitcases.

"I'll go find us a pair of seats."

Arthur nodded, but as Parker set off, the conductor called out the departure and signaled emphatically at the three of them. "So," he heard Arthur say, "you look out for yourself, you hear?" Parker didn't turn around; he didn't want to intrude on that parting. He was thinking of his own farewell to Erika, which had also taken place in a train station, and of the reassurances they had exchanged. He would come back, he promised her—and why not? The two of them had felt a roominess of choice, a freedom to fashion their own romantic destinies, but none of their hedges against sorrow seemed available to a black man from Biloxi taking leave of his Flemish girl. Kin's travels were probably ending for good, and he must have felt as though he were being driven from the garden to return to the ground of his birth, its dust and enmity. Parker thought that he knew as well as Arthur himself what Arthur returned to: "After all," he said to Amsy, "I was a part of what Arthur returned to."

"What about Erika?" Amsy asked, her tone less strident now. "Are you ever going to tell me about her?"

"There's nothing to tell?"

"Nothing?"

"Nothing."

"Do you still write her?"

"I never did."

"Why not?"

"I've been having my troubles with love," he said.

"Haven't we all?"

After a pause he asked, "Am I permitted to leave her out, then?"

"Continue. You're on your way to Rhein Main to catch your plane."

"We weren't exactly welcomed with open arms."

The driver from the Rhein Main motor pool, a low-grade airman whose job was to shuttle back and forth from the Frankfurt train station to the base, rolled his eyes incredulously when they asked for transportation. "Don't bullshit me. You may be Americans—you sound like it, I admit that —but it's no way I'm gonna believe that anyone looks like either of you is in the Army, no way." They produced copies of their separation orders, which the airman studied dubiously, and finally Arthur convinced him by executing a few snappy drill movements. At the base itself, once they'd found the appropriate clerk at the flight center, they met with a familiar bureaucratic attitude. "Yep," said the aggrieved airman, "your orders are just about as fucked up as most of em are." He sighed; he felt persecuted; he told them they'd just have to wait for him to get the proper amendments to the orders before they could be put on the standby list. How long would that take? He didn't have the first fucking idea. Did he have any idea when they might get on a plane? He wasn't a fucking prophet. Where should they bunk? He wasn't the fucking welcome wagon either. But they didn't dare talk back to him, since he could easily hold them up for days if he took offense; they commended his patience. He softened enough to direct them to the enlisted men's transient barracks, which was, of course, on the far side of the base, and when they at last arrived there by post bus service, the charge of quarters wouldn't issue them bedding or meal tickets until the adjutant was reached by phone and approved.

"This is awful familiar," Arthur said as they made up their bunks in a moldy, dank barracks that was regularly shaken to the point of disintegration by the racket of incoming planes. "Not the earthquake, but all the rest of it. It's worse'n familiar. We didn't have no latrine that ripe at Badstein."

"Smells about the same to me."

"Same is worse when you're out of the habit."

He was right, and the sense they both had of alienation from the military—and the Army had been their only previous bond—joined them in a new, more resilient partnership. They took common note of the short haircuts, the uniforms no self-respecting Swiss trolleyman would have worn, the mess-hall cuisine, the general officiousness, the prevailing mania for the implementation of rules and procedures (the barracks wall was plastered with methodical counsel that covered all situations from nuclear attack to the brushing of teeth). Arthur decided to get a haircut —"survival and evasion tactics," he called it—and they took part in a number of reconnaissance missions to locate the post amusements.

Even though they found the theater and the EM Club, they spent most of their time in the transient, tremulous barracks over interminable games of gin rummy and blackjack. For his part, Arthur disclosed the circumstances of his stop in Amsterdam, accounting for the sadness Parker had suspected in the café. Katrin had got pregnant; Arthur sold his car to pay for the abortion. The strange thing was that she wanted the baby, and Arthur had to talk her into giving it up. "She didn't want to get married," he said. "She just wanted to have the baby. 'How we going to raise it?' I asked her. 'What kind of job am I going to get in Holland? You see me as a cheesemaker? Or a fisherman? And how long you think you going to be able to stay in that university when you got a black baby to look after and you not even married?' No way she could have that kid.''

"Maybe you both could have come back to the States," Parker said.

"Me with no money? Her with a baby? And wanting to stay in school and get her degree? And where we going to live when we get back? Biloxi?''

Arthur knew all the questions without prompting. "I couldn't do a thing for her except get her in one kind of trouble or other, give her a baby, make her quit school. Thing is, I kinda wanted to at first. You know, I thought that would be something, leave her with a little black kid to look after, a little black mothuh name of Hans, wearing wooden shoes and talking Dutch. That tickled me.''

And though he smiled, he seemed to believe he deserved his loss. It was clear, too, that he'd taken up with Katrin as he'd taken up with other white girls, but he'd made a mistake. She was serious about her studies, and when Arthur moved into her apartment, he found that he was jealous of her university life. She seemed so engaged in her work that Arthur suspected her of using him. "Listen. I know about that stuff, cause I was using her when it got started, see? But she was always booking, and she had just so much time for me, like I was a pet, some kind of bad dog she kept so she could show me off to her friends at school.'' And Arthur decided, as a kind of revenge, that he'd like to knock her up. When he did, and she said that she wanted the baby, he was ashamed. He hadn't even planned to be around when she found out, and he certainly hadn't expected her to see as a blessing what he intended as a scourge and a punishment.

"What'd she want my kid for? That's what I couldn't figure out. Seemed like she would have been upset, but she was happy about it like we was an old married couple and had been wanting one for years."

What Arthur never said was that she loved him and he loved her—that was the mystery which encroached upon the data, and it was as much a mystery to him there at Rhein Main as it had ever been. It was a mystery to Parker too, yet one whose presence he could feel, and he accepted Arthur's account without any reluctance. It did not seem improbable to him that an ambitious and brainy girl, a grocer's daughter and a scholarship student of economics, would fall in love with Arthur Kin, whose father was a yard man in Biloxi and whose mother operated the Realistic Beauty Shop. At intervals, some of them terrifying, he recollected that Arthur was black and Katrin white, but that didn't prevent him from wishing they'd managed to stay together.

Parker sometimes mentioned Erika to Arthur, but he balked at telling much, for he did not feel that his loss was commensurate. He had by then, in one of those intervals, realized what topic answered Arthur's candor. He thought, inevitably, of his father and Esther and Andrew, but he was not prepared to reveal that family secret. About the rest of his Alabama past, which he represented as extremely grisly, he was very forthcoming, and Arthur listened to him with unflagging irreverence. On the single subject of his father's adultery Parker was reticent; that issue was too fearful. Yet when Arthur spoke of the child he might have had, Parker's memory pressed upon him the image of his half-brother,

Andrew's face and the shape of his head, dented at the temples by forceps, like a pair of question marks facing one another. That boy might be Arthur's, or like Arthur's boy, or perhaps like Arthur. It was as if Arthur's story brought forth the boy thousands of miles away in Ewell and set him down on the bunk with them where the playing cards were spread, a brother or a son, a half-brother or potential son —some relation, anyway, through whom kinship flowed.

Parker broke off his story with an uncertain laugh. "I didn't say a word about any of that to Arthur," he said to Amsy.

"I can understand why," she replied. "He'd have thought you were cracked."

"I don't know how I could have explained it to him. I didn't know how to explain it then."

"Do you know now?"

"Not really." How could he explain, even to Amsy? He knew that his father had had a son by Esther in much the same way that he knew he saw. Vision rayed out from his head; he'd never been obliged to consider its source. "I think I would tell him, though, if I had another chance, without trying to explain. It was a ghost—who's ever been able to explain that? It was haunting our barracks, making it shake, just like those overflights did. Sometimes it flattened out on the wall with those posters telling us how to save our lives in different sorts of attacks."

Amsy stirred on the bed, but she didn't laugh at his fancy. She made a show of looking around the white walls of the newly painted room. "He's not here now, is he?"

"No."

"But you didn't leave him behind, either."

"No."

"What about Arthur? Have we lost him too?"

"I have. I don't know if you have."

Again Amsy looked for spirits. "I don't see him—but I don't have your imagination."

"It's not imagination that creates ghosts."

"What is it, then?"

"They come when they're wanted or when they're called."

"Call one, then."

"Amsy, Amsy, Amsy," he chanted, closing his eyes. "And look: there you are. I've invoked you."

"Parker, Parker, Parker," she answered, "and here we are, the two of us."

Fifteen

The parlor had been designated the recovery room. The sofa was shoved into a corner to make space for Iva's wheelchair, a gleaming contemporary model in chrome, seated and backed with a leatherlike material of robin's-egg blue. This arrangement located Iva near the heater and gave her a point-blank view of the television. Mose and Andrew had cleared furniture and rugs so that passage from there to the back of the house was unobstructed, for Iva's necessities were ordinarily unannounced. She had regained the use of her tongue—the most promising sign of improvement—but either her hemiplegia had so numbed her bladder and bowels that she could not detect their operation or she simply refused to give warning. They didn't know which, but in any case the room smelled like a nursery. There was a sour odor reminiscent of diapers, and the balms and ointments which seemed to give Iva relief (Dr. Price thought they were useless) had the soothing fragrance of lotions used to prevent babies' rashes.

At first, because of her frequent messes, they had tried

to persuade Iva to wear backless hospital gowns which simply fastened at the neck; these Mose and Andrew could change without levering her about. Iva submitted for a few days, but one of her first complete utterances was, "You freezing my ass off," and thereafter she insisted on having fresh flannel orthodox nightgowns. Mose bought her a half-dozen of them in different floral prints, and Trudy, one of her daughters-in-law, came by daily to fetch the washing. Dr. Price thought there was an element of vengeance in her incontinence: if she had to suffer indignity, so would everyone around her. He upbraided her quite tartly for not co-operating, and she calmly puddled the floor while he spoke. Her behavior distressed Mose and made him too fretful to be an efficient attendant, and so Andrew was a godsend; the boy had discovered a vocation in looking after Queen Iva. It was he who applied the patent ointments to her stiff limbs in light massages, he who made her eat the prescribed diet and attempt the recommended exercises. And while she yielded to his ministrations, she always regarded him with her magisterial and staring eyes—her left eye still had the trace of a squint and was as wild as an animal in a trap—as though he were a flunky who'd overstepped his commission but she, alas, was at the moment obliged to endure his firm attentions.

All her symptoms were, according to the doctor, characteristic enough, but Parker had carried away from each visit an impression of acute and preying consciousness. Iva's memory was addled in jarring ways; she interrogated Parker closely about the provisions of her will, apparently mistaking him for a lawyer as his father had been, and then she recalled in exacting detail events he had forgotten altogether—how, for example, Amsy had once gotten angry at him, retired to her room to heat up her curling iron, come out swinging it by its cord, and chased Parker clear out of the house. Iva occasionally asked him how many children he had, and when he answered that he had none, she said, "You'll get em, you'll get em. You can't keep from getting em." She made Mose strap a wristwatch on her right arm, and with every change of program on the incessant television she announced the time. The game programs inspired fits of avarice, and when contestants were asked to debate whether to keep the prizes they'd already won or to risk them by playing on, she encouraged them to "break the bank." She lost interest entirely in her several cats and referred to them as "dogfood." On some days she was wrought by religious urges and she wore a chain of rosary beads about her neck, though where on earth she had procured them Parker could not imagine. Yet her blanks and her enthusiasms, her collapses and her fits seemed to Parker not the results of madness but the manifestations of an inscrutable passion, and she had arrived at an imperious manner and despotic bearing, a condition which seemed too absolute to have anything to do with bodily decay.

Parker had tried to convey to Amsy some of the difficulties of calling on Iva, but when they visited on that Wednesday morning, the day before Thanksgiving, Amsy was carrying a bought bouquet of snapdragons and lilies. Iva did not acknowledge any greeting, but glared at the flowers with some disdain. "Put em in water," she croaked, and dismissed them with a nod of her head. She made a short, jerky sweep with her right arm to signal Amsy to step aside; her view of the television screen, where two women were competing for a speedboat, was blocked. Amsy did move, and Andrew offered to take the flowers from her. Mose invited them to sit down, and then they all waited until the next commercial break interrupted Iva's concentration.

"Wish I had me a motorboat," she muttered.

"Miss Amsy's here to see you, Queen Iva," Mose said. "You ain't even said hello yet."

"I'm glad to see you sitting up and enjoying yourself," Amsy said. "It must be nice to be home after the hospital."

"Can't tell em apart," Iva said to Mose. "She done cut all her hair off, and she had the prettiest hair I ever combed."

"It's still pretty," Mose said gallantly. "It's just less of it."

Iva turned to Amsy. She didn't move her head, but the rotation of her eyes seemed to require immense muscular effort, as though she lifted and moved the whole room with her vision. "Where you been?"

"At school, Iva. I just got home yesterday afternoon. It's our Thanksgiving vacation."

"Turkey and stuffing. Squash. Cranberry jelly. Onions. Sweet potatoes. Mincemeat pie. Punkin pie. Once I had to fix them stinking oysters for your daddy. Don't tell *me* Thanksgiving."

"I don't know how we'll manage without you," Amsy said. "That's why Mama couldn't come with us to see you this morning. She's doing the shopping. She said to tell you she'd stop by this afternoon if she had a minute."

"Miss Eleanor been real good to us," Mose said. "She sholy has. She come by here nearly every day."

"I hope you all are going to have some kind of Thanksgiving."

"Oh yes," Mose said. "Our boys gone to look out for us. They gone to bring all the grandchildren here for Queen Iva to see em. They'll bring us something to eat too."

"Those children don't care about nothing but shoving

270

me round in this chair," Iva said.

"Queen Iva not feeling her best this morning," Mose said.

Andrew returned with the flowers in a blue-glazed Ball jar. He hesitated where to put them and decided upon the table behind the television. Amsy got up from her seat and spread the arrangement, and Iva followed her with her eyes.

"Miss Busybody."

"Miss Amsy brought you those pretty flowers," Mose said. "Don't she know how to make them look nice, though?"

"She ain't her mama," Iva said. "Her mama'd make those flowers look like they grew in that jar. And he ain't his father neither."

"He knows that without you telling him."

"Parker! How much money you got in your pocket?" Iva demanded.

He reached for his wallet. "Not much. Three or four dollars. Let me see."

"He had exactly ninety-four dollars and some odd cents. I remember the sum."

"Who had, Iva?"

"Your daddy when he died. How much you say you got?"

"Four dollars."

"Then you ain't rich enough. You ninety dollars short. Time you went to work and quit living on milk and honey."

"What you talking about?" Mose said. "You not making a bit of sense to anybody."

"He had his pockets turned inside out. Told me, 'All I got is hers now.' And your mama already gone to the hospital with her bleeding. He was lying out in the middle of the floor on his back and he was covered up with dollar bills."

"I'm afraid I don't know what you mean," Parker said. "When was this?"

"You was there, but you was in bed. He had done called up the hospital and they told him there wasn't no more baby. Miscarry. I asked him where he'd been all night that nobody couldn't find him, and he said, 'Esther's.' But it ain't no ninety-four dollars for you, Andrew."

"What kind of crazy talk is this?" Mose interrupted. "Queen Iva, you got company here now."

"So drunk he couldn't count it up. Made me do it for him and stack it all real neat. He asked me how long she been to the hospital, and I told him I called up Hub's Taxi to take her. He gave me two dollars and said, 'Here's for the fare and the tip.' I told him I wasn't going nowhere that night. 'You go to bed,' I told him. 'You not doing any good lying on the floor.' He got out his pen, but it wouldn't write upside down, so he rolled over on his belly to make me out a receipt. Made me sign it. Said, 'You gone to have to look after em now.' I signed it Queen Iva Freeman and I been doing it."

"Queen Iva," Andrew asked, "you want to go back and rest some?"

"She give you the flowers and then she mixed them up. Got to clip the stems crossways and they live longer. Need a fern to make it full. Don't stick em in cold water right off because they'll draw up."

"I think we ought to go," Amsy said to Parker. "We're upsetting her."

"I picked him up and set him on his feet. He couldn't walk no better than a little baby. I helped him up the stairs. He said, 'Mind how you handle me.' I didn't turn loose of him till he was in his room and then I went and gathered up that money and carried it out to the kitchen and put it in an envelope."

"And then what happened?" Parker coaxed.

"The gun. Banged two times. You were in the room before I got there. Nothing to do but drag you out of there. Ninety-four dollars don't go as far as you think, not when you got doctor bills."

"This ain't like Queen Iva," Mose complained.

"Parker, we really ought to go," Amsy said.

"Who called the hospital the first time for your mama? Me. And who called the second time for your daddy? I did it. Who took care of you all till the ambulance come and got him? Me again. Who looked after you till your mama got home? Me, Queen Iva."

"And they looking after *you* now," Mose said. "Miss Eleanor seeing that you get all the best."

"I'm sitting here in my own piss and smelly shit."

"Are you nasty again? How come you won't say when you need to go?"

"I'm finished. I'm finished. That's what they used to holler. I wiped those little white asses many and many a time."

"I'll change her," Andrew said.

"I'll do it again."

"What's wrong with you, woman?" Mose said indignantly. "Take her out of here, Andrew."

But Iva gripped the spokes of the wheel with her good right hand and refused to be banished. Gently, and to no avail, Andrew tried to unpry her fingers.

"I ain't gone to be bossed," she said. "I already got my money hid."

"Queen Iva, turn loose," Andrew said.

"Where you all coming from? What you looking to find?

Bringing me flowers and candy to sweeten me up, but I got nothing for you. I'm keeping what's left for me."

"It's no use you staying," Mose said to Parker and Amsy. "Maybe she'll be more fit for company another day."

"I'm sorry we upset her," Parker said.

"Not your fault."

"You going now? You leaving?" Iva asked.

"Yes, Iva. We'll come back another time. I hope you'll be feeling better."

"I feel fine."

"Bye, Iva," Amsy said, circling the chair at a generous distance. "Please don't be angry. We didn't mean to aggravate you. We're so grateful for everything you've done for us. I'm sorry this had to happen."

"Listen at that," Iva said.

"We'll come back another time," Parker said.

"When you got the money, I got the time," Iva said with glee. "I got the hiding place and I ain't saved enough for my old age."

"Turn loose," Mose said, and that was the last thing they heard. They were on the porch, the door slammed behind them, and Amsy sobbed on her brother's shoulder.

"I just felt so helpless," she said later in Parker's room. Her eyes were red and she still hadn't mastered her breathing. "There wasn't anything to do but stand there and listen."

"I know."

"She was so resentful of us, and, Parker, she didn't seem crazy—that sounded like what she wanted to say, like she meant it. Do you think she'll ever get better?"

He didn't answer. Would Iva get better? Dr. Price predicted that her ability to control her body would improve, but Amsy was asking if Queen Iva would ever become again the familiar Iva. *No,* he thought, because even if she recovered and forgot, they could not.

"Is she always like that? How can you stand it? How can Mama go there every day to see her?"

"It's easier for us than it is for Mose," he said bluntly. The audience with Iva had moved him, but it was not the first time he had seen her in a reckless, revelatory mood. Squinting at her own ruin, Queen Iva seemed to have a steady vision of her condition and theirs, and she communicated by injuring. Wasn't that why she'd spoken of his father? And wasn't that how his father taught? Drunk, fallen, ransacked, his father had made Iva his executor, guaranteed the conclusion she was now meeting—but she'd accepted the duty.

"Was all that true?" Amsy asked.

"All what?"

"All that Iva said about Daddy and what happened the night he killed himself."

"I think it must be true."

Amsy lay back on the bed and put her hand over her eyes. "I guess it's time I knew for sure. That boy Andrew really is Daddy's son, isn't he?"

"Yes."

"Well, I'm glad he is. I mean, I'm glad it's one of us taking care of her."

"It was taking care of him that brought on Iva's stroke."

"Of him? Or of us? There doesn't seem to be much difference, does there?"

He didn't speak.

Amsy said, "I've never even thought about suicide, about Daddy's suicide. It always seemed to me that it was just another way to die, not much different from an accident or a fire. Is that stupid of me? Did you ever think of killing yourself?"

"No."

"You don't sound very sure."

"I found Daddy's pistol this fall."

"Well?"

"I couldn't have done it. Too much in love with my own precious life."

"But you thought of it?"

"No," he insisted.

"Daddy was the real coward, wasn't he?" Amsy said, not oblivious of her words but convinced they both could stand them. "He left all of us, me, you, Andrew, Mama, to sort out the mess he made. Why?"

"How do I know?"

"What happened that night? Did you know that Daddy was at Esther's?"

"Only when Iva told me."

"Do you think he came home the way Iva said, and pulled out his money and just went upstairs and shot himself? I can't remember anything about it. I was confused that night because Mama was already at the hospital. Did they tell me the truth then? What did you see?"

"I was in bed asleep until the gun woke me up."

"Did you know what had happened to Mama?"

"I knew she'd gone to the hospital."

"Tell me."

"Don't you remember that day at all? How Daddy came to get us after school?"

"No."

"He was looking for us. He'd come to pick us up."

"Had he been drinking?"

"Yes."

"Where was I then?"

"Mama was at school too, and you'd already found her. You were in the car with her."

"Did you go off with Daddy?"

"No. I ended up in the car with you. Mama and Daddy had a sort of quarrel when he came to the car—you don't remember?"

"It must have seemed normal to me. What was the quarrel about?"

"About whether or not I was going with him in his car. Mama didn't want me to, and it wasn't really a quarrel. He agreed right away."

"But Daddy was probably angry, and that's why he went to Esther's."

"I don't think so," Parker said. "He went to Esther's . . . for the same reasons he always went there, I suppose."

They were both silent. Amsy sat up on the bed and watched Parker intently, apparently nerved to face this once for all.

"What were the reasons? Was it just that black-woman– white-man stuff?"

"I don't think so."

"Well, what, then? Would you please tell me?"

He wasn't sure. The things he wished to say to her remained beyond the reach of his ability to translate into language. Essentially he knew what his mother had told him two months earlier as they sat together on the lawn. Philip Livingston had sought to increase his family, to offer himself as husband and father, and thus as equal in love, to any who would have him. No motive but a compulsion he didn't survive. It didn't save anyone, least of all himself. Yet to his heirs he bequeathed early and continuing lessons in grief —maybe the necessary lessons after all, since grief is love freed of object, and in that freedom love may become for an instant general and renewing.

He said, "Mama told me that he treated Esther and Andrew just as he treated us, like a second family. You remember how he was gone so much of the time? He was with them."

"Did Mama know all along?"

"Yes."

"When did she tell you that?"

"This fall."

"Anyway, he went to Esther's that night," Amsy prompted him, "and when he got back here, Mama had gone to the hospital in a taxi."

"If Iva's right."

"Did anyone try to get him at Esther's?"

"They must not have."

"You don't think Mama—" Amsy stopped, apparently considering and discarding a possibility too appalling to mention. "That must be why he shot himself," she plunged on, "and why he took out all his money. Just . . . providing," she said, lighting on the word with sorrowful certitude.

"Yes."

"But you didn't see him until he'd done it."

It was half question; she wanted a description. He told her that the first shot had awakened him, and he thought, *Marauders,* since that was the use his father had specified for the only weapon in the house. Imagining thieves were at large, he was frightened, but it didn't occur to him that they had shot; he was sure that the report which he'd heard was from his father's pistol. He waited, listening for sounds of scuffle or flight, but he heard nothing. He let himself cautiously into the hall, and he heard Iva beginning to climb the stairs; her heavy tread reassured him and he went to his father's room. He was in the nursery when the second shot was fired, nothing but the thin panel of a door between him and his father. He ran those last steps. When he opened the door he thought the room was burning. The smoke was blue and aromatic, and the blood on the white wall looked like flame. His father's legs were still swaying; he'd fallen backward onto the bed, or perhaps he'd been sitting when he shot, but his feet did not touch the floor and they still had motion. The cuffs of his trousers were hiked up and one of his socks had fallen to his shoetop. "He dead," Iva declared, and Parker hadn't even heard her approach. He took a step forward and was stopped by her hand on his shoulder, but he saw that the blood had splashed out of his father's head and surrounded it on the bedspread like a rooster's comb.

"I never saw the pistol that night," he told Amsy. "I thought someone else had shot him."

And he had struggled in Iva's hands, but he was held firmly. "Don't fight me," Iva said. "You not gone to get loose."

"And she brought you back to my room," Amsy said.

"And made us stay there together while she did what she had to."

They stopped. Parker and Amsy sat facing one another, conscious, both of them, of the silence which fell upon the house when they ceased talking. They listened expectantly, but all they heard was the unsubdued past occupying their clamorous hearts.

Sixteen

Thanksgiving Day. The sky was a unanimous blue, and the air was cold enough to inspire the birds to their winter manners. They fed ravenously at the brimming stations. Parker, in the course of his appointed tasks, several times found himself watching the display from the windows of the house; he saw not merely a decorous riot but the air's chromatic grace, and he fancied that the birds which stirred the air were a heavenly broadcast, like the fluttering bits of propaganda dropped from the vaults of bombers. He noted with pleasure that the wintry temperature had elicited the birds' avid song.

He'd been assigned the silver, which he exhumed from its coffer in the sideboard. It was ancient stuff that had come down through the Livingston family, very elegant and delicate—small, he would have said, the implements of a well-formed but stunted race. At least its simplicity of pattern made it easy to polish, and he brought it up to a shine in which he could see his own distorted face trapped in the tendrils of an exquisitely chased L. The polish was a pink corrosive, and he rather liked the odor and the scouring properties of the liquid; he rubbed the tarnish off on a cloth and the silver sparkled like creation.

He was charged also with the preparation of the table. After he laid on the felt and leather pads, he covered them with a linen cloth so heavy that it seemed to have silver depths. So draped, and even without leaves, the table was too vast for their diminished family, and the three place settings at the north end of it looked as provisional as the inroads of squatters. Parker arranged the best china, upon which red-and-blue imperial dragons glared through fabulous interstices, but he remained discontented with the bare opposing expanse of the table, and he raided the breakfast room for flowers and greenery. They helped.

The women were in the kitchen amidst plenty, and the fragrant turkey was in the oven. The stuffing was the only recipe that had been entrusted to Parker, and he now hung about watching as the squashes, sweet potatoes, onions, and cranberries were made ready for the meal. He managed to get his fingers into most of the dishes in progress, but it was Amsy, not he, who said to his mother, "We're making enough to feed starving India."

"It won't go to waste," she said.

One by one the containers were added to the warming oven. Mrs. Livingston dismissed her children and told them to make themselves presentable. Parker underwent a rigorous scrub and dressed with more care than he'd taken in months, even plumed himself with an ascot his mother had given him during his college days but which he'd never, before now, found occasion to wear. Feeling gaudy, he was relieved to find Amsy in a long bright dress. They met in the hall; they inspected each other; they smiled at how readily they'd embraced domestic ritual.

They showed themselves to their mother and she approved. She herself went to change, and when she appeared, she'd outdone them both. She was as vivid as one of her birds, and her tentative smile seemed an apology for such gorgeousness. "What ritz," Amsy said, and she replied, "I don't get to wear it often."

When, so adorned, they carried the food to the table, they had to think of Iva, but they did not mention her. Mrs. Livingston produced two bottles of champagne; she was not sly, she protested, although she was pleased that the children had not discovered them. Parker opened one of the bottles and filled the three glasses, but they did not drink at once. They seated themselves, and the children lowered their heads when their mother did. "We are thankful that we are able to be gathered on this day."

The glasses were lifted then, and Parker felt an emotion like gratitude. Despite the excesses of grooming and the proportions of the feast, he was among family. They were, for that meal at least, balanced upon ancestral things, as if the whole of the past flowed through historic artifacts— silver, glasses, china, linen—to unite them within this present, the way the brilliant clarity of the afternoon poured through the window. They were three and they were joined; it kept the house from tumbling about their heads. They needed only to multiply and fill the empty places at the table with kin.

75 76 77 10 9 8 7 6 5 4 3 2 1